Dedalus Origi

THE REDEMPTION CUT

Pat Gray was born in Belfast.

He is the author of five novels:
Mr Narrator, *The Political Map of the Heart*, *The Cat*,
Dirty Old Tricks and *The Redemption Cut*.

He has worked extensively in Eastern Europe, but now lives
in London.

Pat Gray

THE
REDEMPTION
CUT

Dedalus

Supported using public funding by
**ARTS COUNCIL
ENGLAND**

Published in the UK by Dedalus Limited
24-26 St Judith's Lane, Sawtry, Cambs, PE28 5XE
email: info@dedalusbooks.com
www.dedalusbooks.com

ISBN printed book 978 1 912868 66 7
ISBN ebook 978 1 912868 90 2

Dedalus is distributed in the USA & Canada by SCB Distributors
15608 South New Century Drive, Gardena, CA 90248
email: info@scbdistributors.com   web: www.scbdistributors.com

Dedalus is distributed in Australia by Peribo Pty Ltd.
58, Beaumont Road, Mount Kuring-gai, N.S.W. 2080
email: info@peribo.com.au   web: www.peribo.com.au

First published by Dedalus in 2022

Printed & bound in the UK by Clays Ltd, Elcograf S.p.A.
Typeset by Marie Lane

TO JANE

Acknowledgements

I am indebted to many authors whose books have helped me in writing *The Redemption Cut* and its forerunner *Dirty Old Tricks*. Particularly to Martin Dillon for 'The Dirty War' and 'The Shankill Butchers: A Case Study of Mass Murder', and to Patrick Radden Keefe for 'Say nothing: a true story of murder and memory in Northern Ireland'. Memoirs of RUC men were also useful, in particular Edmund Gregory's 'Not waving but drowning: the troubled life and times of a frontline RUC officer'.

As always my brother John has tried to keep me straight where fictional imperatives diverged from historical accuracy. *The Redemption Cut* is a work of fiction and any errors are my own.

THE REDEMPTION CUT
Pat Gray

Chapter One

Belfast, 1976

Because it was raining there was not much for the man that hosed the dust to do, except to watch rubbish cascading down the chute. Occasionally he would use a broom to sweep up anything that fell from the compactor while the seagulls wheeled and fought for scraps around him. The man was almost mesmerised watching the rotting food, newspapers and cardboard, bottles and discarded clothing. His senses were blunted by the noise of the machinery, so much so that he did not at first realise that he had seen what looked like a human arm amongst the refuse. He hit the red button, a hooter sounded, the machinery stopped. He leaned over the railing, squinting down into the jaws of the compactor. A bloodied red hand seemed to be clutching at the air down there, as if reaching up for him.

The men from the nearest refuse truck were called to help. One of them volunteered to clamber down amongst the garbage to get a closer look. When he came back he was carrying the arm like it was something delicate and placed it gently on the concrete wall by the compactor, wiping his hands on his overalls to remove any trace of contact with the dead human flesh.

McCann was awakened by the sound of the phone jangling in the hall. When he got to the receiver a voice he knew but couldn't place asked was that Inspector McCann?

'Aye,' he said, peering out at the weather through the window, scratching his head.

'Mr Arbuthnut asked me to call. You've to be in right away.'

Irritated by the early hour, the lack of breakfast or even tea, the cold in the hallway, McCann became short, officious even, despite himself: 'Who am I speaking to here?'

'It's Deirdre here, Inspector. Did you not recognise my voice?'

Deirdre! The Superintendent's secretary. And Arbuthnut of course was the new man who'd taken over from the Poet.

'Ah Jesus, Deirdre, of course. I'm sorry, I've been that long away.'

'Did I wake you Inspector? You don't sound yourself.'

'Not my best first thing. Yes right, I'll be there as soon as I can.'

When he put the phone down he stood for a moment thinking, watching the silver birch trees outside bending to the wind off the lough. Then he went back to the bedroom, opened the cupboard, pushed the hangers back until he found his uniform and took it out into the light. He rubbed a patch of dust from the lapel, laid the uniform out on the unmade bed. Then, whistling a noiseless but cheerful tune, he went to the bathroom, cleaned his teeth and shaved. He peered at himself in the mirror; the heavy brow, black eyebrows sprouting and in need of a trim, mouth turning down at the corners, eyes quizzical. He tried a smile and wondered was it the same McCann there in the mirror as it had once been. He wondered why they'd bothered calling him. Four months ago they'd let it be known they'd be happy if he stayed on gardening leave, meaning they hoped he would never come back at all.

The minicab driver was surprised to see him in his uniform, opened the rear door for him like he was some kind of VIP, or was putting a safe distance between himself and his passenger. McCann ignored the offer and climbed into the front seat next to him.

'Not a bad day to get back to work Billy,' he said.

'Not seen you in a while, Inspector,' said the driver, getting some of his clutter out of the way so McCann could stretch his legs in the front.

'How have you been yourself?' asked McCann, to stop the prying.

'As well as could be expected.' McCann smiled at the classic Ulster answer and watched from the window as the car accelerated down the motorway into the city, the flat grey water of Belfast Lough leaden under a cloudy sky. Then onto the Shore Road, Carlisle Circus, the no man's land between the tribes; burned out gable ends, half demolished Victorian streets, an army patrol droning past, two Saracens with their drivers peering through armoured slits at the commuter traffic. They drove up the Shankill Road, festooned with fading union flags and then left and up to Division, a high wire palisade around it and a heavily sandbagged sentry point watching the road outside. The driver pulled up short and let McCann out to walk the last few yards, like he'd reached the edge of the land of Mordor and would go no further.

'On the tab, OK, Billy?' said McCann, stepping out.

Outside the police station there was a familiar figure with a sandwich board handing out tracts. 'Repent ye because the judgement is near,' said the message on his back.

'That judgement of yours not come yet Bertie?' quipped McCann, as he went past. The fellow had bottle-lens spectacles, with wire frames. Behind them his brown eyes were huge and round. Despite the mild weather he was bundled up; the vee of several jumpers showing under his tightly-belted gabardine mac, a thick pair of Donegal tweed trousers the turnups of which hung over his very highly polished black shoes. They'd always got the polished shoes, as if God had explained to them that they'd not be let into heaven with dirty boots.

'It'll come soon enough Inspector. Can't be far off,' he said with absolute confidence, like he was predicting more rain before the end of the week. 'Here's a little something for you,' and he tried to give McCann a pamphlet.

'I've no need for that, Bertie, thanks all the same,' said McCann. He knew that Bertie had been a featherweight boxer, twice married, time in the forces, five children, an alcohol problem, until suddenly he had discovered God and everything had made sense. How could all that chaos suddenly make sense just through the application of a bit of mumbo jumbo? McCann tried to give the pamphlet back, but the man's hands were clenched, so McCann had to stuff the pamphlet into his own pocket.

'You'll be needing that Inspector, not now maybe, but one day.'

McCann hitched up his trousers and walked past the sentry point into the Division.

Once inside, he leaned through the hatch into the duty room, taking in the scuffed furniture, peeling walls, the pin board overlain with layer upon layer of notices. The Desk Sergeant seemed flustered as if she wasn't sure he was authorised, one eye glancing at the rota to see if they'd been notified he'd be back on duty, but pleased nonetheless to see him again.

'Hullo stranger. Not seen you in a while.'

'I've not been here in a while. I've been called in to see Mr Arbuthnut. Deirdre gave me a call,' explained McCann. 'How are things anyway?'

She made a long face and McCann laughed.

Back at C Division everything seemed the same; the stairs with the linoleum taped down with gaffer tape in the same spot, the overhead strip light that flickered a nicotine yellow glow over everything, the smell of sweat and the swab of the cleaner's daily disinfectant. That ripple of anxiety as he climbed the stairs, pausing to catch his breath before passing along the top corridor to the Superintendent's office. They had nicknamed the new man Paper Clip, or so he'd been told. McCann grinned. There was something great about the Province that Mr Arbuthnut had hardly taken over and already the men had summed him up and cut him down to size.

Halfway along the corridor a Constable crossed McCann's

path. She was youngish, unfamiliar, smartly turned out in her uniform like it was new, not frayed or faded or shapeless yet with over-use, like she was maybe still proud of it. She looked at him closely, as if wondering who he was, hesitated in her step as he passed.

'Morning!' said McCann.

'Sir.'

'You new?' It was always good to have someone new, someone fresh, a new set of eyes. It was because they didn't last long that there were always new faces. McCann made it his business to know them all in the hope they would stay.

'Sinead Flannery, Sir.'

'Flannery!' McCann was taken aback at the Catholic name, unusual in a police force that generally wasn't.

The woman seemed to find his surprise amusing.

'Inspector McCann,' he introduced himself.

'Oh, so you're Inspector McCann' she said, like she'd already heard all about him.

'Not sure if the Inspector bit still applies,' he said. 'Just going in to see Paper Clip to find out.'

She smiled at his use of the Superintendent's nickname.

'Well, good luck with that then,' she said and tripped away lightly up the corridor.

There was silence as Deirdre ushered McCann through into the Superintendent's office. Head bent, Arbuthnut's fingers moved a paper from one side of his desk to the other, selected another paper and held it in his hands. He had a narrow face, with high cheekbones, a small, precise mouth and protruding chin, grey hair almost the same colour as his face. No one knew his first name and since the epithet 'Paper Clip' had become attached to him, most had forgotten his surname too. He returned the compliment in dealings with his men, by failing to remember their names too.

Then he looked up and said: 'There is something useful you could be doing you know. We're short of people, forty percent down on establishment, forty-two percent as of yesterday. We've had a very nasty report in of a severed arm at the waste transfer station.' McCann nodded, gave him what he hoped would seem keen attention. Paper Clip peered at the missing person's report in his hands, read the first few lines: 'Raymond Small. Young lad from up the Shankill Road, up near Woodvale Park. No body as yet but the mother's very insistent. It could be related.' McCann reached up, took the report, a single call logged by the Duty Officer. It was hardly the recall he'd been expecting, but beggars couldn't be choosers.

'You told the military yet?' McCann asked. Paper Clip sucked in his cheeks at that, waved his hand at McCann as if it had been stung by a wasp.

'Can't do that. There's a new initiative at HQ to bring the police back into the front line. Let the army pull back, a return to normal policing. It's called 'The Way Ahead'[1] and it's why we need every man we can get.'

'Oh aye,' said McCann, as neutrally as he could manage.

Normal policing? That would be the day, with Ulster sliding into some kind of desperate civil war, the death toll mounting.

---

[1] 'The Way Ahead' was a new strategy paper written in 1975 that introduced the policy of 'Ulsterisation' that aimed to reduce dependence on the regular British army.

Where would they find the normal policemen and women to do the normal policing?

'There's restructuring that's going on, new crime teams at Castlereagh which will be better integrated, with better forensics.'

'I know. I applied and wasn't shortlisted,' said McCann. Paper Clip would have known that, having been on the panel. He'd have known about McCann's last case; the two murdered girls and the way he'd tried to charge a fellow officer. That hadn't made him popular. That had given them a reason to restructure him out.

Paper Clip's eyes flicked back to a heavy folder on his desk which McCann now recognised as his own service file.

'So you'll be waiting for redeployment.' It was not a question, but a statement of fact. No reply was expected and McCann gave none, letting the silence lengthen and deepen. 'What age are you now?' he flicked into the folder. '43? Too early to take severance then, but a fine age for a serving officer. There'll be a process of course. Officers who haven't been appointed to the new structure may still be interviewed for any remaining vacant slots that may come up.' Paper Clip looked at a point in the middle distance, to the left of McCann and about a foot above his head, as if admiring a heavenly organisation chart from which McCann would be absent. 'A job like this could show us what you can do. Give you another chance until a position comes up.'

'And when will that be?'

'Now McCann I'm afraid I can't tell you that.'

'Who'll I have with me?' asked McCann, fearing the worst, that there'd be no one, or worse than that, a few of the station's other cast-offs, B-men[2] absorbed into the mainstream like some kind of virus.

'I could give you a Constable, bit of a wild one though I gather, a Catholic too. You could get her on this for a start. It would break her in.'

'What happened to Sergeant Thompson?' asked McCann, wanting a friendly face he could trust. Thompson had supported him and kept him going throughout his last investigation. Starting without her was a disappointment.

Paper Clip's hand searched autonomously around the desk, like that of a blind man, found a sheet with a list of names on it.

'Moved to one of the crime teams at Castlereagh[3] under Taylor. He's a good man. I gather it was well deserved.'

'That's great. She's a good officer.'

'I'll ask Deirdre to show you down.'

Paper Clip reached forward, pressed a buzzer on his desk and almost immediately Deirdre's head appeared around the door.

'Oh Inspector. Are you back now?' she asked outside, her nose twitching with the scent of gossip.

'Seems like it,' said McCann.

Deirdre unlocked the room for him, handed him the keys. The room was narrow and smelt damp, with one small window

---

[2] B-men were the so called B Specials, part-time police drawn uniquely from the Protestant community, and reviled by the Catholic population. They were disbanded in 1970 but some subsequently joined the full-time police force or the Ulster Defence Regiment.

[3] Castlereagh was where police headquarters were based.

set high up in the wall. There were four chairs and two tables
pressed together between the shelving that rose on either side.
Dead files bulged and buckled from them. McCann thanked
her, sat down, read the note of the call about Raymond Small
that had come in, frowning, turning the page over. There was
scant information, but concerning enough. No firm evidence
yet that the arm and Raymond Small had been connected
though. Then a knock came on the door and he opened up to
Constable Flannery.

'The Superintendent said you might need a hand down
here.'

'Did he now?' said McCann, moving back to let her in.

She was scrubbed almost bright as a new pin, thought
McCann, her hair tied back neatly with a green hair band that
matched her uniform. Short for a policewoman, but he'd heard
they'd relaxed the rules to fill the vacant posts.

'This doesn't look right,' said McCann, passing over the
report on Raymond Small. 'Got all the signs: disappearance
out of character, would normally have kept in touch his mother
says. Been gone three days. Just check it out, talk to the family.
Get a list of contacts and we'll see if there's anything in it.'
Flannery took the report, scanned it, looked up at McCann,
then around the narrow room.

'It'll get you out of here,' said McCann. 'We'll sort things
out later.'

She looked down at the address and McCann knew what
she was thinking, that it would not be safe for a Catholic officer,
up the staunchly Protestant Shankill Road. But she had to start
sometime. It might even be safer if she didn't mention her

name at all when she was up there.[4] But people were entitled to their names and the respect that went with them.

'I'll do that straightaway, Sir,' she said. As the door closed behind her McCann thought maybe that's why Paper Clip had sent her to him along with Small's file, knowing she'd have to go up the Shankill Road where a Catholic officer might be in danger. That would maybe be the final push for him, a young recruit lost on his first day back, two jobs done in one day. But it wouldn't do to start the day on the dark side. Maybe he should have gone with Flannery, but you couldn't be mollycoddling. So he followed her out into the wet Belfast morning. He'd to get onto the arm at the transfer station before it started to fester, before anyone messed with it. Flannery would have to face up to the reality of Ulster alone, like they all had to, if she was to be of any use to him.

The smell of garbage was everywhere, even though the office door was closed. Looking down, McCann could see the line of Corporation lorries belching diesel backing up on the quayside leading to the compactor, waiting to go up the ramp and deposit the day's rubbish. A week's garbage from one street reduced to a cube of filth, then another cube, until there was enough to fill a container and enough containers to fill a small ship, to be taken out into the Irish Sea and dumped in the deepest trench that could be found. The forensic team were already down by the chute in their white suits, sifting through the waste. One of the lorries was parked up alongside and taped off awaiting inspection.

---

[4] Names are one of the main clues to a person's religion and political affiliation in Ulster, though the name alone is not always a guide.

'How long are you fellows going to be?' asked the head of refuse. He bulged out of a tweed suit, with a face like a beef tomato, sweat gleaming on his forehead.

'We'll be done soon enough, Sir,' said McCann.

'Aye, but how long will that be?'

'It'll take as long as it takes.'

'No doubt I'll have the public health people all over me too, after this. And if you boys hold us up much longer there'll be half of north Belfast on the phone, their councillors too.'

'We need the arm,' said McCann. 'And to check there's no other bits and pieces.'

'Legally, it's all the property of the Corporation.'

'Is it now?' said McCann, standing by the window, studying the scene outside for a moment before turning to him. 'There'll be putrefaction to consider if there's delay. You'll be destroying evidence and that could be hindering the police in their enquiries. You could be jailed for five years for that.'

'Five years!'

'You've had body parts here before?'

'Not that I'm aware of, Inspector. We've had other things though. You'd be amazed what people think they can get away with.'

'Such as?'

'Pets.'

'Pets? You'd think they'd bury them.'

'You've got to be joking. Once had a whole donkey in the trade waste. That's an offence against the fallen animal regulations.'

'Is that so?' said McCann, encouraging the fellow to

ramble while he watched the forensic team outside seal the arm in an evidence bag.

'What time did they find it?'

'About half eight when they came back in to do the first dump.'

'And the round? When did that start?'

'Let's see, its Reggie Simmonds' turn, so that would have been round number twelve. Would have been off the yard at half six, on the round by seven.'

'Show us the route,' said McCann. The big man walked over to a map of the city hanging on the wall divided into districts, each district divided into refuse rounds identified by coloured boundaries, the boundaries mapped onto the religious majorities in each zone.

'Round twelve, Shankill Road mainly. Here, I'll give you the exact way they go.' He reached over to his filing cabinet, pulled out a duplicated sheet, handed it to McCann. They were familiar streets, his beat as much as theirs, up one, down the other.

'So let's say they started at Shankill Parade at seven and they were back dropping the first load at half eight, that would have been the whole route would it? Seems quick, doesn't it?'

'It's up to them how fast they go. They're paid for the round, the sooner they're finished the sooner they can knock off. Now if we're done here, Inspector?'

McCann thanked him, asked him to keep a watch out, to keep in touch and climbed down the steps to the forensic team. They had four fellows still working on it, had brought everything up from the compactor. They had emptied the lorry contents out onto a big tarpaulin. The air was thick with flies.

21

McCann flicked a squashed tomato off the sole of his shoe.

'Filthy job boys.'

'You can say that again.'

His eyes ranged over the festering jumble sale that lay on the ground before him.

'Find anything else?'

'Nothing Sir. We're nearly done.'

'And where was it? The arm? Where in the load?'

'We've blood on a few items, just here.' The officer took McCann over to a place where the first of the compacted bundles had been opened up. 'Stands to reason it'd be where they stopped the machine.' McCann looked back to the beginning of the line of uncompacted refuse, estimating something in his head.

'Thanks anyway,' he said, strolling away to the gates of the yard where his Land Rover was waiting, turning the pages of the route he'd been given as he walked, noting the small gap between where the arm had been collected and Raymond Small's home.

Why had she joined up? Sinead Flannery had wondered as she did every morning; showering, removing make-up from the night before, dressing like she was going to some office job at the Electricity Board or at Anderson and Macauley, then breakfast alone in the police-house kitchen. Better than at home though, with her Mother there at breakfast with her face strained by anxiety: *'Why couldn't you do something normal? You're a bright girl Sinead? You've you're GCEs, seven of them.'*

She had first considered becoming a civil servant or maybe

a teacher or librarian, while pulling pints part time in a local bar. There had been constant harassment: a wee touch here, a feel there, furtive but somehow entitled to whatever they wanted because it was a man's world and more or less lawless. She'd stood apart from the marches for Civil Rights, though schoolfriends were sucked in, became strident, outraged by the turn that events took. And there had been encouragement for Catholics to join the police, recruiting officers had been to her school with their glossy brochures, their promises of sport and excitement. By the time the Army came in it was just too late for her to back out: she had already joined the police, almost perversely, to show she'd an independent mind and an eye on a solid career.

She took the bus through the City centre. In the morning it was a normal, busy scene outside, like any city with its double decker buses, nose to tail commuter traffic, pavements thronged with bustling and jostling crowds. But there were queues at the security gates for bag searches and above the shopfronts the windows were taped over against the blast from bombs. At Division she completed a transformation in the locker room, peeling off the jeans and top, her suede jacket, swapping them for the thick woollen tights, the green serge skirt, the sludge coloured shirt, gradually buttoning herself into the person she had become.

And this morning it was Raymond Small she had to find. She had one of the patrols drop her at the end of his street, jovial men beside her, secure in their territory, pulling over, opening the door to let her out, the smell of diesel heavy in the damp morning air. The uniform was always a help, like she was one of them, like it was some kind of armour. But the moment the Land Rover pulled away, she felt the protection of her colleagues slip away, found herself alone on a street that felt strange to her, in a place where she was unsure if she would be welcome, though she'd grown used to that, been trained for it. She had always supposed it was the same for RUC men who were Protestants entering Republican areas.

'If you worry about that, love, you might as well give up,' as her training officer had told her when she first started.

On her first posting she'd been out on patrol with two UDR[5] men – both brothers. Big, friendly lads, one of them just married, with the kind of bluff decency that farmers had. They'd shown her the wedding photographs; not a big family, but close, she'd seen that. His new wife was smiling with her wedding dress held just off the ground so it wouldn't get dirty, himself with a huge brimming smile overflowing across his face, his brother in the best man's rig-out with the white carnation in the lapels.

'How long you been married, Will,' she'd asked.

'Two months.'

'Big change, eh?'

And then his brother had butted in, leaning across the floor of the darkened Land Rover as it swept out up the Coagh road.

'Getting it regular, eh, Billy?'

And he'd smiled shyly.

'Come on, there's ladies present,' he said, checking the

---

[5] UDR – Ulster Defence Regiment – A part time Regiment of the British Army that was locally recruited.

magazine on his gun, pulling the bolt back, peering out the front at the road ahead, white in the headlights, twisting up and away under the darkened trees, the land either side infinitely pitch-dark. In daylight she knew it was a mess of tumbling hills, brooks, clusters of beech and alder. At night the Land Rover was an island of light, sailing through that sea of darkness.

They had stopped at a dip in the road between Killylea and Caledon. It was a good straight section of road, with a view of cars coming either way, nowhere they could turn when they saw the patrol.

'OK?' said the driver.

'Looks good.'

She'd got down and was checking the field one side, then the other while the two brothers set up the roadblock. She remembered the smell of the grass, the sound of cows munching softly in the darkness. Then the bomb went off underneath the Land Rover.

There'd not been much left of the vehicle – the driveshaft was found in the far field, the chassis had been thrown into an oak tree and hung there along with bits of both brothers, their torn uniforms fluttering like death flags.

Flannery shook her head to try to clear the memory, took a breath, wished she'd had a cigarette on the way up in the Land Rover. But now the street lay in front of her; a Protestant street which should be safe for any RUC officer, provided they'd not get her Catholic name. The house was in the middle of a long terrace, with slate roofs, coal smoke leaking from the chimneys, the front doors leading straight onto the street. The homes were well-kept and neat, with scrubbed doorsteps, painted boot scrapers set in the wall, pavements swept and washed clean. Bunting had been strung back and forth from the streetlamps, fluttering over the cobbles. Flannery hesitated before knocking on the door.

It was opened by a small woman in curlers under a paisley headscarf, an apron tied around her waist, duster in hand. She peered at Flannery. She flashed her warrant card, withdrew it before the woman had a chance to read the name.

'I've come to talk about Raymond,' she said. 'To see if I can help you find him.' Trying to divert any suspicion, to close in on what would matter more to Mrs Small. She seemed grateful, ushered Flannery through into the parlour, offered her tea, said she had been demented with worry, her words bubbling out as she clattered the teapot, cups and saucers.

'When did you last see Raymond?' she asked.

'Saturday night. He just said he was going out.'

'That would be the 10th, then?'

The mother's hands kneaded the duster she held as she sat on the low sofa.

'Aye, about seven.'

'And no word since?'

'Nothing.'

'Did he say where he was going?'

'He just said he was going out with his mates.'

'I'll need a list of their names,' said Flannery, going through the missing person's routine, relaxing as she did so, sympathising with this woman. The mother nodded, sniffed, pulled a handkerchief from her apron, her distress welling up. Flannery paused, let her compose herself, trying not to let it

26

affect her because that wouldn't be helpful. She made a neat and careful note of the names.

'And you've rung round, contacted everyone.'

'Of course, I've been desperate.'

'Has he ever gone off before without telling, staying away?'

'Never.'

'Where did he work?'

'He was a fitter at Harland and Wolff.'

'So, were they his mates then?'

'Some of them.'

'He had others?'

A faint look of distaste lingered around the mother's mouth, turning the corners down.

'He'd been hanging around with some lads from the Sceptre. That's where he was the night he disappeared.'

'The Sceptre?'

'It's where the hard men go.'

'Did he mention any names, of people he met down there?'

'He kept all of that to himself.'

'I'll need names, any names he might have been with on the 10th. And I'll need to see his room.'

Flannery followed her up the stairs which were so narrow her shoulders touched the walls on either side on the way up. At the head of the first flight of stairs were two bedrooms and a further flight.

'We had him up in the attic because of the noise. He likes that music you know, hard rock or whatever they call it.' She paused on the landing. 'I try not to go up there, to leave him alone.' She made a gesture that Flannery should go first. The stairwell was dark, a thin panelled door leading off into the attic. Flannery moved up carefully, called out as she rapped on the door: 'There'll be no one there. Haven't I told you he's gone?'

Flannery pushed the door open, reached in and turned on the light. Across one wall hung an Ulster flag, a Linfield scarf over the mirror, football cups on the chest of drawers.

Flannery moved further into the room where there was an unmade bed, khaki fatigues thrown on top, black boots underneath.

'He liked to wear the kit. They all did, God love them.'

Flannery bent down, looked under the bed, then turned to the drawers, pulling them open one by one. There was a slew of socks and pants inside. She reached in and rootled around, finding nothing but loose coppers, a match programme, a boxing glove. Then she turned to the cupboard, pulled at the door, but it was locked.

'Do you have a key?' The mother hugged her arms, as if feeling a chill in the empty room.

'I've no idea.'

Flannery went back to the drawers again, pulled each of them out, searching underneath and in the wooden frames, then along the top and side of the cupboard, the mother frowning now, until she found a key. When she opened the door the cupboard was full of clothes, shiny blue-grey men's suits, crisp white shirts. And behind that there was an electric guitar and plug in amplifier. Flannery took it out.

'Fender Stratocaster. That will have cost a bob or two,' she said, then realised that the mother was baffled too, because she had leaned forward to touch its shiny chrome and plastic body, like it was a spaceship that had just landed.

Downstairs, she took a couple of photographs from the mother, including one of the lad in his last year at school, uncertain in his expression, standing in the backyard with a brick wall behind him, his tie half off, his school blazer draped over one arm, shirtsleeves rolled up.

'It was the end of his last term. He was so happy, so pleased to be away from school at last.' As she held the photograph, the mother's fingers lightly stroked his image.

Looking closely Flannery could see the faint shade of his moustache around his upper lip. There was a later one of him wearing brown flares, a Fair Island jumper, a denim jacket. By then he had a long shock of black hair, strong eyebrows and a flourishing well-trimmed moustache. She reached over, picked a black and white photo in a silver frame from the mantelpiece.

'Went down to the News Letter specially, to get a print,' said the mother.

Flannery peered at the photo. The boy seemed taller, maybe he'd a pair of Cuban heels under the bandsman's trousers.

'Loyal and ancient number five' she read the inscription on the big drum.

She was on unsafe ground here, on their ground, not hers, but she'd to investigate nonetheless. How did it work, she wondered, the Orange Order?[6] They kept all of that secret, so

---

[6] The Orange Order was founded in 1795 to uphold the Protestant religion, and 'Orangemen' are a secret society which Catholics cannot join. There were overlaps between the membership of the Orange Order, the police, paramilitary groups such as the UFF and the main Unionist parties.

only the members knew.

'It gave him a structure. The poor lad was desperate for some discipline and these fellows, well it's what they do, isn't it?'

'Aye, I'm sure it is,' said Flannery. She could remember bandsmen, marching and banging along the end of her street, every year, like they owned it. Stopping there to hammer and batter their drum. But it didn't justify someone killing the lad, if that was what had happened. So she thanked Mrs Small and stepped outside into the grey morning air. She called in for the patrol to pick her up, strolled to the end of the street where it was busier and had a quick cigarette in a doorway, sucking the smoke down deeply into her lungs while she waited for the Land Rover to arrive.

'For God's sake, McCann! What do you expect me to do with this?'

The pathologist had the arm up on the dissecting table, like it was a fine ham ready for slicing. 'What have you done with the rest of it?' Her blue eyes were unnaturally large and bright behind round tortoiseshell spectacles, her unruly auburn hair bursting from beneath her cap. For some reason she had used mauve lipstick, reminding McCann of some character in a horror film. Her white laboratory coat seemed freshly laundered, but despite that still carried the stains of past dissecting encounters, the pockets bulging with tools of her trade; the cable from her dictaphone trailing out, a packet of disposable rubber gloves and what looked like the familiar bulge of her favourite electric saw.

'Thought you'd be pleased to have less work to do. Get

away early, the way you like it.'

'Ah now McCann there's enough to be getting on with here to take me way beyond lunch. You'd be surprised what you can tell from an arm, especially if you've got the hand. If you've fingers you've got fingernails, fingerprints. It's a regular treasure trove.' She leaned forwards, peering at the nails. 'If you're lucky you'll get bits off the assailant stuffed up under there. The fellow what done this wasn't an expert; normally they'd have the fingers off to stop us getting any of that, normally they'd not even put the remains in the refuse.' She was smart, thought McCann. He'd not even told her and already she knew where the arm had been found, though the smell was an obvious clue. 'Refuse is way too obvious. Far better just to vanish a fellow, then you can't have the likes of me poking about.' That would be better for spreading fear too, thought McCann. Better to leave the gaping question of where a fellow might be, with everyone speculating, not sure if he'd run off or what, sowing doubt, blame, terror. Teaching people to keep their heads down, that was probably the name of this particular dirty game.

'I need the prints first,' said McCann.

'Can't get you all of them,' said the pathologist, pointing at something, taking a professional interest. 'Very clean.'

And then McCann realised that the ring finger was missing.

'Not an accident then?'

'Dear god no, Inspector, it looks almost surgical, very recent too. Until I've finished I can't tell you if it was done at the same time as he was killed, or probably just before.'

'Why'd they do that?'

'You tell me. It's you who is the Inspector isn't it?'

Torture maybe, thought McCann. What had the fellow known that they had wanted? And it needed two to torture, one to hold the fellow down, the other to do the chopping.

'Anything else you can see? Jewellery, distinguishing marks, any inkings, injuries?'

'Hold on Inspector, I'm doing my best for you.' McCann waited while she went through the formalities, weighing the arm, recording details on her dictaphone, examining every inch of the arm through a magnifying glass, photographing. He stared at the ceiling, tried to look out through the frosted windows, imagining if it might have turned into a sunny day outside.

'How long ago was the fellow alive?'

'Well, it's hard to tell without the rectal temperature. You've your blowfly here already though, they're useful little fellows.' Then she was into the arm with the tweezers and the eyeglass, collecting specimens, shaking out the bag the arm had come in, a couple of live flies humming away in the bright lights of the autopsy room, swatting them away.

'Interesting little beasts, dirty habits though. I'd not think the flies in the bag are relevant, being as this came from a refuse tip where there'd be flies everywhere. But this here wee maggot, that's a different affair.' She held up a tiny squirming maggot between her tweezers that she'd extracted from the arm. 'I'd say it's a centimetre long and that's a two-day-old maggot. Just as well you got me this today, another couple of days him and his mates would have ate the lot and there'd be nothing for me to look at but a pile of bones. So in answer to your question Inspector, I'd say he died the weekend just gone,

Saturday or Sunday.'

McCann was starting to feel faint, that hot and cold feeling, the buzzing in his ears louder even than the flies that were still droning around him.

'I'm not making you ill am I, Inspector?'

But McCann was making for the door and the outside world.

'Think of it as the hors-d'oeuvre. I'll get you the main course later,' he said over his shoulder.

'OK Inspector. You've whetted my appetite now.'

And McCann pushed out through the swing doors, gulping down the air outside, the doors closing behind him with a near-silent swish.

And by the next evening when the fingerprint team had visited Raymond Small's home, they'd no doubt the arm belonged to him, which put him right up McCann's list of priorities. It was a case with the blood and the memories still fresh. A missing person with a chance to find a killer. A careless maniac just might give them a lead on the room full of dead files. It might even be the missing bit of the puzzle of his last case, which still nagged McCann like a bad tooth every time he tried to smile.

The café was half empty in the evening lull, preparing to close as the City shut up early for the night and locked its doors. McCann pushed through the entrance and found Sergeant Emily Thompson waiting for him.

'Emily! How's it going?'

'Inspector. You're looking very smart.'

'You too,' he said. Today, out of uniform, he thought it even more so. Thompson was in her thirties, divorced like McCann, had a daughter in her teens, a few years younger than McCann's own daughter who was away at Uni in England.

McCann ordered sausage and mash, with beans and a pot of tea, while she settled for a sandwich.

'What was it that you wanted to see me for?' he asked, when they'd sat down and he'd poured the brown sauce over, put a dab of mustard on the side while she checked the tea was brewed before pouring them both a cup.

'I just thought it'd be nice to catch up.'

'Nice?'

'Yeah, nice,' she repeated, cutting into her sandwich, tapping her foot mysteriously. 'Or maybe you don't think so.'

'Of course I do. It's always brilliant to see you Emily. Division's not the same since your elevation.'

'Some elevation,' she said. 'Under Inspector Taylor.' He laughed at that.

'Give the fellow time.' said McCann, though he'd not given Inspector Taylor much time himself when they'd first met. 'And how's it going, this new job of yours?'

'We've been on a big robbery this month, the Ulster Bank. You'd not believe the money involved. Taylor's being cagey, but it's massive. They reckon it was organised to a tee; held the manager's wife hostage till he opened the vaults for them.'

'Aye, I saw the reports when it happened.'

'And you, Inspector? Anything resolved yet?'

'Up in the air,' said McCann, embarrassed, ashamed even to talk about his last case. 'Even though Deevery had as good as admitted what he'd done with those two girls, the forensics didn't come through so we'd not enough to go to trial.'

'And Deevery himself?'

'The force had him down to Purdysburn for a psychiatric assessment. I gather he's still up there on sick pay.' McCann tried not to let his frustration show, not to talk shop, not to go back but to move forwards.

'I'm really sorry. So, what are you doing now?'

'Fellow called Raymond Small, loyalist from up the Shankill, chopped into bits.'

'That'll keep you busy then.'

'Got a new Constable on it, name of Sinead Flannery.'

'Jesus, I know her. She's a character.' He looked at her questioningly from over a forkful of beans.

'We had a few nights out when we were on a course together, kept in touch since then.' McCann nodded, knowing that you'd need a sound stomach for a night out with Thompson, that she could drink any man under the table and still turn out sharp as a knife in the morning.

'And Clarke? Do you see anything of Clarke?'

'He's on the Ulster Bank team too, attached to us from the Special Branch to give it some depth.' She paused, then added gently: 'Me and him are going out together.'

'Going out?'

'Took me out for dinner, a film. We've been up to the Lyric Theatre. There's a great play there you should see. *We Do It For Love*, by a fellow called Patrick Galvin.'

'Well that's good, Emily.'

'We'll see where it goes.' There was nothing wrong with her and Clarke going out of course, thought McCann. It had been on the cards from the start. Clarke was a handsome lad, quick, would rise up in the new order. He'd been useful to McCann in the past, slipping him information when he needed it, but selectively, never the full picture. Like all the Special Branch men, he could spin an idea like a bright new sixpence, always seemed to win the toss. Better sometimes at guessing which way the coin would fall than McCann ever was. Emily Thompson was bright too, a star in fact and she'd be safer keeping her love life in the force. McCann would need Clarke on his side too, so he didn't let his hurt show.

'Hear tell he's a big wheel at Castlereagh now?'

'To be honest we don't talk about that much. He keeps a lot of that to himself.'

'What do you talk about then?'

'Kitchen units,' she said suddenly and laughed the old infectious laugh he remembered so well from their time together back at Division.

'You two moving in together then?'

'No way. We're both doing our places up. It's the overtime that pays for it, the war dividend so it is.'

'Ah dear God,' said McCann, unlocking at home later that evening, stepping in to the darkened hallway, pausing to listen for a moment with his head on one side before flicking on the lights and going into the galley kitchen, dropping the heavy bundle of files he'd still to read down on the counter, switching on the electric kettle. He made himself a last pot of tea, slipped through into the living room and turned on the television to catch the news. There was more coverage of the bank job. They had finally managed to find the place where the robbers had held the manager's wife. The camera panned across a living room in a chaos of unwashed plates, newspapers, empty bottles, before homing in on the chair where she'd been tied up, with gaffer tape still clinging to the arms. He watched as Inspector Taylor spoke confidently to camera, his hat almost too big for his small head.

'Twelve Million!' said McCann, out loud to himself, thinking it was more money than anyone had in the Province. Enough for whoever had done it to buy themselves tanks and aeroplanes.

He switched off the TV, the screen fading and dying to a tiny point of light.

Then he returned to the old files he had brought home, going through them again. Cases unsolved and abandoned, investigations wound down for lack of staff and time. People had disappeared and there was neither rhyme nor reason to it. Or their bodies had been found, often horrifyingly mutilated. It was as if they'd been caught in some great historical mincer and ground to a pulp. He went to the cabinet, poured himself out the last drop from a bottle of Black Bushmills and started to sift the files again, looking for cases with the same precise, brutal cruelty, the same trademark as that in the case of Raymond Small. Late in the evening he let out a groan of despair as two familiar files once again fell open on the table before him, of two young girls brutally murdered, their cases unsolved. He had been almost there – but fallen at the last hurdle that would have linked the suspect and the crime.

Chapter Two

Inside the Land Rover was still foetid with the cigarette smoke of the night shift, chip wrappers stuffed between the seats. McCann revved the engine, brought the vehicle up to the barriers and tooted the horn, edged into the gates the moment there was an opening, then away into the City Centre traffic, Flannery still silent beside him. Then she said: 'God, the finger off and the arm? That's disgusting, that is, the poor lad.'

McCann scrabbled in his pocket, rootled out a cigarette, lit up.

'You say he'd boots under the bed? Involved with the paramilitaries?'

'His mother said he'd been drinking up the Sceptre the night he vanished, said it was where the hard men go.'

He looked over at her as if he was concerned.

'It's no place for a lady right enough.'

They crossed the bridge. The brown waters of the river Lagan swirled below. On the other side, they swung out onto the dual carriageway towards the Harland and Wolff shipyard, the traffic queuing ahead, the two giant cranes – Samson and Goliath – astride the skyline.

The reception had parquet floors, mahogany desks, a high

ceiling and tall windows throwing sunlight across the paintings of famous ships that adorned the walls.

'I'm Inspector McCann and this is Constable Flannery. We're here to see Mr Ponting.'

The receptionist ushered them over to a waiting area with deep leather sofas, then worked the switchboard till she found the right man. She chatted while they waited for Mr Ponting to arrive: 'Will you be here for the launch? We've the Leonia launching on the 2nd July. It'll be a big day.' They said they'd seen the ship taking shape, that it was great the yard was so busy, agreed that it was something to be proud of in the City.

Eventually they were interrupted by the slap of leather soles across the parquet and a man in a blue pinstripe suit halted in front of them. He was a young man, barely thirty, but already the big Ulster breakfasts were showing in the fullness of his face and the flapping of his unbuttoned suit over the developing paunch. They followed him up some stairs with polished bannisters and ornate newel posts and on through a room with a vaulted ceiling that was filled with men at their drawing boards, a Union Jack hanging across one wall. Beyond the drawing office lay a hangar overlooked by travelling cranes and echoing to the sounds of fabrication. He led them through into an office partitioned off from the main workshop, but with glass windows so he could see everything that was going on outside. Once they were settled, McCann explained why they had come.

'Raymond Small! That's terrible news. I'm very sad to hear that. Murdered, you say? The lads will be devastated. Devastated and angry too.' Ponting explained that Raymond had been a fitter in the machine shop, that his last shift had been the Friday of the week before. He gave them the names of the men on his shift. Flannery leaned forwards frowning, somehow dissatisfied with his response.

'What kind of a fellow was he?' But her question didn't make much sense to Mr Ponting who seemed to have the engineering manager's studied myopia where personal matters were concerned: 'How do you mean?'

'Was he a good worker?'

Ponting pulled his attendance records from a filing cabinet, said that lately he'd been warned for absenteeism, days sick, was edging close to the threshold where formal warnings would be due. But he had no idea why. It wasn't something they were interested in, as a rule. Either a fellow was at work or he wasn't and if he wasn't he'd to take the consequences.

'Any trouble with workmates? Any fights, disputes, complaints?' McCann let her ask the questions, interested, impressed even as Flannery hoped he would be.

'He was a quiet lad,' said Ponting, 'As far as I'm aware.'

'Did you know him well?'

'I know all the lads, all the men too,' he said. 'Keep tabs on all of them.'

'Did he have any special friends? Was he popular?' Ponting thought hard, hesitated.

'There was one incident though,' he said. 'When the lad finished his time. It was just stupid really, one of the initiations they like to do that got a wee bit out of control, so it did. You know boot black, dressing up, broom handles and buckets, Swarfega and that kind of thing. We all had to go through it.' He looked ashamed, trying to avoid explicit descriptions of what had happened.

'And was there ill feeling afterwards?'

'Hard to tell. I'd be surprised if there hadn't been. As I say he was a quiet lad and these kind of fellows tend to pick that up. I put a stop to it, warned the lads involved.'

'What kind of fellows?'

'I don't know, bullies. You get it all the time in the engineering shops, you've to watch out.'

Yes, and everywhere else too, thought Flannery, thinking back to her own experiences as a Catholic police cadet at Armagh; if Swarfega had been available, no doubt they'd have used that on her too.

'We'll need their names.'

'Ah well now it was only a bit of fun. There'd be no offence committed.'

'All the same it'd be a help if we could have the names,' Flannery insisted.

'I'll see what I can do for you. I'll need to get on to personnel for that.'

'Well we can just wait while you do that,' said McCann, wading in to back her up.

When they had the names they thanked him and he led them back out through the machine shop, men pausing in their work, their eyes following Flannery as she passed, their comments inaudible above the noise of the machinery. McCann scanned the names he had been given as they walked along, passed them over to Flannery.

'Means nothing to me,' he said.

'Peter Kemp,' said Flannery, 'And Patrick Kidron too. Raymond's Mother mentioned them both as friends that went up the Sceptre with Raymond.'

41

'Some friends!'

Just as they moved towards the stairs he paused, catching sight of someone in the shadows.

'That fellow over there,' he murmured, inclining his head in the direction of a big man, bare-chested under his blue overalls. 'I know him from somewhere.'

'Where?'

'It'll come to me.'

Outside in the car park, Flannery took a deep breath.

'Thanks for that, Sir,' she said. McCann grunted, not sure what he was being thanked for, and lit up a cigarette. As they were climbing back into the Land Rover he slapped himself on the forehead.

'Crunchy Bar, that's that fellow's name.'

'Why Crunchy Bar?'

McCann hesitated, trying not to describe the noise a body made going through rollers designed to bend shipyard steel.

'Because he killed a fellow in the plate bender.'

And later, back out on the road to Division, he turned to Flannery and said: 'You done well there, good questions, useful answers. Well done.' And Flannery felt a rush of gratitude that someone had recognised her for what she did rather than what she was. It was bad enough joining any police force, but joining *this* police force. Even the name seemed designed to irritate any nationalist; the Royal Ulster Constabulary, with its cap badge with the crown on it. The police had not covered themselves in glory since she had joined up and the worse it got, the more her people took it out on Catholic officers. They were shot at home in their beds, on their way to work, like Protestant RUC men too, but maybe more so because they'd

42

be easier targets, living in Republican areas, seen as traitors, spies, turncoats. In the year since Flannery had joined there'd been many killed or intimidated out of the force, so McCann's praise meant a lot.

'Raymond! That's proper tragic. He was a lovely lad,' said Mrs Kemp, her face softening a little around its granite edges as she settled in one of the chairs that were clustered tightly round a stone grate. Family photos were arrayed across the mantelpiece. A small occasional table with a doily on it and some dried flowers in a vase stood in one corner, but the room smelt musty with underuse. On the way in Flannery had glimpsed a lad in a tracksuit in the kitchen, smelt frying bacon in the hallway.

'They were at school together you know.' She went to the mantelpiece and picked a photo out from amongst the clutter. 'This here's Raymond,' she said, 'With my Peter.' A football team of lads in their striped shirts, long baggy shorts, legs still thin and knobbly with their arms around each other's shoulders. 'They were in the first eleven together at the Model School.'

'Do you mind if I have a word with Peter then?'

'No problem,' she said. But when she went to fetch him, the back door was open and the lad had gone.

Flannery ran out after him into the back alley, ran to the street corner and radio'd for the patrol that had brought her there to drop back and pick her up. As she stood waiting on the doorstep, Mrs Kemp asked: 'What did you say your name was?'

'I didn't,' said Flannery, relieved as she heard the squeal of tyres on the road and the Land Rover swung to the kerbside.

The patrol caught up with Peter Kemp walking fast up the Shankill Road. She asked the driver to pull over and stepped down, the open door blocking his path. He was out of breath, wearing just a T shirt and jeans, with a pair of unlaced trainers without socks.

'Peter. Just a word,' she said. He glanced up and down the street, as if gauging whether he might be able to run for it or look for assistance.

'Peter, I want to ask about Raymond Small.' The lad hesitated. Two passers-by had halted to watch the confrontation. 'We can have you brought into Division for questioning, or we can just go for a wee drive somewhere nice and quiet. Which of them is it to be?' One of the members of the patrol had climbed down too, was hitching his trousers ready for any rough and tumble that might be needed. She nodded towards the open door and Peter Kemp climbed in, Flannery following, sitting beside him.

'I'm sorry to hear about Raymond,' she began. 'It must be upsetting.'

'Aye it was.' It was what she would have expected, from a lad that age unable to process such a terrible event. But also what she might expect from someone with something to hide.

There was silence, other than the noise of the engine and the windscreen wipers going backwards and forwards, the driver staring straight ahead. Flannery was conscious of the two other men listening, waiting for her to slip up, maybe even amused at her first steps as a detective.

'So, you were friends?' Then there came a grunt that could have been either yes or no.

'I saw you boys played in the same team. You must have

won a cup or two?'

'We did.' More silence, while they turned off up the Antrim road, more suburban, one of the few neutral places left.

'We could take a walk,' she suggested. 'I'd be grateful for your time.'

She told the driver to park up under the shadow of Cave Hill, at the end of a long street of prosperous houses, overhung by plane trees, told the patrol she'd call when she was done. Together they strolled up towards the castle grounds.

'Do you ever come up here?' she asked him. Now that he was alone with her he had become shy, she was amused to see. It was not just the natural reserve he would have with a policewoman but the shyness of a man with a woman he didn't know. Away from his people, his gang, he was strangely unmanned. That had been her intention in taking him away from the Shankill. 'We'll go up to the castle and then we can talk as we go.'

He said nothing, their feet scuffing on the loose stones on the path. He had a shock of unruly ginger hair, a big, formless face, fleshy and freckled, with a thick nose, a small puckered mouth, with large hands that swung by his side as he walked, like he found it hard to keep at Flannery's pace. He was a good foot taller than her, so he had to lean down to hear what she was saying.

'After you left school, what did you two lads do?'

'We both went down to Harland and Wolff.'

'What do you do for them?'

'I'm a riveter.' So that explained his physique. He walked with a slight prehensile stoop.

'Hear you were involved in some rough and tumble up

there, is that right?' He shrugged, and said: 'Ach it was only a joke. A wee bit of fun.'

'And how did it end?' Flannery started to dig, to let him know he was a suspect, put him under pressure, not to let him off the hook.

'One of the older fellows stepped in and told us to wise up. Then it got reported and Ponting got involved.' His voice had risen at the memory of that injustice, at the prospect that his involvement in it might put him in the frame.

'You still go out with Raymond though, I gather?'

'From time to time,' he said.

'And on the night of 10th April? Saturday night?'

'We went up to the Sceptre,' he said, halting to light a cigarette, his hand cupped against the wind, head on one side, eyes crafty through the smoke before he straightened up and took a deep draw.

'What time did you get there?'

'Half seven.'

'Who'd you go with?' But he didn't answer. Belfast Castle, with its grey walls and turrets, loomed over them and the view beyond, as its builders had intended.

'This is some place,' he said. They took a seat outside against the wall, from where they could look down on the shipyard.

'George Turnbull, Robert Thatcher, Bill McNicholl, Patsy Kidron,' he suddenly reeled off a list of names, as if the fresh air and the unfamiliar location had cleared his head of some rheum that had prevented him speaking, like he was opening up an address book for her.

'And you have any idea what could have become of him?'

'No Missus, I don't,' he said, and he took another deep draw, holding the smoke in, squinting down at the distant green of County Down and the blue grey of the Mournes in the distance.

'That last night you were up at the Sceptre with him did anything happen that seemed out of the ordinary?'

His right foot began to tap up and down nervously.

'Was Raymond with you all night?'

'He was.'

'What did you do?'

'Played pool, watched the footie, had a few pints. Finished at closing and then we went home.'

'What time?'

'Closing time. Eleven o'clock.'

'And where did you leave Raymond?'

'At his corner.'

'And that was all was it Peter?'

'I've told you. I've told you,' he repeated almost angrily, flung his cigarette away and started to walk away from her.

'Was there an argument Peter? In the Sceptre?' She hurried to catch up with him, throwing her questions at his back. 'You've not to say anything. Just nod if there was.' His pace accelerated as he tried to shrug her off, but in his hurried exit she thought she saw a faint jerk of the head, downwards as if in agreement and then he broke into a run and left her behind.

'There's two people been waiting to see you,' said the Desk Sergeant. McCann peered through the one way mirror into reception. A well dressed middle-aged couple were standing there, unwilling to share a bench with the ordinary punters, both looking directly at him like they could see straight through the glass.

'Mr and Mrs Deevery,' said the Desk Sergeant. 'They were most particular that it was you they wanted to see.' Of course, thought McCann, who'd recognised them with a dull shock as the parents of the man he'd tried to put inside for the murders of two girls. It was the case that haunted him, that sense of unfinished business; if Deevery hadn't killed the girls, who had? He stepped forward, opened the door, reached out a hand in greeting: 'Mr Deevery! Mrs Deevery! There's a surprise now.'

'How are you son?' The man shook his hand, perfunctory, limp, like contact with McCann's flesh could have spread some disease. Behind him stood Mrs Deevery, dressed in a smart black suit, high heels, a wide hat with a veil, lipsticked, like she'd come from a funeral. She came up to McCann, lifted her veil for him, her eye glassy as it dared him to kiss her powdered cheek. They were familiar folk from his home town, but aged and distanced from him by events.

'Come on inside and I'll get you both a cup of tea,' said McCann, his mind speeding meanwhile as to why the parents of a man he'd tried to put inside should be so keen to see him.

Then when they were settled in the canteen, with the tea he had poured left untouched on the table before them they started to explain: 'You should go and see our son,' said Mr Deevery. 'He asks for you, you know.'

'Asks for me?'

'He's a changed man now. Getting the treatment he needs. He says he's something he could tell you.' Mr Deevery sighed. 'We can all go down the wrong track, you know.'

And McCann saw Mrs Deevery watching him like she was checking her husband was saying what she had told him to say. He could smell her perfume, a cloying artificial odour across the table.

'You'll go and see him? He's in Purdysburn right now. Ward 2B. They've visiting every Tuesday and Thursday.'

'Changed in what way?' asked McCann, trying to keep the disbelieving sneer out of his voice.

'Go and see him, then you'll see,' said Mr Deevery

'Please,' said Mrs Deevery. 'There's not many will visit after what you said he'd done.'

'It'd be a reconciliation, some kind of peace,' said Mr Deevery. 'For the stress you put him under with those allegations of yours.'

'I didn't put him under stress,' snapped McCann. 'He done that himself and was already in free fall when I got onto him.' Were they asking him to apologise? He wouldn't do that because if Deevery hadn't killed the girls himself, he'd been involved all the way through.

'All the same son, we'd be pleased if you'd see him. He's maybe got something he'd like to say to you.'

Deevery? A fellow with links to the most grievous of crimes, a bent copper who had gone over the edge. Maybe he'd know a name or two of someone prone to chopping and dicing, some ideas about who had attacked Raymond Small? Maybe he would have changed, had time to reflect, to discover and deal with his conscience.

'OK, I'll do it,' said McCann and ground his cigarette out in the ashtray, stood up, thanked them for coming in.

Afterwards McCann bought himself a pint in Hannigan's and took out the evening Belfast Telegraph, perched on the high bar stool with a reflection of the top of his head with its bald spot looking back at him from the angled mirror behind the bar. He flicked over the front page, to find a picture of Inspector Taylor at a press conference on the Ulster bank job, looking the part in his full uniform, making some point decisively. They'd issued a statement with the serial numbers of the stolen banknotes. It would be like a reverse lottery, thought McCann; if you got a note with one of the serial numbers as like as not you would end up a suspect too. So he tore the page out with the numbers, folded it in his wallet. Then when he'd downed the pint and had a final cigarette he strolled out to get the bus home, like a normal person on a normal night, except that McCann didn't do normal nights, didn't look forward to them; the baleful flicker of the television in the empty living room, waiting for sleep to release him. So he caught the number eleven bus instead of the number two and went to the Sceptre instead.

The Sceptre stood at the end of a half derelict street like some kind of fortress holding out against invaders. The windows were boarded up, the paintwork peeling, barbed wire wound up the drainpipes. At the top of the flagpole a fresh Ulster flag hung limp and damp, twitching in the cold stray gusts like a fresh corpse on a gibbet. It was dark by the time he got there, rivulets of rainwater falling from the broken guttering above his head. The three men on the door were huddled back under the porch. He had a glimpse of bulging black leather jackets and white faces before the flashlight in his face blinded him.

'What d'you want?' The biggest of the three stood

forward, blocking his path.

'Sammy McGuigan said I'd to be let in.' McCann knew that Sammy's name usually did the trick in places you'd rather not be in. He was a big fish in the murky Shankill sea, and McCann still had business with him from time to time, most of it unfinished. There was an invisible nod in the darkness, the sound of a double tap on the door and bolts being drawn back, a burst of noise and light and McCann was shoved forwards as if through a human airlock into the brightness of the bar inside, like inside some tropical fruit that was hard on the outside, but soft and exotic inside with the bar at its centre, brightly lit, besieged by drinkers pushing forwards with banknotes held aloft. The white-coated bar staff were working furiously to deal with the early evening rush. McCann moved in cautiously, hoping to merge into the back of the crowd, to observe things before he was recognised, to have a moment to collect his thoughts, but no sooner had he slipped himself into the back of the queue than a voice said in his ear: 'You've some balls coming in here, Inspector.' And on his other side, someone had gripped his arm just above the elbow. 'If you'll come upstairs there's a free drink waiting. We've always a free drink for Sammy's men.'

He found himself propelled up the stairs and through into a darkened room with a well-lit stage. The moment he stepped inside McCann knew he'd made a mistake. A table had been set up on the stage and as he entered three men with balaclavas climbed up and seated themselves behind it, as if the first act of some play was starting, and McCann was the main actor who hadn't learned his lines, didn't even know which play was being performed. In the shadows an audience was already assembled, an expectant hush descending, a crush of latecomers from the bar below crowding in behind.

'What do you want?' A rude, hard voice from beneath the balaclava.

'Inspector McCann. C Division. What's going on, lads?'

'What kind of name's that? Sounds like a Fenian name.' This from a voice on the left.

'We're looking into the disappearance of a lad called Raymond Small,' he said loudly enough for everyone to hear.

'What's your first name, Inspector?' From a voice on the right, ignoring his question.

'Michael.'

'Michael as in Mick? Inspector? Am I hearing you right? An Inspector in the Royal Ulster Constabulary called Mick McCann?' The master of ceremonies had adopted a sarcastic, disbelieving tone. The audience began to titter.

'What're you lads up to?' said McCann, but his voice had a tinny quality. It was as if he hadn't spoken at all.

'No, Mick you don't understand,' said the man on the right. 'It's us that ask the questions and it's you that answer them.'

'We're just having fun,' whispered a helpful voice in his ear, from right up close.

'Are you hot Inspector or what?' said another voice.

'Maybe the Inspector needs to take his coat off and make himself comfortable' His coat was suddenly pulled down over his arms, pinning him.

'Aye, and his trousers!' a voice from the audience, a gale of laughter. McCann found himself upended, his shoes pulled off, then his trousers, struggling, trying to hold onto his dignity.

'Come on fellows,' he started, but it was too late.

'Not too bold now McCann. Let's see your bollocks.'

Pulled towards a seat at the front, facing the men in balaclavas, caught in the brief flare of a camera flash, McCann turned his face away.

'Tell us about Raymond Small. Did he get caught up in this circus too?' he growled.

'Ah now Mick it's not a circus. That's not what it is. Do you see any lions, any giraffes, any tigers? Any performing animals at all, other than yourself, that is?' Another gale of laughter.

'What have you done to Raymond Small? Night of the tenth of April.' McCann repeated doggedly.

'There's been no one of that name here at all. Has there, fellows?' A murmur of agreement greeted the chair's question, a ripple of 'nos' and 'never seen him.'

'So now you've got your answer Mick, why don't you just get the fuck away from here and let us honest decent law-abiding folk go about our business, without molestation and harassment?'

And then there was a huddle of men around him and he was manhandled away down the stairs, pushed out into the street without his shoes, before he'd any chance to identify anyone in the throng, his trousers thrown out after him into the wet.

Outside, McCann pulled on his trousers, pulled his coat over his shoulders and plodded along, the rain soaking through his socks. It had been a stupid thing to do, taking risks, but without the risks, you'd get nothing, thought McCann. They were taking risks too, overconfident they were. If they thought there was impunity, they'd soon slip up. He sheltered in a doorway, pulled his hat from his pocket, found his lighter and cigarettes. It wasn't complete impunity though; they'd not killed him, not harmed him yet, only his pride and there wasn't a great deal of that left. He drew on the cigarette. They would think they were hurting him, but didn't know that he was beyond hurt. Someone beyond hurt knew no fear, only hope of his own release.

'What happened to your shoes, feller?'

He was glad of the warmth in the back seat of the black cab, glad when it swung away out of the Shankill and joined the traffic flowing away out of the city along the motorway. The taxi driver eyed him warily through the rear-view mirror.

'Big night,' explained McCann, feigning intoxication. He peered down into the gloom – mock unsteady, mock baffled – at his sodden feet in their wet socks. The driver smiled consolingly at him in the mirror, well used to such late night losses.

'Well I'll get you back in a minute Sir,' he said, flicking the radio on, playing 'Don't go breaking my heart', the dark water of Belfast Lough briefly glinting in the occasional reflected glare of headlights from the motorway. It was all nearly normal, apart from the wet feet and the loss of the shoes, thought McCann. Good pair too, kept the winter wet off, with Goodyear soles. He'd get himself a new pair at the weekend, if he ever had one. Make do with his number two's, the brown pair for now. He'd had enough of the black anyway.

The cab swung round onto the gravel in front of his house, the headlights showing the rain still slanting down, the driver pulling up as near to the door as he could manage so McCann didn't have far to go barefoot. He paid the driver and dipped out of the cab, found himself standing on the step under the porch, fiddling for his keys and swearing under his breath while the cab swung away with a cheerful toot of farewell, leaving him in darkness. The door swung open and he stepped over the circulars that had come in during the day, through into the kitchen, flicked on the light and put the kettle on. Sat down, peeled the socks off his feet, shrugged the coat off while the kettle boiled, went to the cupboard and got out the tea bags, sugar, sniffed the milk from the fridge. And when he'd the steaming mug on the counter in front of him he turned to the phone, getting a number from his black book.

'Sammy?' he said, hearing the unfamiliar sound of an answerphone. 'You and me have some urgent things to discuss.'

Chapter Three

McCann awoke before the day was fully up, a grey light filtering through behind the cheap curtains, the wind tapping something against the window as if requiring his attention. He opened his eyes in the gloom, fumbled for his watch on the bedside table, flicked on the light. It was six in the morning. He was still tired, but unable to rest. So he swung his legs out over the side of the bed, stood, stretched to take the tension from his spine, made his way into the kitchen for a cup of tea and the first cigarette of the day. He had to see Paper Clip to ask for support to clear out the Sceptre and show those boys who had the upper hand. Then he'd to catch up with Flannery, get an update on progress, check she was coping, before getting out to see Sammy McGuigan. Sammy should know what had gone wrong at the Sceptre, maybe had even ordered it himself.

With a mug of tea in hand and a cigarette smouldering comfortingly nearby, he smacked a chunk of lard into the frying pan, watched it sizzle and melt on the hot stove, dropped in three rashers and a couple of pork sausages, let them crisp up while he finished his cigarette. Then he slipped them out onto the plate he'd set to warm, did a fried egg and two slices of bread in the fat that was left. Still in his dressing gown he carried the plate through to the dining table, opened the curtains on the new day and ate, watching the clouds piling past the window, hearing the occasional splatter of rain on the glass.

McCann caught Paper Clip on the stairs at Division, told him he'd something urgent to discuss with him. The Superintendent half turned, without pausing on the steps up to his office: 'See if Deirdre can give you a slot.'

'It'll only take a minute,' said McCann, hustling up behind him, on his heels on the narrow stairway. When they reached Deirdre's desk that guarded the door to Paper Clip's office she wasn't there and the Superintendent fumbled for the keys, McCann still standing close.

'She'll be in at nine,' said Paper Clip, then grudgingly relented. 'OK, come in then man if you must, but make it quick. I've a full morning on the quarterlies to get through.'

McCann felt the chill as he entered the room, as if the heating had been off for months, as if Paper Clip required no normal human comforts. He hung his coat, went to his desk, began to unpack papers from his brief case, arranging them neatly across the surface of his desk.

'Well?' he said.

'Just to let you know we're making progress Sir,' McCann started with the good news, knowing there was a thirst for that amongst the brass. 'We've identified the arm, linked it to that Raymond Small like you suggested. That was a good hunch you had Sir, that the two were connected.' Trowel it on, the flattery, before hitting him with the bad news next.

'That's one good thing then, at least that Mr Small will be off the missing persons tally now. It'll make the figures look a bit sharper.' And Paper Clip's nose went down, McCann could see his fingers tapping away at a desk calculator, already making the necessary adjustments to the data.

'Seems like the lad was last seen up at the Sceptre Bar on the Shankill. I've got Flannery out tracing his movements the night he vanished. But when I went up there to investigate myself last night I was assaulted. It seems like there's a big paramilitary operation going on up there that's getting out of hand. We'll need to close it down, bring in witnesses, get forensics in.'

'Assaulted, McCann? How did that happen?' McCann described his visit to the Sceptre, but Paper Clip stopped him halfway through. His hands flicked around on the desktop, finding the folder he was looking for, expertly riffling the corners of the pages.

'You mean you went up there by yourself without support, without completing a risk assessment? There's no RA2 come across my desk, nothing here at all McCann.'

'Would it have been OK for them to beat me up if I'd had an RA2 Sir?'

'It would have made it better, yes, if there were questions afterwards. If you'd been killed for example, we'd have been able to show that we'd followed procedure. In the event of any action against us by your bereaved relatives, well our solicitors would have had a leg to stand on. But without an RA2 you see what a difficult position we would have been in, McCann. We could have seemed negligent in matters of your safety, quite unfairly of course because it's you that's been negligent in this case. But I as senior officer would have been held responsible for your recklessness. I don't suppose you even thought of that.'

'So you'll approve a raid if I fill in the RA2, Sir?'

'I'm not saying that, McCann. The RA2 application will be a first step. We'll need to clear it with Taylor and the crime team at Castlereagh. As it's a murder enquiry now they'll need to take over. We'll need to clear it with intelligence too, maybe request military backup. But that's the last thing I'll be doing as 'The Way Ahead' is quite clear about the need for the RUC to handle frontline policing I'm afraid.'

'You mean that's what the British want, to have our people killed rather than theirs?'

Paper Clip ignored McCann's remark: 'And that means we'd better handle Mr Small ourselves.'

'So there's to be no support for a raid? We're just going to let these guys get away with it are we?'

'Put up a case, McCann, talk to Taylor. Follow procedures and I'll be the first to back you up. It may take a little time, but it'll be better in the end. And don't forget, I'll be right behind you.'

Yes, thought McCann, that's where he'd always be.

McCann burst out of Paper Clip's office, clattered away down the stairs to the dead files room, pushed open the door to find Flannery already at work, a mug of tea steaming on the table in front of her. She had acquired an electric kettle set up on a steel tray, together with a couple of plates, a packet of biscuits, and a freshly laundered dishcloth hung over the back of one of the chairs.

'See you've made yourself comfortable?'

'Someone has to Inspector,' she said, sipping her tea,

looking over the rim of her cup at him, maybe sensing his mood.

'Went up to that Sceptre Bar,' he began. 'Not a pleasant night either.'

'Find anything out?'

'Never got the chance, they gave me the heave-ho,' said McCann ruefully, rubbing his chin with bewilderment at the memory, even a little ashamed. 'And you?'

Flannery filled him in on her interview with Peter Kemp, the details of Small's last night she'd managed to glean. She explained she was still working through the other contacts: 'They seem afraid,' she said.

'Well, who isn't?' said McCann, then asked if she was coping and when she said she was fine, he told her to keep working through the contacts while he went out to see Sammy McGuigan.

'Who's Sammy?' she asked.

'Sammy?' said McCann. 'Sammy's a monster.'

Sammy McGuigan's villa was built in the Spanish style, single storied with shuttered windows, white walls, a low red-tiled roof. The villa was set in two acres of land that sloped down showing a wide view of Belfast Lough. The garden was newly planted on either side of a flight of white marble steps leading up to the front door, the path illuminated by fake Victorian lampposts. A new Mercedes was parked in front of the house. McCann paused for breath before ringing the bell, noticing the razor wire along the perimeter fence and scowling up at what looked like a camera fixed on his face.

'Well, well Inspector, long time no see.' Sammy McGuigan

had lost some weight since the last time McCann had seen him, had added hair to his pate, but the flesh under his chin still hung white and loose like from a chicken wing.

'Nice place, Sammy. It must have cost you a bob or two?'

'Hundred thousand, Inspector, actually. Come in and take a look,' he said, ushering McCann in, shouting out: 'Amy! Can you get us two coffees?'

'Ok.' A woman's voice came from a kitchen far away at the back of the house. The living room was long, with windows at either end, dominated by a modern granite fireplace in which shimmered an artificial log fire. McCann settled himself with a squeak and a slither on the leather sofa. A naked ceramic woman lounged on the coffee table between the two men. When Amy came in, she moved it to one side to make way for the tray with the coffee. She was tall and maybe half McGuigan's age.

'Amy's a grand girl,' McGuigan said, when she had left the room.

Did McGuigan think of her in the same way as he did his artworks, wondered McCann? Were they both objects to be acquired and handled for his pleasure, to be admired by his acquaintances, to demonstrate his importance, trophies from his apparent dominance of the jungle in which he lived?

There was a brief silence while they sipped their coffee.

'I got your call, McCann, been expecting you.'

'I been down the Sceptre looking for a lad called Raymond Small and they gave me a roughing over. It wasn't what I was expecting,' began McCann. Though he was still angry, he tried to keep it light so Sammy was at his ease, pretending it was some kind of social call. McGuigan adopted a professional manner, watching McCann's face as he spoke, like a general practitioner considering what prescription might work for a patient. He seemed concerned, like McCann had mentioned a symptom of some serious disease that he'd not been expecting.

'And you gave my name at the door?'

'I did,' said McCann.

'Ok,' said McGuigan, like he'd grasped the details, knew what was wrong and knew the right medicine too.

'But what about that other matter first?' McGuigan lowered his voice, though there was no danger of his being overheard, leaning closer.

'Depends,' said McCann.

'There's no prosecution possible with the girl dead. My solicitor said so.' McGuigan's face was close to McCann's now, his mouth close to McCann's ear, his voice intimate in McCann's head, stirring painful memories for McCann; of Sammy's abuse of one of the victims in his last case.

'You may be right, for now Sammy,' conceded McCann, like he was sucking bitter lemons.

McGuigan shifted his empty coffee cup back carefully onto the tray, seeming unhappy with the way McCann was bringing him problems when it was meant to be the other way round, or a two-way exchange at the very least.

'Raymond Small, just a young lad, last seen up the Sceptre Sammy. Someone chopped his finger off, then his arm, some dirty beast that had it in for him. I thought you were the fellow in control down there?'

McGuigan didn't answer. McCann seemed to calculate something for a moment and then stood up as if their business was concluded.

'Aye, all right Sammy, we'll turn the Sceptre over for you, deal with the fellows down there if you can't.'

'You'd need City Hall on your side.'

'I'm going up there next,' said McCann, standing up. 'Make it a licensing matter.' McGuigan started to smile, a quick, eery twitch that he quickly stopped. 'But that'll be a first won't it? You and me on the same side.'

'Makes your blood run cold, doesn't it McCann? You and me, strange bedfellows.'

'I'd never get in bed with you, Sammy'

'Nor me with you, McCann. I'm no bender, me.' And McGuigan released an earthy, crude chuckle, putting a hand on McCann's elbow, guiding him towards the back door.

'Here, McCann I've something to show you before you go. It'll only take a minute.' McCann allowed himself to be led back out through the kitchen, with its floor of white limestone slabs, its country pine cupboards, the new extractor fan humming in the ceiling. Amy was already putting the coffee cups and saucers in the dishwasher, giving McCann a brief glance that was hard to read as they passed by.

Sammy unlocked the back door, pulling back the bolts, the fortress he'd built doubling as a prison. McCann found himself standing outside at the back of the house, the wind chilly on his face, the trees along the boundary fence tossing like horse's manes. He followed Sammy up a newly laid concrete path to the garage, entering through a side door. He was already ascending a wooden ladder ahead. McCann suddenly smelt a familiar smell as he climbed up behind him.

'Y'see there's a few things I've taken from my old life,' said Sammy, gesturing around the pigeon loft, the birds purring and cooing in their cages under the felted eaves.

'It's all brand-new McCann. I'm in for the North Coast Classic you know? Y'see this one?' And he opened a cage and softly cradled a bird in his big hands, bringing her out for McCann, the bird ducking its neck away from the light, McGuigan soothing its feathers. 'She's a beauty McCann, a real racer. I call her the Maid of Ulster.'

'She's a fine bird right enough Sammy,' said McCann, not quite believing the transformation he was seeing. Maybe the pigeons soothed McGuigan's urges, or blurred the memory of evil acts with acts of kindness, albeit only to birds.

'And there's this too,' said McGuigan and reached under a cloth, pulled up a .45, flicked off the safety catch and pointed it in McCann's face.

'Jesus,' said McCann and ducked away involuntarily. McGuigan laughed.

'Come on McCann. You and me go way back. I'd only use it if I was pressed.'

McCann took a few minutes before his meeting was due, to start to stroll around the garden outside the City Hall, which reared in gleaming marble untouched by the surrounding mayhem. While some Republicans called it 'tin-pot dictator pomp', it was nonetheless impressive, never mind that the building had almost bankrupted the city. He paused for a moment to look up at the bronze statue of Harland, one of the founders of the great shipyard. A waistcoat and watch chain was buttoned under his morning suit, a ship perched in the crook of his elbow like it was a favourite pet. Harland had been an MP and Mayor of the City. That had always been the way with power in the Province, it tended to multiply itself, then coagulate, then finally solidify. McCann shook his head to clear the thought and ground a cigarette out beneath the heel of his boot, realising the time had slipped by and he was running late.

He jogged up the steps and into the City Hall, the pigeons wheeling and ducking overhead. At the top there were two fellows in a parody of police uniform going through bags, patting people down for weapons and behind them out of sight another two fellows from close protection in flak jackets, armed with automatic weapons. McCann recognised one of them, nodded familiarly over to him as he presented his warrant card, but there wasn't a flicker of recognition back, just a blank middle-distance stare that passed a couple of inches above his head.

'Councillor Rabbie Smith? He'll be up the stairs, committee room A. He's waiting for you.'

The central corridor was like the nave of a church, with stained glass in every window, punctuated by marble statues, solid doors leading off into the committee rooms. There was a low murmur of conversation, groups of men holding beige files, briefcases, the mutter of their whispered discussions could have been in some ancient City State where worthy burghers resolved all issues of concern. But McCann knew it wasn't quite like that now. Outside the City Hall the place was in permanent turmoil. For the moment the Unionists still had a grip over every decision, but inexorably, year by year the numbers were slipping as the Catholic population grew. The structure was still there, but its time was coming to an end. Hadn't their Parliament at Stormont already gone, been swept away in an act of reforming madness by the British? And hadn't that given the green light to Republicans to press on, each concession only stoking a thirst for more and a harsher and harsher push back from those who didn't want to lose control, from men like the new Chair of the Licensing Committee that McCann was due to see.

'Inspector McCann, hullo, hullo, come on in,' said Councillor Rabbie Smith. McCann was surprised to find that he was barely half his own age, with curling black hair already receding over a high forehead, but thick set, with square shoulders that pushed at his grey suit, red socks vibrant over tight, highly polished shoes. He shook hands in a business-like way, almost cursorily and McCann noted his heavy gold ring and the tattoos across the knuckles.

'We need to have a wee chat, Inspector,' said Smith, turning on him suddenly, before he'd even had a chance to explain anything. McCann had heard the phrase 'wee chat' too many times. It was a phrase he'd used himself, when he'd bad news to impart, or a warning to give, sometimes both.

'We've been asked to investigate serious crime at the Sceptre on the Shankill. We've had an assault on an officer, a lad disappeared.' He started fast like a salesman about to put his foot in a door that was already closing.

'I'm sorry about that, but I'm afraid it's going on everywhere Inspector,' said Rabbie, a touch too cocky for McCann's liking, perching himself on the edge of his green baize desk, swinging a polished toe, like he'd already heard what had happened and didn't care.

'We'll need to take action,' said McCann 'And we'll be wanting your support.'

'What kind of action?' Rabbie's tone had sharpened, like inaction was much preferred. The old ways died hard in Belfast.

'Immediate withdrawal of the licence as a first step.'

Rabbie slid off the desk at that, towards McCann.

'If I was you I'd be looking up the Falls Road first. There's shebeens aplenty up there Inspector, illegal drinking, raising funds for the IRA. And you fellows are turning a blind eye to that. And what do you mean about it being a first step? What other step had you in mind Inspector?'

'I'm afraid I can't tell you that.'

'You'd better not fuck with any of our businesses.'

'Businesses, is it?' said McCann. 'Is that what you call them?'

'What else would you call them?'

'I'd say they were rackets,' said McCann. 'Plain and simple rackets. Why else would they assault me when I was up there?'

Smith laughed.

'Ah come on, McCann you can't just waltz in there and expect everyone to co-operate. With that attitude it's no wonder they took offence and gave you a hard time. You've to have due process, just suspicions, a warrant maybe.'

'We think a fellow was killed up there.'

'How do you know that?'

'We found an arm.' McCann began to explain, but realised that it still didn't amount to much; just Peter Kemp saying Raymond was last seen up at the Sceptre, his arm later found in a bin lorry that had done the rounds of all of the Shankill. So he backed off: 'Have you had other reports? Concerns being raised at licensing?'

'Come on now Inspector, what is this, some kind of fishing expedition against a legitimate business? The licensed trade is a big employer in the city. We in the Council have a strong partnership, which brings mutual benefits to everyone. There's little enough work to go round, little enough entertainment.'

'And Sammy McGuigan? You and him still on good terms?'

'McGuigan? Why wouldn't we be?'

'What's going on up there at the Sceptre, Rabbie? Why are you covering for them?'

'I'm not hiding anything, the licensed trade are just aware of their rights, McCann. And it's you that should be protecting them, not giving them grief. It's hard enough to do business in this city, to make an honest buck, without the likes of you interfering, poking your noses in.'

'Well it's more than poking I'll be doing, Rabbie,' said McCann. 'And I'd prefer to do it with your say-so. We've a lad vanished up there, assaults on an officer. I'll not let that pass. You're either on the side of order or you're not.'

'There'll be no order, McCann until there's victory for our people. Ulster is under threat and every loyal and decent person has to join that struggle.'

'That doesn't change the fact that a lad has vanished up there and an officer's been assaulted. We'll be going in one way or the other,' repeated McCann.

'You just do that and see where it gets you.'

'Where will it get me? Is that a threat?'

'It's not a threat, it's a realistic assessment. I'm trying to help you Inspector. I'd not like to see the Constabulary losing good men needlessly.'

'Needlessly, is it?' said McCann. 'Would you say it was needless if it was your son or daughter that we were looking for?'

'The defence of Ulster and its people comes first,' Smith said pompously, glancing at the clock, then stepping back behind his desk, already starting to check his diary for his next appointment.

Afterwards McCann slipped through into a café tucked away amongst the City Centre shopping streets, ordered a pot of tea and selected a nice piece of fruit cake with icing on top, lit a cigarette. But he hadn't the appetite, the way the day was going was not what he'd expected.

When Clarke appeared he was brisk, snapped out an order for a coffee, sat himself down opposite McCann, almost sprawling in his seat. He wore a casual, short raincoat over a new suit with a waistcoat tightly buttoned, a crisp new shirt, new black brogues that glinted in the café's fluorescent lighting.

'I've not got long McCann,' he said, flicking his cuff back to check the heavy watch on his wrist. It looked to McCann like the kind of watch James Bond might have, capable of working on the moon and at depths of thousands of feet.

'How's tricks up there with the Branch in Castlereagh? See anything of Munton?' asked McCann, the old way, slowing the pace, bringing it down to the personal before starting on the real business, the rural way that came naturally to him, to put them both at ease, though ease was the last thing McCann felt on that particular afternoon with Clarke.

'Cracking on, Inspector, I'd say. And Munton, he's fine.'

'And how's Emily getting on?'

'She's well.' McCann tried to gauge the meaning of that, to get through Clarke's jaunty confidence. 'I hear tell you two are an item these days?' Inside, he was wound up at the idea that Emily Thompson too was slipping away from him, not that she had ever been his.

'Ah well I'd not say that exactly,' said Clarke, a master at the art of saying nothing.

Clarke looked around himself at the almost empty coffee shop, too late in the day to be crowded, checking they'd not be overheard, fiddling with the packets of sugar in their holder on the tabletop.

'Look, what can I do for you, Inspector?'

'There's a lad disappeared up the Sceptre, on the Shankill.'

McCann saw Clarke slip into professional mode, like some steel shutters were being pulled down over a shop to keep it safe at night. 'Who're the boys up there now? You had any dealings?'

'Well there'd be a lot of activity there, your friend Sammy McGuigan for a start.'

'He's not a friend now,' said McCann.

'Isn't he?' said Clarke and started to fiddle with McCann's box of matches, flicking it round on the tabletop end to end, till McCann took it off him. Clarke's eyes narrowed and he moved closer to McCann. 'We've been told to play them along, like play the long game.'

'The long game, what's that?' McCann didn't like the idea of the long game, though he knew what it meant. It was a game played when you'd lost every other game, but maybe it was the only game possible.

'Had a lad go missing on a night out. Chopped up, just got the arm out of the transfer station.' In the corner the Juke Box started up, McCann wincing with irritation, but it gave the opportunity for Clarke to lean closer still.

'I'd say that would be the IRA, Belfast brigade. They've an intelligence section that's upped their game now. No more disappearances, that's bad for morale. Like to send a message, they do. They think it's better if you've a body to show everyone, suitably marked. After they've extracted what they need to know.'

'And who's in charge of doing that in Belfast?'

'In the IRA? Can't tell you. That's way above my pay grade.'

'Would Munton know?'

'Maybe but he wouldn't say.' The song wound on. Two teenagers swung their heads in time to the music, mouthing the words behind McCann. He could see the footfall in the street outside dwindling now, dusk falling, the streetlights coming on.

'Any chance it's the other side, the UFF[7] doing their own? He was just a young lad, decent life ahead of him. They chopped his finger off, then the arm, whoever done it. Stunk like hell, Straight up, Clarke, that's what these fellows done. Now will you let us have any names?' Clarke was silent, even a little shocked, just as McCann had intended.

'OK. I'll see what I can do for you Inspector,' he said.

'So you'll know the UFF boys, but not the fellows in the IRA?'

---

[7] UFF – Ulster Freedom Fighters. They were the military wing of the Ulster Defence Association, associated with many sectarian killings.

'I didn't say that, McCann. I just said I couldn't tell you who's in charge of the IRA nutting squad.' He stood up, fumbled for a note in his wallet, scrunched it up and tossed it down on the table in front of McCann.

'No need for that,' said McCann, pushing it back towards him.

'Keep it,' said Clarke, 'I'm sure I owe it you,' and walked away leaving McCann staring after him. A woman who was washing down the tables with a grey cloth unlocked the door to let Clarke out. Except that Clarke had thought of something else to say, clicked his fingers, spun round and came back towards him: 'Just don't be letting your new Constable have any names I give you, OK?' And then he turned on his heel and was away out into the night. McCann ran after him, but when he got out on the street it was in time to see him slam the door on a black BMW which screeched away into the gathering darkness.

Back at Division he caught up with Flannery at the end of the day.

'There's a group of them went up the Sceptre, Sir. I've nearly done them all now and the fellows he worked with.' Piles of her notes, neatly tagged, lay across the desk. The air was hot and dry in the brightly lit room. 'They're sticking together, all got the same story: *up the Sceptre, played pool, watched the footie, had a couple of pints.*'

McCann stretched. Flannery looked tired, her hair astray.

'You must be knackered? Fancy a bite?' he offered.

They found a space at the back of the canteen. The dinner service had ended and there was a clatter of baking trays being rinsed, plates stacked in the washers, the tables cleared and wiped down with just the sugar and napkin dispensers there for tea through the night. McCann got himself a jam doughnut and a pot of tea for them both.

'You got the list of Small's contacts there?' he asked, biting into the doughnut, holding a napkin so the jam didn't go everywhere, while she rummaged out the list from her bag. The names were neatly crossed off, dates and times alongside. McCann paused in his eating long enough to smooth it out on the Formica tabletop.

'Would any of these fellows merit another call, d'you think?' he asked.

'What do you mean, Sir?'

'Good cop, bad cop, all of that.'

'What makes you think I'm the good cop?'

'I didn't say that, Flannery, did I?' McCann chuckled. It was true, he'd been making assumptions about her and she was right to pick it up. 'Just a wee change in emphasis might open up one of these lads for us. Now which one is it to be?'

Flannery thought hard for a moment, then reached and pointed out a name to him.

'Patrick Kidron? OK, I'll rattle his cage for him,' said McCann.

The lounge bar of the Regency Hotel had recently been refitted and the security improved. No expense had been spared inside; dark wood panelling was set off by the velvet curtains and red leather upholstery, gilt on the legs of the tables, gold around the long marble bar top. In the early evening it was already full when Flannery entered and looked around for Emily

Thompson in the crowd, before perching herself on a bar stool to wait. A moment later Thompson appeared and Flannery felt a wave of pleasure, relief even that she'd not be left alone there in the throng, that at last she'd be able to have a proper night out.

'Jesus you're looking very nice,' she said. Emily Thompson had transformed herself, with short skirt, hair dyed blonde, high heels.

'You too,' said Thompson. Flannery was shorter, but she'd fitted herself into tight white jeans, black boots, a silk top. Friends since they'd met at a training event in Enniskillen, Flannery looked up to Thompson for advice, guidance even in dealing with the force and its men, but more than just that, for fun as well. They found two seats together, sat down, called the waiter over.

'What'll you have?'

'Give us one of them Black Bombers.'

'Jesus, whats in that?'

'Black Bush, vodka, gin, rum, blackberry, lime. It's brilliant.'

'Bad day then?'

'You could say that,' said Flannery, unable somehow to shake the memory of Raymond Small's room, the grim silence of his friends, wanting to put work behind her.

'Mines a double Jameson, just ice, no water mind.'

And when the drinks came she said: 'Anyhow, we're out of it for now,' and glanced round the bar like it was the entry point to some fantastical intergalactic journey, taking a deep breath like she was sucking on the oxygen needed for the trip.

After Flannery's third drink, the bar became suffused

with a warm, enveloping glow, an aura of possibilities. The place was rammed, everyone talking so loud it was a roar that drowned out the canned music from the speakers.

'My name's like waving a tricolour isn't it?' Flannery let out a peal of laughter. 'I've been posted to C Division and ended up working the Shankill Road where the name won't endear me to anyone.'

'Do you see anything of McCann down there?'

'McCann? Do you know him then?'

Thompson leaned forward to take a deep slug from the whiskey, while Flannery sucked her cocktail through the straw, draining it down to the cherry at the bottom.

'We were on a hard case together.'

'Looks like he needs some TLC,' prompted Flannery.

'Well who doesn't dear?' Thompson made a joke of it, defensively.

'Everyone seems to steer clear of him, like there's a bad smell off him.'

'Didn't work out for him the way it should have.' She looked around for the waiter again amongst the packed tables, snapping her fingers, ordering up another double Jameson.

They talked about other matters for a while; Flannery's family, Thompson's daughter, until Flannery became wistful: 'I was always good with children,' she said, shrinking everything down to the reduced bar English that could be both heard and understood. 'Not got the fellow yet that I could trust to make me one though.'

'Anything on the horizon?'

'There's always fellows aren't there. It's getting the

right one.'

Thompson laughed and nodded agreement. And then as if on cue two fellows who'd been at the bar watching them sidled up drinks in hand.

'You girls mind if we join you?' asked one. Flannery moved aside before Thompson could protest and the two men sat down either side.

'And what are two lovely girls like you doing all alone on a night like this?'

'We're not alone, thanks,' said Thompson briskly.

'Can I top up them drinks for you ladies?' said the other.

'So, do you come here regular like?'

'Jesus you've to get some better chat-up lines fellows. How about what kind of books do you read? Or a decent joke?' snapped Flannery.

'Books? Ah come on girls, we were just being ironic. We're serious fellows, us.' The fellow beside Flannery was older than her, slightly overweight or maybe it was all muscle that bulged and pushed at his blue suit that shimmered in the light as he moved his hands over the drinks, lighting their cigarettes. He'd strong, heavy lips, a shaving shadow, hair so black it could only have been through the use of dye. A vain fellow maybe, or just someone that liked to look good, liked to look after himself, Flannery thought as she glanced at his hands, looking for the marks left by a wedding ring that maybe even then was secreted in his waistcoat pocket.

'So what's your name?'

'Annabel,' said Flannery.

Both women flashed a collusive smile at each other.

'And what do you do for a living?'

'Have a guess.'

He looked her up and down, his eye running up her legs, lingering on her chest.

'I'd say you're a bookkeeper.'

'Bookkeeper! Is that all? What about you boys. You look like the likely lads on a night out.'

'I'm a solicitor's clerk,' said the tall one. 'My name's Liam.' He held out his hand and they both shook it.

'I'm Dermot. I'm a pipe fitter for the gas board,' said the man.

'And what kind of pipes do you fit, Dermot?' Flannery asked, trying to suppress a giggle that threatened to erupt.

When the man with the dark hair moved closer to her and started to tell jokes, Flannery suddenly found him extremely funny. She was no longer in the RUC. She was someone else completely, not Sinead Flannery either, but some other girl, without the Catholic attached. She was out having a good time, with a capital G and a capital T.

'You fellows are a joke,' she said, catching Emily Thompson's eye giving her a warning look. But Flannery had realised now that everything was temporary, which made it all somehow light and without risk, not worth investing any of herself in, that you'd to seize things while they were there. Emily had warned her once about the mistakes you could make thinking like that. Flannery wondered now if it had been with Inspector McCann those mistakes had been made.

Then Liam came on strong, asking if she'd like to go on somewhere else and she had felt a sudden desire, an abandon. It was what you came out for after all, beneath all the chat and bravado, all of the dressing up and the make-up, what you were after was a fellow that would hold you, protect you, make you safe, then love you over and over until you forgot all about everything else.

Afterwards, she had woken up somewhere up the Antrim Road. She was in a flat Liam shared with a couple of other fellows. He'd a tiny room, so small her feet had touched the wall. She'd had to get dressed in the toilet too, because the bed took up all the space and he was still asleep with one white arm folded across his face, like he was dead too, except for his breathing.

She spoke to Emily on the phone later in the morning.

'How did you get on then? Those fellows were right "head-the-balls" weren't they?'

'More balls than head,' said Flannery, fingering the slip of paper with Liam's number on it.

Chapter Four

'Patsy Kidron is it?' McCann was standing just out of sight, not on the step exactly, but looming up as Kidron came out of his house, ready to give a grip of the elbow if he started to twist away, McCann's other hand pulling the front door closed behind him so there'd be no interference from inside.

'You and me are taking a walk.'

'Says who?'

'You can walk the other way any time you like,' said McCann. 'But I'll be back with a warrant and I'll be in a worse mood. We can lift you in a van or an armoured car, stir things up. Hold you for how many days is it now we can do that Patsy? Can you remember? Under the Emergency Powers?'[8]

'That's for Micks.'

'Is it now?'

McCann's grip suddenly tightened on Patsy Kidron's elbow. Kidron was the last of Dezzie's so called friends that Peter Kemp had named, that had been at the Sceptre with him, one of the lads involved in the bullying at the yard too. Flannery had questioned him and thought he was the one most

---

[8] The Emergency Powers Act 1973 gave police and courts in Northern Ireland additional discretion in handling terrorist offences.

likely to be hiding a story and likely to crack were the pressure to be put on.

'You've not told us the full story. You've not been honest,' said McCann

Kidron found himself walking along beside him, watching the rainwater form small silver droplets, trickling down off the shoulders of his cape, down the arms, off the peak of his cap, like the surprise arrival of some watery God.

'Tell us again what happened up the Sceptre, that last time you saw Raymond.'

'I've told your woman already.'

'What time you due at work, son?' asked McCann.

'Eight.'

'We'll get your bus then, shall we? Wouldn't want you to be late, would we?'

They halted at the bus stop, joining the queue that was shifting and grumbling under their umbrellas. Kidron spoke wearily like it was a line he'd been made to learn: 'We played some pool, watched the footie on the telly, had a few pints.'

'How many pints? What match was on?' McCann piled in with the questions, back and forth, like testing shaky ground with a heavy boot. 'What was the score?'

'I can't remember.'

'Who was playing then? Can't remember that either? What was the point of watching if you can't even remember the score or who was playing? Come on son, let's not mess about. Who did you lads speak to?'

'No one.'

The bus arrived and McCann followed him to the top deck, sat beside him, continued the questioning in a low, urgent murmur in Kidron's ear.

'Some night out, eh? Good *craic* all night down the Sceptre and you all spoke to no one, watched a match that was so rubbish you've no recollection of who was playing nor the score. You must have spoken to someone.'

'I guess so.'

'Guess or you did speak to someone. Who was he? Describe him.'

'There was a fellow spoke to Raymond.'

'Go on, you've got my interest now.'

'A fellow tapped Raymond on the shoulder and Raymond turned round. Gripped him by the elbow, like you just done to me, said: "Raymond, you're needed upstairs."'

'Did Raymond seem afraid?'

'Aye, maybe.'

'And you've no idea what it was about?'

'That's it. That's all I know.'

'And did Raymond go upstairs?'

'He did.'

'And come back?' McCann had the scent of it now, like a hound at the head of the pack.

'He did,' said Kidron, but there was too big a pause, the tone flat, not nonchalant, like he had started to go off the script and didn't know what came next.

'Had you seen the fellow before?'

'Never.'

'What did he look like?'

'Didn't get much of a look at him.'

'Was he short or tall?'

'I'd say middling.'

He let a pause lengthen. Kidron tried to see where the bus had got to, wiping the condensation off the window with the sleeve of his coat, peering outside. Queen Street, Albert Square, a line of Saracens behind the barriers on Royal Avenue. The bus jolted to a stop. There was a trample of feet getting off, then the press of new passengers getting on.

'You'd be protected, son. There'd be nothing to connect you, we'd make sure of that.'

Kidron swallowed, still thinking. 'If he's that dangerous he's a fellow that needs to be off the streets,' murmured McCann. 'Don't you think?' He grappled in his mind for the final nudge that would tip the balance. 'Does your mummy know you've been threatened? Does she?'

'It's not threats Inspector, its discipline.'

'A bit harsh, to kill a fellow. He must've done something bad for that? They must have thought he was beyond correction.'

'He's not dead.'

'How do you know that?'

McCann had a sudden crazy doubt, a hope even that Raymond might not be dead, that it was all a nightmare or delusion; the arm, the fingerprints. Kidron was denying it because he didn't want to believe it either.

'He's dead,' said McCann. 'There's nothing from him; no letters, calls, sightings. There's things he was due for that he wouldn't miss.' Leaving out the arm, because there was definitely nothing to be gained by letting people know how far they had already got with their inquiry. 'And it's your man that gave him the tap to go upstairs that maybe holds the key.'

He could feel the bus slowing again, Kidron bending to

collect his bag, trying to get McCann to move but McCann sat there immobile, hemming him in.

'What's the rush, sonny? We can go round again,' he said. 'You'll be late for work but you'll help us put a killer behind bars, the fellow that likely killed your friend Raymond. Could kill you too, could kill anyone, even kill your Mummy and how would that feel, knowing it'd be you that had let it happen?'

'He just said he wanted a word with Raymond, upstairs.' Now his tone was sad, regretful, guilty even. Because they all must have been feeling guilty, that they'd let Raymond Small go, let him slip through their fingers, when they could have challenged it. Kidron seemed to give the word 'upstairs' a special emphasis, like upstairs was maybe the gateway to hell or somewhere worse.

'What went on upstairs?'

'I never been up there. Some of the lads meet there of a night.'

'What lads?'

'Lads out of the brigade.'

'The UFF?'

'Aye.'

'When he came in the bar you could hear the hush,' said Kidron.

McCann sat forward. Those were the kind of men you'd to watch out for; men with a big black cloud over their heads, men that sent a chill over a crowded room like there was cold rain coming.

'What was his name? Come on son, give us a clue?'

'I think it was Billy.' Kidron whispered. 'Now can I go?'

'Billy who?' He started to push out and away from

McCann like a strong young heifer, his tight muscles easing McCann to the edge of his seat, McCann holding firm.

'Tofer or Thomas or something, I don't know.' Then he pushed clear and stumbled past McCann. McCann started to get up to follow but Kidron was already away down the stairs. A moment later, twisting in his seat, McCann saw him on the pavement outside looking right and left like a scared dog that didn't know which way to run.

'At least we've some kind of a name now,' said McCann, pushing open the door to the dead files room. Inside, Flannery paused with a teabag in one hand, the kettle beginning to boil on the table behind her.

'You ready for a cup of tea Inspector?' McCann waved her away impatiently.

'Billie Telford, Telfer, Toner, Tofer something like that, begins with T. Get us his records, please. A regular up the Sceptre, he'll have done time maybe, minor league hoodlum, becoming major, a guy with aspirations I'd imagine.'

Soon the records lay on the table between them, in their brown police envelopes, a pile of them, six or seven men whose name began with T that had done time and whose first name was Billy or William.

'This fellow's still inside,' said McCann, discarding one, throwing it back at her. 'And this fellow's sixty-two.'

'You never said I'd to get youngsters.'

'Dominic Toner. He's an RC,' said McCann, tossing another one back. 'No way he'd be part of a UFF squad, no way he'd be drinking up the Sceptre.'

'If you say so Inspector.'

Then there were only three records left on the table. When the papers of the rest had been put back carefully in their folders, McCann laid out the three photographs, side by side.

'What do you reckon Flannery?' He gestured at the images of the three men. One of them had a prison haircut, brutally reduced to a near skinhead, a lopsided formless face, a narrow mouth, the lips turned in a cocky grin that showed bad teeth. The second man had shoulder length hair, was handsome with an almost Italianate face, dark intelligent eyes that looked directly at the camera. He was wearing an open necked check shirt. The third man had a small head, receding hair and a forehead that was prematurely lined. He had looked down as the shot was being taken, as if he were holding something in his hands. McCann wondered which of the three men had the capacity for viciousness, for fanaticism, for gang rivalry, the capacity to go beyond the extra mile to achieve their aims. Or maybe the opposite, the weakness that meant that in the right circumstances when they were triggered, whatever was wrong with them would take control. Or maybe faces couldn't even be read that way; wasn't it often the case in Ulster that the man of whom people would say: 'a nicer, more decent man you could never hope to meet,' might turn out to be the very worst?

'What do you think?'

She peered carefully at each picture in turn.

'Well I couldn't rightly say, Sir. We could ask Patsy Kidron or any of the mates that were there for a positive ID couldn't we?'

'No point. He'd barely admit anything happened at all. Patsy would never stand up in court and point the finger. Not unless he wanted to go the same way as Raymond. So, what's your hunch? Your guess?'

'This fellow,' said Flannery, tapping the picture of the man with the Italianate face.

'Why'd you say that?'

'Counter-intuition, whatever feels right is generally wrong.' she said.

McCann laughed.

'Jesus Flannery, that's some life you must have had to think like that at your tender age.' He pulled the man's records towards him, looked at his watch.

'Ballymoyle Road. Let's bring him in.'

As he turned into Ballymoyle Road, McCann was surprised by the sudden change from narrow terraces to semi-detached houses in red brick, a steeply rising street with the mountain behind. A street where the air was fresher too as he stepped out with Flannery by his side. The front garden was set to roses that had been carefully pruned, now covered in fresh spring buds, a crazy paving pathway running up to the front step. Parked in the road outside was a new two litre Rover in dark blue, with a pale grey speed stripe and gleaming hubcaps.

He rapped at the door, rang the bell, a tune tinkling inside.

'You sure this is right?' Flannery asked, just as the door opened and a woman with a young child at her hip opened up, another slightly older one pulling at her skirt.

'We're looking for a William Tofer,' said McCann. But before he could say anything else he heard a door slam at the back of the house, the sound of footsteps in the side alley and a man appeared, caught a glimpse of uniforms, seemed on the point of running.

'William Tofer? I need you down the station Sir, to answer some questions about the night of Saturday, 10th April.'

'He was here,' said Mrs Tofer. Then more shrilly: 'He was here watching the telly.' The child, let down on the floor, began to cry.

They drove back to Division in near complete silence, Tofer in the back seat with Flannery for company.

'What's this about?' Tofer asked, as they turned in towards Division. 'Are you charging me with something?'

'That's for us to decide, Sir,' said McCann. 'Depending on what you have to tell us.'

Down in the interview room, McCann started gently enough: 'Mr Tofer. I'm sorry we're keeping you. Is there anything we can get you before we begin,' The room was hot, the overhead strip light buzzing and crackling. A single steel legged chair stood behind a bare wooden table, two chairs on the other side for McCann and Flannery.

Tofer looked up. Under the bright lights it was clear that he'd changed since the prison photograph had been taken. Though his features were still fine, the long dark hair had been replaced with the remnants of a brutal prison haircut and dirty lines were etched in his forehead as if some kind of time machine had accelerated his life in the year since he had left prison. But more than that, a long white scar now ran across his lower lip and down his chin.

'Tell us what you do in the upstairs room at the Sceptre,' said McCann tiredly, like he already knew and didn't expect an honest answer.

'I'm not telling you anything without my solicitor,' said Tofer.

'Duty solicitor all right?' McCann offered.

'No way. Give this fellow a call,' and Tofer slipped him an embossed card with a well known name upon it, which McCann passed over to Flannery. 'Give him a bell will you?' he said. 'He'll enjoy being dragged in for the likes of this fellow.'

McCann took a break while he waited for the solicitor to arrive, went down to the canteen which was deserted, a few shrivelled meals baking under the hot lights, just the low rumble of the extractor fans as background to his thoughts. He got himself a coffee from the machine – milky white – and boosted it with three sugars, tapped on the steel counter with a coin till the woman on duty came out and knocked him up a bacon sandwich the way he liked it; sliced pan and four or five crispy rashers that he slathered with ketchup and brown sauce.

It was all a balance of terror, a fine adjustment, McCann knew that. For Small to be punished he would need to be deserving it in some way, the cruelty appropriate. Misjudge the punishment and people would start to talk, to be concerned. Unless you went right over the top so the punishment was so far above what was needed that it terrified everyone. Was that why it was so hard breaking through to get anyone to open up?

But something about Tofer already didn't seem quite right. He couldn't put his finger on it exactly. Maybe it was the soft merino wool sweater he wore, the fact he didn't appear to have any tattoos. Maybe it was the house he lived in on Ballymoyle Road with its neat semis, the new car in the driveway. Somehow Tofer didn't seem to have the angry, tense drive, the focus that was required for murder, though psychos came in many disguises. Maybe it was because Tofer was lower in the food chain than the man they wanted? Lower down and frightened of someone even worse. Just a messenger tasked with bringing Raymond Small to meet his master? Maybe he wasn't the right man at all? He bit into the bacon sandwich, washed it down with a gulp of coffee. Then he moved back to the interview room.

Tofer's solicitor was waiting by the door. George Brindley had on a big heavy Ulster overcoat that he'd thrown on and when McCann unlocked to let him in he pushed past breathing good whiskey like he'd just returned from a trip to a distillery.

'Afternoon George,' said McCann.

'May I ask how long you have had my client detained?'

'About as long as it took you to get here. And he's not detained, he's assisting us with enquiries.'

The interview resumed, Brindley lowering his bulk down with a groan on a steel chair next to Tofer like it was seriously substandard compared to the class of furniture he was used to, his large face covered with liver spots sinking into his neck like a toad deflating, his eyes hooded, just the faint glint of weary intelligence showing below the eyelids.

'What goes on in the upstairs room of the Sceptre then Billy?'

'It's the social club, fundraisers for the cause, social support, we've a food bank comes in, support for the elderly, dominoes,' said Tofer.

'Knitting? Embroidery too maybe?' McCann cut him off before he could add more.

'That too,' said Tofer, grinning a bit, which made the scar

on his lip seem to open, like he'd another off centre smile that echoed the first.

'Tell me, where d'ye get that scar?' McCann leaned forward and reached out his hand as if to softly touch Tofer's deformed lip with his fingertips, until Tofer pulled his head back with an angry jerk. 'Sensitive about it, are you?'

'It was in the Crumlin Road. They stitched it up but it must of got infected, because my face swelled up the size of a pumpkin. It was desperate, so it was. They had me on the antibiotic drip, more pipes in me than come out of the Belfast waterworks.'

McCann nodded sympathetically.

'And afterwards, when you come out, how come you came to be up the Sceptre with that rabble?'

A low rumble came from Brindley: 'I can't see what this has to do with anything, McCann. You've not even explained what you've brought him in for.'

McCann ignored him.

'We're investigating the murder of Raymond Small. We want to know why you brought him upstairs on the night of 10th April, the last time he was seen. We want to know what happened to him up there?'

'I didn't. Who told you that? I was in all night, watching the telly. You heard what my wife said.'

McCann didn't answer, took out a cigarette for himself, tapped it out, lit up without offering one to Tofer, blew the smoke in his face, wafted it away with mock politeness.

'I think I met you the other night Mr Tofer, you and your pals. I believe you've got my shoes. Nice pair of black brogues.' And McCann bent down to look under the table.

'Don't suppose you'd be stupid enough to be wearing them?'

'I don't know what you're talking about.'

McCann reached into the folder he'd brought with him, pulled out the pictures of Raymond Small, spread them across the table one by one, chronologically like it was 'This is your life,' though it wasn't a life now.

'You seen him before?' Tofer gave the task his full attention, studying each photograph close up as if magnification would improve his memory.

'Nope, can't say as I have.'

'Then how come he's in 3 Batallion, UFF?' said McCann. 'Your company, that meets at the Sceptre. You'd have known him. And I gather you were the Intelligence Officer.' McCann took out the list that had come down in the post from Clarke at Castlereagh, just as he'd promised. He made a show of taking it out of the envelope, unfolding it, running his finger down the list of names. 'William Tofer, Intelligence Officer. Raymond Small, soldier.' Then he leaned back like he'd just pulled his best party trick, raised his eyebrows daring either man to disagree. 'So what happened to Raymond, Mr Tofer?'

'I don't know,' said Tofer. 'Maybe the IRA took him out, maybe he's a victim of one of their murder gangs? How would I know?'

'Any other ideas, Billy? Like maybe the wee green men landed on the Shore Road and beamed him up to the planet Zog?'

'No.'

'And you're not concerned?' Tofer was silent for a moment too long, came back with an overemphatic: 'Of course

I'm concerned.'

'Well, Billy, that makes two of us,' said McCann. 'In fact there's more. His mother is concerned too, beside herself with worry and not able to grieve.' McCann stood up, paced round behind Tofer, so close to his ear that he winced when McCann whispered: 'But then I suppose a coward like you doesn't care much about that.'

McCann turned his back on Tofer for a moment, then returned to his other ear to whisper: 'I've a wee birdie tells me your Raymond had been a bad boy.'

'What wee birdie?'

'Actually, several wee birdies,' McCann added a layer of exaggeration, knowing Tofer wouldn't know if he had witnesses or not. 'Tweeting birdies that were there on the night of Saturday, 10th April, 1976 when you done for him. They tell me punishment was being handed out. You can't be a popular man, Mr Tofer, with people telling tales like that about you.'

'Just hearsay, McCann. If you've the evidence you should charge my client or let him go.' Brindley blustered. 'I'll have to insist I'm afraid, you've absolutely nothing at all here. If you have, go on, bang him up man, else let us all away to our supper. He's a family man, with a home to go to.'

McCann hesitated, smiled, placed his hands flat on the table: 'I'm keeping Mr Tofer in. There'll be no charge as yet. It's my right under the Emergency Powers as you well know.'

And he led Tofer down to the cells.

'Give him a wee fright and time to think,' he said to Flannery later as he turned out the lights in the dead files room and they both made off in their different directions into the Belfast evening.

After the first round of drinks, which Liam had paid for and brought from the bar – a pint for himself and a small white wine for her – Flannery stood up and offered to get the next.

'What'll you have?'

'No, no,' he said. 'This one's mine.'

'No way. You sit there,' she said. 'I always pay for my drinks.'

'No, no you sit yourself down,' he insisted, standing to block her way.

'It's my turn.' She took his hand off her arm, where he was holding her back. The bar was packed, warm, friendly, noisy. She felt hot even in her red shoulderless dress.

'Give us another pint of Guinness then,' he relented.

She pushed up to the bar. A big throng, but parting as it always did when they saw a woman there in a short skirt and heels.

'Let the lady through, lads.' There was a barricade of red-faced men, sleeves rolled up, with heavy pressure at the front row as new customers pushed away at the back. She ducked through like a scrum half, emerged at the bar. The barmen were frenzied, the taps jammed on, diving to place a fresh glass under as each was filled, cutting the foam and topping up from another tap, chucking empties into bins, all simultaneously as if each had four sets of hands, but somehow not seeing her until the fellow standing beside her took pity and said: 'This wee girl's been waiting first,' when the barman turned to him for his order, the man smiling at her condescendingly in an act of unwanted chivalry.

'Thank you,' she said, when the drinks came and paid

with a twenty pound note from her purse.

She held her wine glass against the pint, the men parting again as she pushed her way out and back to her table, with an accompanying murmur of: 'Mind your backs now, there's a lady coming through' and 'Can I help you with any of that missus?' and 'You'd need a tray for that, love,' until she was back with Liam who jumped up to take the drinks from her.

'I'll let you into a secret,' she said, taking a gulp of her drink.

'What's that?' Liam was relaxed, shirt unbuttoned.

'I'm not actually called Annabel.'

'What are you called then?'

'Sinead Flannery.' And there it was, the name bit had come out – his and hers – and they were OK because it wasn't going to be a problem; Sinead Flannery and Liam O'Rourke would be fine together, both Catholics so no one could object to that. What they could object to was if they found out she was a policewoman drinking in the bar of the Gaelic Athletic Association.[9]

'Why did you say you were called Annabel then?'

'You can't be too careful, can you, on a night out?'

'That's right,' he said easily, smiling, watching as the band came in through the door with their instruments, began to set up on the small stage by the bar.

After a few more drinks listening to the music and chatting, she settled beside him hearing the clatter of the snare

---

[9] The GAA catered for traditional Irish sports like Gaelic Football, Hurling and Camogie, as well as supporting Irish music and dance. At the time these sports were played almost exclusively by Catholics and there was a strong overlap in some areas with active Republicanism.

drum, a harmonica, wistful, plangent, the room suddenly quieting, some of the fellows almost standing to attention beside her. The Soldier's Song was followed by a man taking the microphone saying there was a collection coming round. When the collection box arrived at her table Liam put a fiver in, but she sat there with her arms crossed, the fellow waving the tin under her nose.

'That's for both of us,' said Liam, helpfully, but really it wasn't helpful as she'd never give money to their cause, to any of their causes. Why would you give money to blow people's legs and arms off when you were having a night out?

Out on the street later, they argued: 'It's the social fund, to support the widows and their families.'

'If they weren't fighting there wouldn't be any widows, no orphans neither,' she said. Outside it was cold, hard to walk in her high heels, hard to follow him. Why couldn't she just fall in line, she wondered? It was like there was nowhere she could be that was safe.

'Tell that to the Brits. Tell that to the UVF,' said Liam, putting his arm round her shoulder as if to comfort her, keep her warm till they got the cab that would take them away.

He made coffee in the galley kitchen for them both, two cups of instant in earthenware mugs.

'Sugar?'

'Aye.'

'How many'

'Two. I can't be doing with coffee without sugar, its way too bitter for me.'

'Me too,' he said, tossing the unwashed spoon back into

the tin of instant.

Flannery looked around the kitchen. Under the fluorescent light it looked different to the first time she had been there: brown Formica doors on the units, hinges sagging below what had once been an orange worktop. A pin board plastered with cards for minicabs, takeaways, the occasional postcard of some improbably blue sea, snaps of lads together. The fridge was cluttered with novelty fridge magnets, one holding a shopping list that had turned yellow and started to curl. She perched on the edge of the dining room table.

'Do you never want a place of your own? I mean being a solicitor and all you could pay for it.'

'Solicitor's clerk. Not a solicitor yet,' he said. 'Anyway, I can't be bothered with all of that doing your own repairs, paying the rates, too many other things to do.' He sat down opposite her, restless, pushing yesterday's papers aside to make room for his cup.

'How about you?'

'I don't earn enough to get a place of my own though, even if I wanted it.'

'Where is it you said you worked?'

'Buntons, the toolmakers down Donegall Quay,' she said swiftly, already having arranged the story. It was a big firm, mixed workforce. Even if he knew someone who worked there it would be legitimate for them not to have heard of her.

'Which department?'

She'd worked that out too, done the necessary research.

'I'm in accounts.' Something boring, something she knew just enough about to be able to spin a line, were she unlucky enough to meet an accountant who asked questions.

'Many people in the department?'

'It's one of the biggest. There's bought ledger, accounts payable, treasury, payroll, audit…' His eyes seemed to look through her, then suddenly he took her hand and pulled her to him.

'You're never an accountant are you? You don't work at Bunton's either, do you?' It wasn't threatening, but a kind enquiry, an invitation to be honest with him. She wasn't sure how he'd worked it out, but he had somehow. She felt sick, empty at the deception. He was a nice guy, funny, strong, good looking, kind, he'd a good future ahead of him. He was even the same religion, which pretty much trumped everything else and here she was lying to him because it had seemed the safest thing to do. It was what they all did. Because it wouldn't do for her to be in the RUC with the views he had, the people he supported. It had maybe been a mistake all along to join, one she'd almost grown used to until now.

'Actually I'm in the police, in the RUC. I'm a Constable.'

'You what?' He began, but couldn't finish the sentence. 'Ah come on now Sinead you're having me on.'

'I'm not, its straight up the truth,' she said, leaning down to the bag by her feet and pulling out the warrant card, sliding it across the table towards him like some sort of peace offering, where it lay face up in front of him. He glanced at it, like he couldn't quite believe it was there, then leaned down, checked the likeness in the photo. There was a long silence, then he said: 'If I'd your job I'd not want people to know either.'

'I'm sorry,' she said.

'Sorry for what? You must have your reasons?'

She didn't let it fester. She told him her reasons for joining the police and the trouble it caused her, the danger she was in all the time because of it. Later she even told him about Raymond Small, the case she was working on, so that he'd understand. She described Raymond's empty room, the way his mother's eyes had ranged around his abandoned things as if he might still be there, or on his way home, the arm that inspector McCann had recovered and how they knew he was dead. She talked about the fear that seemed to grip everyone she spoke to. While she was speaking Liam nodded and said: 'Yes, yes, I see that, yes,' taking it all in like small sips of some new and unfamiliar drink that he was having trouble digesting and wasn't sure he could come to like.

'Disappeared up the Sceptre Bar, last seen,' she finished.

'Have you been up there?'

'Wouldn't be allowed. Inspector McCann says it's no place for a lady.'

'The Sceptre?' he said. 'Aye that's a rough place I'd not go to now. But it's a boozer just like any other. I've been in there a few times when I was lad, before the Troubles kicked off, just for a dare. Lunchtime it was quiet and you could drop by.'

'All the same I'd like to get in there. Maybe a woman with a man would be less conspicuous.' She left the sentence hanging there and Liam's eyes seemed to twinkle with the idea of helping her in some way, of showing off that he wasn't afraid.

'Listen, maybe we could go up there tomorrow, you and I, just to take a look,' he suggested.

Chapter Five

McCann steeled himself as the cab swung through the gates. Purdysburn was where they took you when you couldn't cope and not coping was where most of them were at, so the walls were paper thin – even non-existent – between the people inside and the people outside. But inside the hospital it was all pleasant enough; a smell of polish, even the scent of roses from flowers that visitors had brought in. There weren't the hospital beds he'd expected, but a large room with table tennis, the radio on, patients strolling around, playing cards, chatting like in a good hotel except that the door was in thick unbreakable glass and clicked shut behind McCann as the orderly led him over to the rear of the lounge. He could see the top of Deevery's head over the back of a big leather armchair. If Deevery was asking to see McCann, if he had changed, or if he was lonely, well maybe Deevery could tell him something he didn't know. Because Deevery had known everyone, known all their foibles, used them when he could. Deevery might even know the kind of man who would take the finger off an eighteen year old boy, then kill him.

Deevery stood up as the orderly approached, turned towards McCann. He was still an imposing figure, with his shock of grey curling hair, but he stood with a slight stoop now and moved with a certain stiffness. His face had somehow fallen in on itself too since the last time McCann had seen him, when he had still been an Inspector at Division. Now his lips had turned down at the corners, so that dark shadows lurked at either side of his mouth. In between the colour had seeped away and the lips were almost bloodless.

'McCann?' he said, strangely hesitant. 'What are you doing here?'

'Your parents said you wanted a visit.'

'Did they now?' A pause then, no offer of a seat, while McCann blinked, saying nothing, acting normal, being normal. 'Tell me why you're really here, McCann?'

Deevery settled himself back in his chair, began to tap out a little tune on the Formica tabletop between them. 'I'd have a guess you're here because there's something you need my help with.'

McCann nodded, surprised by the hint of regret in Deevery's voice, a certain heaviness in the sigh that accompanied the words. Deevery rubbed an angry hand across one eye, gestured that McCann should take a seat. He pushed a packet of Weights towards Deevery, who took one but his hands were shaking so he couldn't light it. McCann held his hand steady to do so. Deevery suddenly looked him in the eye like they were together again, back in the old days at Division. Then he smiled, like a watery sun appearing over a wet bog road, a faint glimmer appeared in his eyes.

'So it wasn't me done them girls, was it?' A pleading tone, like maybe McCann could absolve him.

'It wasn't *just* you,' corrected McCann. 'Maybe there was

someone else?'

'Ah!' Deevery sighed, a long gasp of relief, or surprise maybe.

'I was after who it was same as you were, McCann. That's what I wanted to say. That's what I wanted you to know. I was close to them and could have sorted it out and then you came blundering in as you always did, on your white charger.' He stopped, coughed, wiped his lips, peered out at McCann between narrowed eyes to judge the effect he was having. 'Clippety clop, clippety, clippety clop, McCann, whoah! With your shining armour and your lance, seeking out evil, galloping in with your trusty steed, a fine sight indeed.'

'Close to whom?' McCann butted in. 'Because I'm after a fellow that's not averse to a bit of knifework, a bit of chopping and dicing to get what he wants. Might have done a lad down the Sceptre. Might be a fellow out of control.' He spoke too urgently, regretted it because Deevery suddenly veered off, changing the subject. Whether it was voluntary or his mind had suddenly lurched away, McCann couldn't tell: 'You know the funny thing McCann? Since I've been in here, I've had a lot of time to think, and clever people to help me think, to reformulate as it were.'

'And have you reached any conclusions?'

'I have, McCann. And you know what they are?'

'You tell me.'

'That there's nothing there in the centre of this puzzle of yours. There's just the work of the devil, McCann.' He raised his eyebrows, daring McCann to contradict him.

'And this devil is still out there doing his dirty work up the Sceptre Bar is he?'

'The devil's everywhere, and I'll tell you one thing. It's not in me. I was on the side of the angels. And now I'm in here so there's nothing I can do and nothing you can fit me up with either this time.'

Deevery sat back, like he was playing again to provoke McCann, shape shifting, shadow boxing. Whatever he had been about to tell McCann had been withdrawn, pushed aside by his urgent need to be absolved. He'd been using young girls as honey traps for informers, and somehow they'd been murdered before the truth could come out, but McCann hadn't been able to link him in the end in a way that would stand up in court. There wasn't a limit to Deevery's cunning.

'What devil? What was his name?' Deevery clapped his hands together with delight, almost like the old Deevery, changing the subject again: 'You know what McCann? It's good to see you again. Really good, I really do mean that, I've missed our wee chats, haven't you?' Wee chats? Thought McCann, Deevery's bullying and jeering couldn't be forgotten. He reached across the table and offered his hand to McCann, daring him to refuse it. 'Come on, McCann, don't be a girl about this pal,' and he nodded to his outstretched hand. McCann left the hand untouched.

'I'll shake if you give me his name. You must have had your suspicions? Any names, that were involved along with you. That might still be out there, doing the dirty work. I'm after a fellow that could have been an enforcer. Not afraid of a little light surgery.' He'd not give him Tofer's name yet, he'd let Deevery suggest it first.

'It'd be the Shinners done a lad from the Sceptre, them dirty Fenian bastards don't care who they kill. Cowardly, evil shites they are.' Spittle dripped from Deevery's lip as he leaned towards McCann and he moved back involuntarily to escape the invective.

'Well, here's some names you can add to your list of suspects: Thomas Michael Sheehy, Timothy McDade...' McCann pulled out his notepad, began to write as Deevery spoke, but the names came faster and faster. Deevery began to shout out more and more names, like he had swallowed a whole school register, a register of anyone anywhere that just might be looking to torture boys like Raymond Small for their cause, like he was emptying his head of the contents of some vast and deadly filing cabinet, a cascade of humanity, so many that McCann could only grasp a name here and there until, out of breath, Deevery bent over, his hands on his knees, chuckling and coughing. 'Any one of them, McCann. Take your pick. Tell your story to add to all the other stories, your story about who done what.'

'And there's not a William Tofer amongst them is there?' But there was no response, no flicker of recognition from Deevery. Either he was still a pro, that could let the name slide past, or he didn't know the name. 'And no chance it was their own side, a feud amongst the paramilitaries. Or that he fell foul of the Branch and their dirty tricks?' Deevery drew breath, rubbed his hands together, composed himself, gave a laugh.

'That's more your kind of fantasyland, McCann,' he said.

'And Sammy McGuigan? Maybe he had a fellow to clean up after him?' McCann leaned forwards, trying to get a glimpse of the hint that Deevery might still give him. 'You've not brought me all the way out here just to play with me, have you?'

McCann stood up to go, took off his visitor's permit on its

lanyard, picked up his half empty pack of Weights and lighter. Deevery's expression changed.

'You're not going are you, McCann.' Acting crestfallen, or maybe he actually was crestfallen? Or had something else to say, some other thing to tease McCann with, to keep him guessing. To keep him coming back, him and Deevery in a lockstep together, always dancing, never getting to the truth, always in his power.

'If I tell you, what are the chances they'll let me out of here.' Was he a God that could set people free, not just in a literal sense, but free of their conscience too? McCann felt the pressure of that, weighed against the possibility that this ruined man before him might have the information he needed. The end would justify the means, there'd be no absolutes, just a calculation of acceptable transactions. That would be the way they'd all be at peace.

'Tell us first Deevery and maybe we'll see,' said McCann.

'Ah no McCann. It's not like that. There's not got to be any maybe about it.'

'Let's just say if I get to him thanks to you, there'll be a deal, it'll have a bearing on how you're treated,' said McCann.

'What kind of a deal? That's not a deal at all,' said Deevery, his foot tapping up and down.

'You'll walk out of here without the answer, having turned down an offer of help, an offer of closure.'

'Aye, well, I can do that,' said McCann. 'And you can't.' He began to walk away.

'You'll not be safe,' said Deevery's voice, cutting in, suddenly gravelled with threat.

McCann spun on his heel, reaching across the table,

Deevery dodging back, the chair flying, an orderly moving forwards from his place near the wall from where he'd been watching. 'Easy now, McCann sure you wouldn't want to lose control would you?' Deevery was smiling back, knowing McCann had heard him. 'Just saying no-one out there is safe, McCann, in general, like,' he said smoothly. 'Not like me, in here, no one is.' And he held up his hands in mock surrender, knowing there was no need to surrender, because he thought he'd won. And then he laughed again, like it was an excellent joke he'd played on McCann and the orderly moved back, still attentive against the wall.

'If you put a stop to what you started you'll be out of here,' said McCann.

'That's just it McCann, it's beyond me too. It always was, once Sammy set his dogs loose.'

'Dogs? What dogs?' Deevery smiled wanly, calmly, like he felt better for telling a tiny portion of truth.

'I can do nothing in here. If I was outside, maybe I could help you,' he said.

The glass doors closed noiselessly behind McCann. The wind hit him with rejuvenating strength, a north-easterly breeze carrying a few stray raindrops. He lit a cigarette and looked around for a moment while he inhaled the smoke. The car park was almost full, a couple of health authority transit vans by the door, beside the spaces reserved for senior staff. McCann took one last look back at the red brick building. It was modern in a functional way, the windows looking out over the fields beyond the boundary wall. He caught a glimpse of a grey face behind a twitching curtain, a hand waving to him. Then there was a sudden last blaze of evening sunlight, which caught the glass as if it were consumed with flames.

He walked down past the vans, towards where the minicabs picked up visitors. A name on one of the staff parking bays caught his eye and he paused, then heard the toot of a car horn from behind and jumped aside as a new Volvo estate swung round into the space. A man climbed out dressed in a tweed suit, with a well-used briefcase stuffed under his arm, apologising for giving him a fright.

'Dr O'Leary! Just the man,' said McCann, showing his warrant card to introduce himself so O'Leary had to invite him in.

O'Leary's office was comfortable, with a fine old leather topped desk, the smell of pipe smoke, an old watercolour of the Mournes and an oil painting of yachts racing at Dunlaoghaire on the walls.

'You've an Inspector Deevery as one of your patients, I believe? Wrote the report on him for the RUC, is that right Doctor?' Dr O'Leary confirmed that was the case.

'Did Mr Deevery at any time mention an accomplice, or accomplices?' McCann asked.

'I'm afraid all that is confidential. You may perhaps read the conclusions of my report to the Constabulary, but the actual substance of our conversations cannot I'm afraid be revealed.'

Dr O'Leary sat back in his chair, with his plump hands calmly folded on the desk in front of him. He had a pleasant face and McCann could imagine him treading delicately around the unexploded ordinance of Deevery's mind, drawing inferences, hypotheses, conclusions, but in a professional language that was clinical and devoid of judgement, so different from McCann's own. 'I know it is frustrating for you Inspector,' he said. 'It is frustrating for us too, to be unable to help directly in the way you might like. But you must understand that without total confidentiality, our patients would be unable to provide us with the information we need to treat them effectively. The treatment is the most important thing.'

'Treatment?'

'In men like Mr Deevery it's more a case of containment; the main thing is to prevent them getting in with like-minded people and harming others – there's a term for that – "self-sustaining groupthink" it is. The environment in Ulster can be extremely dangerous for certain vulnerable people.'

'Deevery's not vulnerable.' Deevery had no doubt pulled the wool over O'Leary's eyes, no doubt more wool than it would take to knit an Arran jumper. The psychiatrist wouldn't have seen what McCann had seen; the bodies of innocent teenage girls flytipped into a ditch and a disused coal bunker.

'Well I can't comment on individual cases, but most of them have had traumas in their past.' McCann knew all about that. 'He was an active police officer, would have had difficult times.' Maybe there were grounds for some exculpation there and if not that, then explanation at least, thought McCann. But they all had difficult times and just had to deal with it. 'For some people they are able to shrug things off, behave normally. There may be some symptoms of Post Traumatic Stress Disorder, certain triggers can operate like a key to a cabinet of horrors. A door can be opened on darkness and once it is opened it is hard to close again, no matter how the person tries to do so.'

The psychiatrist paused: 'You worked together you say?' His eyes twinkled in a kindly yet neutral way, ambiguous yet caring, encouraging McCann to talk.

'Yes, we worked together at C Division for a while,' said McCann, becoming irritated now, interrupting: 'So he never mentioned other people, blamed them, never hinted at serious crimes?' It was as if he hadn't spoken. O'Leary asked: 'And you were responsible for charging him?'

'I wanted him prosecuted but other people thought better,' said McCann, trying to keep the bitterness from his voice.

'Meaning me, I suppose?' The psychiatrist smiled wanly. 'And you never asked him about his past?'

'I knew about his past,' said McCann. 'What does it matter what happened to him in the past Doctor? What does it matter what's happened to any of us? None of us has had a good time, a good life Doctor, but we don't all get even by killing people, or even thinking of it.'

'Ah,' said O'Leary sympathetically, smiling a gnomic smile, putting his hands together, the fingers like the steeple of a church.

McCann tried again: 'So, he didn't tell you about any accomplices?'

'He believed in a dream and if you're like that you're loyal to fellow believers who have the same dreams of omnipotence, dreams of power. Every Protestant like Mr Deevery dreams of going back to Ulster like it was, a glorious loyal country, settled for ever in the bosom of the United Kingdom.The Republicans dream of a Gaelic Ireland, free of Brits, themselves alone to make their own destiny, to be themselves.' Dr O'Leary swivelled on his chair, musing, looking out of the window for a moment at the patients working in the hospital garden outside. 'But all dreams are without substance because when will you know you've achieved the dream? And what will you have to do to get there? How can you explain when the dream doesn't come true? You can blame everyone else for their betrayals, for their sell-outs to explain why you've never arrived. Then never arriving becomes the thing itself and you find yourself killing people and people killing your people and the chimera is even further away, the road to it longer, more bloody. That's what is going on in this country.'

'So you're saying there's no way out, is that it Doctor?'

'I'm not saying that at all, Inspector, there's always hope. Because suddenly at some funeral, another bereavement or blood spattered moment these people come to realise that they've more in common than their losses and the damage they've done. It's the fact that they are all addicted to a fantasy, to something that will never happen. I've seen it a lot, in my patients here. Then it's the beginning of a common understanding of our delusions. It's the basis of co-operation, Inspector; recognising in the other not difference, but similarity, not otherness, but sameness.'

McCann was baffled. He'd seen precious little sign of anyone recognising the common humanity of their enemies. But maybe O'Leary was right. Maybe he had seen that in his patients. Maybe the most brutal, the most enraged, might recognise something in their enemies, that in their darkest hour the faintest glimmer of light would begin to appear, just as Deevery had once said it would.

'And do you think Deevery could change in that way do you? Have you seen any sign of a change of heart? Do you think there's a chance…'

'That he might remember something? Tell you what you wish to know?' O'Leary finished his sentence for him. Again came the benign smile, as if from some higher, ethereal ground, in which all meanings were infinitely malleable, a smile that said both yes and no, that anything was possible in the hearts of men.

Chapter Six

'We'll just go in and have a quick one shall we?' said Liam. They were still on the main road looking in a shop window and there was time to turn back. Already they'd walked past the end of the street once, glanced down towards the Sceptre, checking the street was quiet, the bar likely deserted at that time of day. They'd draw attention if they lingered longer, Flannery knew. But if they went in maybe they'd see something inside that would help McCann. Maybe they'd be able to get into that upstairs room he'd mentioned. Liam looked the part; the boots, faded denims, second hand parka with the hood pulled up. Back in the day it had been a laugh, a bit of a dare to cross over to the other side. But now, since the Troubles had kicked off Catholics had little reason to visit Protestant bars – vice versa too – and she was no longer sure she would know the language. Then Liam murmured, 'Let's do it' and swung her left towards the Sceptre. She could feel the panic rising. He held her arm tightly, like they were a courting couple, so she couldn't turn back. 'Walk in like you own the place,' Liam whispered as they drew near. 'Like it is yours alone, yours and your people.'

There was only one man on the door, with a flat tweed cap,

his narrow face shrivelled and wizened, wearing the standard black bomber jacket, a cigarette smouldering between his thin lips.

'Can I help you?' The fellow barred their way.

'We've just moved into the area and wanted to check out the bar,' said Liam.

'Where would that be?' the fellow asked, peering at them with weasel eyes, enlarged by the spectacles that clung to his pockmarked nose.

'Olive Street.'

'Which number?'

'Sixteen.'

'You'll know Bertie Scott then?'

'We've not had the time to get to know anyone yet. Thought we'd make a start down here today. Hear tell this is the best place for a quiet pint.' Flannery found herself doing the talking.

'Oh aye, it is that,' said the fellow doubtfully, like there was still a button he was waiting to have pressed before he would let them in. He peered into her face close up so she could smell the cigarette smoke on his breath. Some people still thought you could tell a Mick from their ears, or their noses, their smell and maybe he was looking for that.

'Come on Mister we're gagging,' Liam used the common language of alcohol and the fellow took pity, convinced enough to reach to pull the bolts on the door and let them in, watching their backs as they entered.

Inside the bar was dimly lit at that time of day, a few drinkers murmuring in the snugs, the barman reading the News Letter spread out across the bar, the stone floor newly swept and still damp from the morning swab. A radio murmured somewhere under the counter. Flannery felt eyes upon her, realised too late that in the day security might be lax and the bar empty, but a woman would be conspicuous. Normally at that time of day the women would be preparing food, looking after the wee ones, or scrubbing, not going out to the bars. As they walked forward and hoisted themselves up onto two neighbouring stools, she was aware of a gathering silence in the room.

'Yes?' said the barman, barely lifting his eyes from the racing page.

'A pint of double and a Bloody Mary for the lady,' said Liam, pulling a pack of Bensons from his inside pocket, offering her one, lighting up for them both, watching the barman cut the foam off the Guinness, mixing the tomato juice with a stirrer, placing the drink on a paper coaster in front of her.

'Nasty day,' said Liam.

'Aye it's a wet one, right enough.'

Liam drew the smoke in, pulled out his wallet stuffed with notes, making a show of it so the barman could see he was a fellow of substance, that didn't care if people saw the money because he was the kind of person no one would dare to rob. She saw the barman's eyes flick over the wallet and then move away, taking it in, but not lingering, not dwelling on it impolitely. Liam pulled out a twenty and left it there on the bar like he didn't even care if he got the change or not.

'Tell me,' said Flannery. 'We're looking for a room for a do. Hear tell you've a function room up above.'

The barman paused in the act of pouring a pint, like she

had rung a warning bell. Flannery sensed it had been a wrong move, presumptuous even, but maybe Liam's wallet full of twenties would carry it.

'Who told you that?'

'It's for a birthday party,' she added swiftly and gave the barman a big smile, holding Liam's arm like he belonged to her. Maybe it had been too brash, a woman shouldn't have taken the lead, but Liam helped her out: 'It'll be a big do for the Model School lads, Annabel's mates from the Academy. We'll need a big enough space. You'd have a cut of the bar. It's been a while since we've all met up.'

'The Model? I was at the Model. Which year were you in?' The barman was suddenly friendly, opened up like a switch had been pulled, except that Flannery knew that Liam had been at St Malachy's, knew nothing about the Model School.

'I was in '62-'67,' said Liam. 'Till I got suspended for thieving, got the bum's rush. Good riddance, says I.' Liam took a big slug of his Guinness, draining the pint glass two thirds down, nodding to the barman to set up another as he'd soon be ready for it.

And the barman was smiling now.

'Well there's a coincidence, the very same thing happened to me.'

And they both laughed. Where was Liam getting it from, she wondered, that imaginary Protestant backstory? It was time to move on before he pushed his luck.

'Come on, what'll you have?' Liam was insisting the barman took a drink. 'A wee double, OK for you?'

'That's grand, I'll take a Black Bush.'

And then when that drink was poured and they clinked

glasses, Liam moved on to Linfield, and their chances, again a grip of detail she'd never imagined any Catholic, any Republican would have. In the same way Protestants would know nothing of Gaelic Football, the Easter Rising. In the background she could hear the low murmur of conversation resuming, showing they had passed as Protestants and would be allowed to stay.

'So, the function room upstairs? Can we have a look?'

'Sure thing,' said the barman, taking the keys from the hook under the bar. They climbed the wooden stairs, turning on a landing, pushed through into a high ceilinged room with a stage at the front draped with the Union Jack, stacking chairs piled against the walls. The air held the musty, sweet smell of stale beer. She walked around, running a toe across the floor, like she was testing its suitability for dancing, while Liam asked a few questions about if they could get Guinness on tap and the price they'd ask for a barrel. But then she noticed the signs of scrubbing on the floor at the front, the tang of bleach, that hadn't quite cleared a spreading reddish-brown stain. Maybe this was where it had started, where it had finished too, the end of Raymond Small?

'What night would you be wanting?' The barman was asking, but she found herself struggling to remember her own birthday and gave the first date that came into her head.

'That's spoken for.'

'Could you not get them to move?'

'You could try but I doubt very much they'd be in favour.'

'Who has the room?'

'The volunteers use it for their meetings.'

'We could have a word, couldn't we?'

The barman seemed reluctant.

'I could give them a call if you've their number,' she wheedled.

He took a beer mat from the bar and scrawled a number on the back for her.

'You could try that,' he said and tossed it down in front of her.

When they walked away from the Sceptre she was elated: 'Jesus, I'm glad to be out of there!'

'Scary, right enough,' said Liam, grinning.

'Where'd you get all that about Linfield? With that line of patter you could be in the Branch yourself, Liam?' He was pleased with the flattery.

'Who's to say I'm not?' Making a joke of it as they skipped away up the street, fast, but not so fast that it could draw the attention of the doorman, who was still watching them even as they turned the corner.

Once out on the main road where he'd left his car, she said: 'You go on. I've to give Division a call. Tell them what we've seen.' McCann would need to know about the blood stains, the volunteer meetings. He'd need to have the number she'd been given. They'd need to get forensics in.

'I'll wait, give you a lift.'

'Not a good plan,' she said, not wanting him anywhere near Division, any gossip, any complications. 'I'll get the bus down after. You go on.'

'You sure?'

'Yeah. Give us a call tomorrow.' She kissed him on the cheek, turned back towards a phone box on the corner.

It reeked of smoke and urine inside, the paintwork scarred and abraded by generations of graffiti, the customary marking of the territory. Except that the slogans were unfamiliar to her: FTP, UDA, UFF,[10] scratched penises and female genitalia, Union Jacks, a crawling iconography more potent than the smell. She jiggled out a couple of coins on the counter, dialled through to Division, heard McCann's number ringing and turned to find a fellow hunched against the outside of the box, just the outline of a heavy winter coat, black boots, shaved head, smoking, as if encouraging her to finish the call.

Now a heavy blanket smelling of dog hair lay over her and on top of that they had tied her down in darkness. How had it happened? Suddenly the man had been in the phone box with her, filling it with his bulk, his hand on her throat, his weight pressing her up against the glass, something over her mouth and everything had gone dark. But she was alive and that was the main thing and so far unharmed which was good because it meant she still had value to whoever it was that had taken her. As Flannery's thoughts skipped and raced in the darkness, Liam's smile came back to her, but not in a reassuring way. That and the ease with which he'd seemed to pass himself off with them, almost as if he was one of them. She then had a chilling, absurd thought: maybe he was trained for it, maybe an IRA Intelligence Officer and not just a supporter putting fivers in their box out of habit? Maybe he'd been scouting out the Sceptre for them, setting up an attack? And even worse than that, in the dizzying anxious spiral of paranoias that

[10] FTP – Fuck The Pope, UDA – Ulster Defence Association, UFF – Ulster Freedom Fighters.

now gripped her, maybe Liam saw the opportunity to get a Catholic policewoman topped, a traitor to the cause? That was why he had jumped at the chance when she had talked about the Sceptre and been so confident, professional, had his story arranged. That was why – the moment the barman's eyes were off him – he'd been looking around, taking everything in in the upstairs room. That was the reason he had so easily accepted her offer to make her own way back to Division. Meanwhile at the Sceptre she had been prattling on to the barman about her birthday party and was there any chance of having time to get the place decorated, almost like she meant it.

A door opened, letting in a sudden blaze of light. Where was she? It was a nondescript room, with a filing cabinet, a small window, cans of cleaning agent and boxes of equipment on the floor, a single light bulb overhead. How long would it take for Liam to raise the alarm? Maybe it wouldn't happen until he rang her the next day or the day after, if he rang at all.

'Just a few wee things,' said a high pitched voice, slightly hoarse, like of a fellow with a speech impediment from too much shouting and sloganeering. 'You said on the door you'd just moved in. Then you had a different story, that you were after a birthday party. And that fellow wasn't at the model school '62-67 because we know everyone expelled, so why did he make that up? Who are you? Who was that fellow you were with?' She swivelled her head to see who had spoken, but could see only a hooded face, two eyeholes, a mouth hole with dry red lips, a bit of a nicotine stained moustache twitching under the black balaclava. The fellow had climbed up on a swivel chair, like he was a dentist getting ready to start work, his denimed crotch at her eye level. He swung back and forth on the chair with his legs wide apart, like a bored child.

'I'm an RUC officer,' she said. 'And so is he.'

The fellow stopped his swivelling.

'Pull the other one, missus. You're no more an RUC officer than I'm the Pope.'

'You can ring Inspector McCann at C Division. I'm Constable...' And she stopped herself just in time because the name Sinead Flannery might be a death sentence, much more than being a policewoman, amongst these people.

'Constable who?' The fellow grinned, sensing something, but not sure why she was reluctant to say her name.

'I'm undercover, can't give you my name.'

'And the other fellow? What's his name?' She thought fast, through the same historic problem, the name like a flag in their faces; Liam O'Rourke was as bad as Sinead Flannery, namewise. He'd react like one of Pavlov's dogs, except the fellow in front of her was a Doberman who'd have her head off if the stimulus was the wrong one.

'Just ring 669333. Ask for Inspector McCann.'

By his slouch and the belly on him she'd have him in his forties, a leader of sorts, a senior man. Just out of vision she could hear someone else moving from time to time and once she was able to sneak a glance at a big lad in ill-fitting jeans, black boots, slightly stooped, with long, prehensile arms and a lower lip that trembled slightly underneath the balaclava before he tried to hide in the shadows, like a conger back into its hole in the rock.

'Is that Peter Kemp?' The lad jumped when she used the name, as if he'd been fearing recognition all along. He cowered away, his back to her, voice deliberately muffled.

'No, missus, no way.'

'It is Peter, isn't it? What are you doing messed up in this?' She had recognised him, the first of Raymond's friends she had interviewed up at Belfast castle. It seemed a long time ago.

'You shut up,' said the older fellow, moving his face closer to her. 'Leave my men alone.'

'Men, is it?' She said. 'Is that what you want to be Peter? To be a man?' This time Peter Kemp didn't cower but came forward from the back of the room and gave her a clumsy slap across the face, a glancing, careless blow like he was trying it out for the first time, doing what a man had to do to be accepted.

Her face stung from the shock of the blow. Then she heard a phone ringing, far off, as if at the end of a long corridor and the leader nodded that Peter should answer, pulled out a cigarette, turned his back on her, filled the room with the smell of smoke. When Peter returned from the call both men stepped outside. A whispered conversation began, but she could hear little of it, before the leader stuck his head back round the door.

'Wait a minute,' he said, switched off the light and locked the door behind him. She heard their footsteps moving away outside, leaving her alone. In the silence she could hear the ticking of her watch, even her heartbeat, but in the darkness she had no idea of time. After what seemed a very long time she heard voices outside again and her interrogator came back in and came towards her. Behind him, haloed in a bright light was Peter, standing still, peering in, as if to witness what might happen next. The leader stopped in front of her, rocking on the balls of his feet, seeming to enjoy her fear.

'We're going on a wee trip,' he said and began to untie the rope that bound her.

McCann had come in early, hoping to question Tofer. He was concerned when he couldn't find Flannery, though her shift had started at eight. The kettle in the dead files room was cold, her things were missing. He checked with the desk upstairs if there'd been any messages come in from her, rang through to her lodgings in the police house, but received no reply. He considered where else she might have gone, but realised he didn't know much about her at all, other than the fact she was an excellent policewoman and a Catholic.

He looked in on Tofer, the Custody Sergeant letting him through into the cells, the smell of sweat and unwashed bodies powerful in the narrow corridor. Tofer jumped up as he entered.

'You got anything to tell me, son?'

'How long you going to keep us?'

'Till you see some sense.'

'How long will that be?'

'Only you can tell me that,' said McCann, hanging at the door, the Custody Sergeant behind him, ready to lock Tofer away once McCann gave the word.

'If you remember anything, just give Smithy here a knock, all right?' said McCann, and nodded for him to be locked up again, stepped outside, walked away, hearing Tofer's muffled shouts behind him fading as he climbed the stairs and away out onto the step for a cigarette in the fresh air.

It was another grey day, not actual clouds as such, but the sky heavy over the rooftops, stray raindrops on McCann's bare head. From the step he could see the redbrick terraces with their grey slate rooves pressing in. When he had finished his cigarette he went back inside and made another call to Sammy McGuigan and arranged to meet.

Sammy McGuigan was wearing trainers and a matching tracksuit. He'd left his Mercedes at the park entrance while McCann had taken a cab over to meet him in whatever kit he could find.

'You'll join me for a wee run, McCann?'

'How far are you going?'

'Twice round,' said McGuigan. 'Helps clear the head. You've got to watch out at our age, McCann.' He broke into a slow run, his arms working, belly wobbling under the tracksuit. 'You've to keep your breathing regular, like this.' He demonstrated with a steady gasp of air, cheeks puffed out and a loud slow exhalation as he ran.

'You heard of a fellow called William Tofer?'

'Tofer? It doesn't ring any bells,' McGuigan said.

McCann pulled out the snap of Tofer he'd taken from the records, already damp with sweat. McGuigan slowed, gave it a quick glance, handed it back: 'I do remember this lad. Right wee cunt he was too. I thought he was sent down for five.'

'He was, for aggravated burglary. Records say we tried to do him for drugs too, though that didn't stick.' The path took an upward turn past an ornamental bandstand. McCann was finding it hard to talk while running.

'We done him for the drugs,' Sammy corrected him. 'Don't think he ever forgave us for it. Wiped the smile off of his face we did.' Maybe that was what explained the cut, thought McCann.

'Did he have a crew of his own?'

'Could have done. Sure I'm away above all of that now, McCann. But I hear tell he was sick.'

'Sick?' McGuigan glanced at McCann's face, now red, his eyes bulging with the exertion.

'Here, we'll take a breather shall we?' He offered. The two men paused while McCann – doubled up with his hands on his knees – caught his breath back. 'Aye, time on the sick bay in Crumlin Road. He'd not have been able to build any kind of gang.'

'What was he in the sick bay for?'

'Stabbed,' said Sammy. 'Some cunt knifed him and it got infected.' Simple, matter of fact, probably on Sammy's orders, thought McCann. Maybe Tofer now wanted to get back at McGuigan's gang at the Sceptre? Maybe that was what it was all about?

'Any idea where Tofer is now?'

'How would I know, McCann. Not seen him in a while. Jesus, McCann you look wiped out. Let's call it a day shall we?'

McCann limped on to the exit and when they reached the end he stood and watched as McGuigan climbed into his Mercedes and pulled away, leaving him standing in a cloud of blue diesel smoke.

Back in the dead files room, the phone was ringing as he came through the door. He grabbed the receiver and a strange, high pitched, almost sing-song voice asked was that Inspector McCann? McCann could feel the hair on the back of his neck tingling, the tight grip of anxiety knotting his stomach: 'We've got one of your officers, a lady that won't give her name.'

Immediately he guessed who that person was.

'And you've our Mr Tofer I believe and we want him back.'

'What! Who is this?'

But already the line had gone dead.

McCann was out of the door and along the corridor like a man possessed. Reception was quiet, just a fellow whingeing drunkenly at the window about a lost girlfriend, a mother propped asleep on the corner bench. McCann shouldered the fellow aside, let himself in through the hatch into the duty room.

'Sinead Flannery. Surely to God someone saw her, knows where she went this morning?'

The Duty Sergeant yawned, stretching, showing dark marks of perspiration against the white shirt under his arms, the room cluttered and heavy with smoke.

'I just come on, Inspector' he said. 'I'll take a look in the day book, see if she left anything.'

'I asked. There was nothing,' said McCann. But the man's gears had engaged anyway and he ambled over to the ledger where everything was recorded. He riffled through the day book, messages pinned there with paperclips, sorting through till McCann just leaned over and ripped them from him, flicking through till he came to one in her handwriting, folded over neatly with his name on the front.

'Why'd I never get this?'

The Duty Sergeant shrugged.

'Maybe they were busy on the desk, didn't get a chance to pass it on, maybe they forgot?'

'Busy is it?' snarled McCann and opened the note, understanding now that while he had been busy with McGuigan and Deevery, Flannery had gone to the Sceptre.

Chapter Seven

Paper Clip for once looked directly at McCann, repeating his own words back to him as if he couldn't find any of his own.

'Abducted? A hostage? Who's got her hostage and what do they want? How in devil's name did that happen? You've a duty to protect your officers. What had you got her doing that they were able to get to her?'

'I'd no idea she was putting herself in danger Sir. If I'd known I'd have protected her.'

'Why didn't you know, McCann? You are expected to know where your men are at all times. That's your responsibility.'

'There was a mix up at the desk, a message not passed on.' Paper Clip's face distorted as if he were in the grip of a minor coronary.

'I've systems and processes in place down there. They've had their instructions, training, all of that.' McCann remembered the numbered day books he'd had printed with carbon duplicates, stacks of which were still being used to prop open the door of the duty room on hot days.

'Where did this happen?'

'She went up to the Sceptre Bar I'm afraid.'

'The same place where you were roughed up? Jesus

Christ, McCann!' Paper Clip's face froze for a moment as he struggled with the implications. 'I'll need to get Castlereagh and the crime team onto this now. We'll need to let Inspector Taylor know and we'll need Army support.'

'Surely that's not in 'The Way Ahead'? Surely it's us that are meant to be handling things, you said so yourself.' McCann couldn't resist reminding him of his own words, that he was now contradicting himself. Paper Clip glared back: 'They're specialised in sieges, psychological support, hostage taking, more than we are. They've the Special Air Service done time in Malaya against insurgents. From what you say about this Sceptre Bar it would be best if we went in there hard. But God knows it's an embarrassment for Division, a humiliation, when we're meant to be handling things ourselves.'

'Is there not a risk in that Sir, to Constable Flannery? Could we not try another way to get her back?'

'Oh yes and what's that McCann? You going to put on your bicycle clips and cycle over there and have a wee friendly chat the way you did the last time?'

'A fellow called Tofer I've got in the cells, suspect for the murder of Raymond Small. It's him they want. They might be open to a deal.'

'A deal? You mean you've been on the phone to them already? That's completely irregular, without my authorisation, without Lisburn and the Branch involved, it's…'

But McCann cut him off, enjoying the spectacle just long enough before he said: 'They rang me Sir. I've no idea who they were.' Paper Clip frowned and shook his head with a degree of expressiveness that McCann had not seen before.

'And how did they know you had this fellow Tofer? Has

there been a breach of security as well, McCann?' McCann wondered about the men that had seen him bring Tofer in, the solicitor George Brindley. They would have been quick to pass on what they had seen.

'It could have been anyone that told them,' said McCann. 'We are all fish in the same sea when we recruit men.'

'No, no, McCann, all of our men are 100% loyal. And anyway, we don't do deals now. There'll be no more dirty tricks. I'd think you at least would understand that. Its plain honest to God down to earth policing will win the day. We've to send a firm message to the men of evil on either side, in both communities. You've listened to the Chief Constable, heard what he's got to say, haven't you? Things are going to change round here, people are going to change. I'll get onto Castlereagh right away and set the wheels in motion for Taylor and the Crime Team to come in. Isn't abduction the modus in the bank job too? Could be you've the same men behind both. And I'll get the army in for back up, to make sure we're properly equipped when the shooting starts.'

The empty room was more depressing even than before; Flannery's neat desk a reproach to him, the walls seeming to close in, the files bulging and leaning from their shelves. McCann turned in the narrow space, the options running out. It was a lose-lose scenario and he was no further on with finding out who had killed Raymond Small. So he picked up the phone and rang Emily Thompson.

'Inspector, so this is your lair is it?' she said, half an hour later, stepping into the dead files room, bringing a waft of freshness from the outside world, shaking raindrops off her cape, straightening her hair blown by the wind.

'Didn't expect you to get down so soon,' said McCann.

'Nice surprise?'

'I need a friendly face right now,' said McCann, and told her his news.

'Abducted! God Jesus poor Sinead. How did that happen?'

'I never guessed she'd be daft enough to go up to the Sceptre.'

'But they'll not keep her there. They'll move her.'

Maybe 'move' was a euphemism; when people were moved they rarely came back, McCann knew.

'Paper Clip wants to send them a message just the same. He wants to bring the army in.'

Thompson frowned at that.

'That'll be a message that we're easily riled. It'll be what the paramilitaries want, for us to do something excessive.'

McCann slumped, like he was weighted with lead, patted his jacket for cigarettes but couldn't even find the energy or interest to light up, so Thompson pulled out two of her own, lit one up for him, passed it over. For a moment they both puffed away, blowing smoke up in the air.

'She'll not have gone up there alone,' she said. 'She was walking out with a new fellow. Very keen on him from what I gather. A nice enough lad, a solicitor's clerk, Liam O'Rourke she said his name was. If I'd a guess I'd say she'd gone up there with him. She's not daft, would never go into a place like that alone. It's a long shot but I'd say it would be worth a look. She'll maybe have his address or number somewhere.' And the two of them turned to her desk, pulled the drawers out, began going through her papers, finding nothing.

'It's Taylor's call now. I gather they'll be coming in to take control,' said McCann.

'That'll be nice, being back here at Division,' said Thompson, looking round the narrow space filled with smoke, then at McCann slumped in his chair. 'We'll need to requisition a couple of rooms, more phones, get a larger space for Taylor's office, get everything cleaned up.'

'He'll not be based down here,' said McCann, then realised – with keen disappointment – that she'd been teasing him about getting everything cleaned up for Inspector Taylor, that she'd not be there with him.

McCann heard a shout that he'd to 'off the lights or fuck off' as he turned into the barracks, but once he'd switched off the headlights the squaddies on the gate were civil enough when he wound down the window. They walked the Land Rover through into the factory where the Green Jackets were billeted, helping him park up alongside four or five army Saracens, and another police Land Rover.

'There's an Inspector and one of your boys from Castlereagh up there already in the briefing room,' the Sergeant in charge explained. Then they were on through some swing doors up a concrete ramp, along a corridor lit by inspection lamps rigged along the walls. Somewhere in the background McCann could hear the throb of a diesel generator.

The briefing room was already packed, fifty men sitting cross-legged on the floor in their battle fatigues, faces blackened, the back rows disappearing in the shadows. At the front he recognised Taylor and Clarke standing next to an army Major with his beret and swagger stick. Taylor had dressed himself in his full uniform, the green unnaturally bright in the glare of the lights, gold twinkling and sparkling on his epaulettes, like a cross between a leprechaun and superman. He glanced over as McCann entered, gave him a small, angry nod, to show he'd seen him and noted his lateness.

'So, we'll have men here, here and here.' The Major was tapping the street plan with his wooden pointer. He spoke with a clipped English accent. 'Inspector Taylor here suggests that the target may have been moved, but we're to secure the whole site for forensic examination and detain everyone inside.' Taylor stepped forwards into the light, his thumbs in his pockets, his complexion bleached by the glare from the lamps.

'Yes that's right Major, I gather we've evidence it's a paramilitary stronghold from where multiple forms of criminal activity may have originated, including the recent abduction of one of our officers.' Taylor spoke – repeating what Paper Clip had no doubt told him – authoritatively, as if he had discovered all of that for himself. He was younger than McCann, fitter too, with an agile, alert manner, taking in the reaction of the men as he spoke, his eyes scanning his audience. He glanced over at McCann. 'Inspector McCann can say a bit more perhaps.' There was already a rumble of disquiet there in the room, at the idea that anyone could lose an officer, a hint of a disrespectful titter from the troops, when McCann stepped up to the lights.

'The important thing is that we get her out alive,' said McCann. It was the only thing he could think of to say, the light shining into his eyes, the men in front of him melting into one dark mass of bodies, the heat and the smell of stale sweat overpowering. 'There's a lad been killed too. Its maybe a crime scene and we'll need to be careful to preserve forensic evidence.' He could think of nothing else to add, so the Major stepped in, took the microphone from him: 'There may be booby traps, you may face resistance but the primary goal is to avoid loss of life and secure the missing officer, the site and its people for investigation. So far the RUC have been unable to do that.'

A titter of actual laughter rippled around the room which the Major stemmed with a glare and a tap of his stick on the lectern.

'Tommy, you'll have 3 Company on the rooftop of the old bakery in Collybrae Street, Johnboy will have 2 Company here behind the wall of the Presbyterian Church, in the graveyard. And 1 Company and myself will be in the Saracens. Our positions will be here, here and here.' McCann slipped gratefully back into the shadows, Taylor coming up beside him like a gilded shark.

'Some shit show here, McCann. How did this one happen?' And beside him Clarke, slight in civilian clothes, almost invisible in his ordinariness.

'These people are loyal British subjects,' the Major was saying. 'We are in support of the police, not fighting a war. When the attack starts, 3 Company will enter at the rear, 2 Company here through Belvedere Street at the front. Once the site is secured a warning will be given. We will establish telephone contact also with those inside, to negotiate a peaceful resolution, but if that is not possible both companies will be equipped with blast bombs to break down the doors if needed and tear gas to flush out the occupants if they refuse to come out. 3 Company under Captain Pollack have hostage training in the event that the Constable is inside, and will report directly to me if operations go down that road. Once we gain control of the site the disposal team will go in to clear any booby traps or devices. After the site is clear my colleague Inspector Taylor will take charge.' Taylor bowed to the Major. 'At the signal from me the attack will commence.' Here the Major pulled out a whistle on its lanyard and blew it sharply three times.

A few minutes later McCann found himself sitting next to Taylor inside one of the Saracens as the engine started up with a thunderous rumble that grew louder as the armoured car began to move out from the barracks, accompanied by the sound of the soldiers inside checking their weapons as it turned up towards the Shankill.

'Here we go,' said the Major. But then – above the noise of the diesel engine – they heard the sound of a huge explosion close by and the interior was lit by a sudden flash from a bomb going off.

All that was left of the Sceptre was a pile of loose bricks and broken timbers, sprinkled with shattered pieces of what had once been a thriving bar; a cash register on its side with the drawer out, plastic beer crates, torn curtains, half of a bar snug with its upholstery bursting through. One end of the building still stood, leaning crazily with its rafters pointing in all directions. There was an eery silence, other than the noise of approaching sirens and the sound of tiles slipping from the roof, water pouring from broken pipes and the crackle of flames from several small fires that had broken out.

The Major was out of the Saracen first, bellowing orders, sealing the perimeter just as the fire engines arrived and began to lay their hoses across the rubble, connecting them to the standpipes. McCann paced behind the army cordon, back and forth, stepping over the snaking hoses, the flames sending shadows dancing like some unhappy Halloween when the spirits of the dead made merry with men's souls.

'Looks like someone got here first,' said Taylor. The Major was drenched in sweat, even through his bulky bullet proof vest, diving here and there, keeping his men under control, controlling the cordon.

'Can we not get in ourselves now, see if she's in there,' McCann pleaded.

'Stand back men, please,' he said, busying past. McCann saw he'd still his whistle, dangling unused on its lanyard like a bad luck charm. Meanwhile passing residents skipped away furtively on the far side of the road or doubled back at the end of the street when they saw what had happened. McCann's eyes tried to see through the smoke which drifted like an evil grey vapour across the rubble, looking for any sign of life. Taylor turned to him and said: 'I'd go home if I were you, get some kip man, you'll be useless if you don't get some shut-eye. They've to get the fire out to protect other properties, then those boys go in.' He nodded behind him where a small tracked vehicle loaded with cameras and pincer arms, was coming down a ramp from a Saracen. He could hear the quiet whir of its electric motor, see the technical boys from bomb disposal fussing around.

'And when do they see if there's any living souls?'

'They're doing what they can.'

After a while McCann heard the ambulances starting up, where they'd been lined up behind the cordon, the short whoop of a siren quickly silenced, the sound of them turning in the road. That could mean two things. Either no one was hurt, or everyone was dead and it'd be for the coroner and forensics to deal with what remained.

Eventually the fire officer in charge came over to them, wiping his hands, his face smeared with soot.

'Seems like there's no one hurt, thank God.' Amidst the wreckage the robot was completing its work; scrunching over the brickwork, poking in corners, gripping fragments in its metal arm, the view from its camera showing in a ghostly flicker relayed to a screen in the back of a Saracen, where the technical men were watching.

The sun was coming up, a purple lightening over the chimney tops turning blood red, then orange, a fine day starting. McCann heard the birds singing as clean air started to sift down the street, sliding off the green mountain above, taking away the smoke and dust. He wondered if Flannery would still be alive somewhere to see the new day.

Chapter Eight

Two Land Rovers arrived with the rest of the crime team from Castlereagh; a couple of PC's and lastly Sergeant Emily Thompson, picking her way across the rubble of the Sceptre straight towards McCann and Taylor.

'Flannery's not here. There's no casualties,' McCann repeated what he had been told, seeking to re-assure.

'But if she's not here, where is she?' Thompson seemed distracted, almost panicked and the feeling was contagious. Taylor turned to McCann: 'Any other ideas, McCann, about who would have her and where they'd be?'

'I had a call,' said McCann. 'They wanted an exchange of a man I'd detained, a William Tofer. He'd be in with the gang that was based here. If you can find the rest of the gang maybe you can find her.'

'Any idea where they might be?'

'That's anyone's guess now,' said McCann.

Clarke was out of earshot, bending down amongst the rubble, turning over smouldering papers with the toe of his boot, as if on some quite different line of enquiry. Taylor called him over.

'Could you trace a call for us, last night into Division, to the Inspector here?'

McCann didn't like the idea of Clarke's people able to listen in to calls. But Clarke said too much time had elapsed to get a trace, while his eyes ranged over the wreckage of the bar, frowning, like he was worried about something other than the fate of Flannery.

'And any names you had of the people here. We can follow up on them.' Clarke nodded, a hint of reluctance there to be sharing valuable intelligence again.

'They must have had a tip-off here, a warning about the bomb,' McCann said. 'Ten on a Friday night? An empty bar? No casualties? As unlikely as a snowball in hell, I'd say. If it was the IRA done the bomb they'd want maximum casualties, to take out a whole unit of the UFF, take the military with them too.' A bomb was definitive; as a show of strength you couldn't argue with it. It was the best message anyone could send.

'Who'd give them a warning?' Clarke queried.

'Maybe someone inside with a bit of humanity gave the tip-off,' suggested McCann. Taylor gave a bitter laugh at McCann's suggestion, but McCann continued: 'Sometimes it happens. Maybe someone close to the IRA Active Service Unit got wind of what was going to happen and didn't like the idea of that many deaths. One of Clarke's informers maybe rang the Branch? And the Branch maybe let the bomb go ahead but made sure they'd have the UFF men alive if they needed them later. Letting the bomb go ahead would give their informer some cover too.' Now it was Clarke's turn to laugh. 'Ah Come on McCann you've been reading too much Republican propaganda. There's no way we'd condone paramilitary activity at the Sceptre, nor put the armed forces at risk.'

'Then how come you have their staff list here if it comes to that? Maybe there's people above you that don't buy into your fine moral patter, that are less fussy than you are?' McCann could feel himself losing it, with the lack of sleep, with Emily Thompson watching, the conversation drifting away from rescuing Flannery into dark speculation about the work of the Branch. He'd be needing Clarke on his side. He tried to get a grip, everyone looking at him as if he was mad: 'But more likely this was a feud between your UFF boys.'

'They're not our boys,' he said. 'And they're not into killing each other,' said Clarke.

'Is that so? Then how come Raymond Small got himself killed?'

'You tell me.'

But McCann hadn't an answer. Had Raymond Small been one of the foot soldiers and done something so bad that he had got himself killed by his own people? Was the bomb Sammy McGuigan's way of saying that if he couldn't control the Sceptre he'd make sure no one else could have it either? Or was it just an IRA hit, the obvious explanation?

McCann bent down to look in the empty cash register by his feet.

'They even took the money before they went. They'd have had time. There's not even small change here. There's nothing here for you, Taylor.'

'There's no way there'd be the bank money here,' snapped Taylor. 'That was a Republican job.'

Maybe it was just the old tried and trusted methodology, to hide a crime with a bigger one, thought McCann; if there had been any forensic evidence most of it would have been carbonised by the blast and the subsequent fires.

Then he saw a black armoured Rover with tinted windows pulling over on the road, the flash of spaghetti on epaulettes as the diminutive figure of the Chief Constable climbed out, followed by Paper Clip and the limber flak-jacketed muscle of the Chief Constable's protection team. They scrunched across the rubble, Paper Clip following behind, like a child about to be shown the consequences of his bad behaviour.

'What's going on here, men,' said the Chief. 'I've had OC Northern Ireland on about this, not to mention the Secretary of State. Nearly wiped out half the Green Jackets I gather.'

'It seems like it was a coincidence, Sir,' explained Taylor. 'Our raid and a Republican attack on a Protestant bar coincided. We were going in after some paramilitaries that had taken one of our officers, when this lot went up.'

'Coincidence! Nothing is coincidental here is it?' And just for once, McCann was inclined to agree with the Chief Constable. Paper Clip meanwhile was riffling in his shiny black attaché case, plucking a paper from amongst those neatly filed inside: 'It's all in order Sir, a full risk assessment and you'll find all the T's crossed and I's dotted, protocols followed. McCann here said a raid was essential and I'd to back him up of course.'

McCann saw there was nothing to be done. He had to get away from the high-ups, circling like seagulls dropping their shit on the people below. He had to think about his next move now that the raid had gone so badly wrong.

'I've to get back to Division,' he said, reversing away,

trying to leave them to it, but Paper Clip followed him.

'You've really dropped me in it here, McCann. Dropped Division in it, your colleagues, everyone. You've made all of our jobs much harder.'

McCann trudged away. He tried to outpace the Super-intendent, who broke into a small run in order to keep up, bouncing along at McCann's elbow, hissing imprecations like a leaking tyre overinflated with his own sense of self-importance.

McCann was dog-tired when he got back to Division, had nodded off in the back of the Land Rover for a few minutes as he was driven back, his mouth dry, eyelids gummy when he was awakened by the driver.

'You snoozing on Sir?' A friendly face peered back at him. He blinked, jumped upright, scrambled out into the daylight, made his way down to the dead files room, like he was drawn to it, back to his own chamber of disappointed hopes.

He'd intended to wait there, but was not sure for what. There would be a call he was sure, after the night's events at the Sceptre, the raid gone wrong. It would not go unnoticed that they'd sent the Army in, that there'd been a bombing. God alone knew how they'd react, but he was certain there'd be a reaction. So he waited by the phone, expecting more bad news. His head felt heavy, his eyes prickled.

McCann dozed at his desk for an hour or so, his head on his arms. But when the call came he was awake immediately and his hand lashed out for the receiver.

'What're you cunts up to?' Said the sing-song voice. Then came the sound of a slap and a woman's scream.

'You get us Tofer and no more of your stupid tricks.'

'I wanted to, but the brass had other ideas. I couldn't stop them. I'll get you Tofer now, I'll guarantee it. I promise you. Just me and him, we'll come anywhere you say. Just leave my Constable out of it.' McCann found himself babbling, making crazy promises. There was a silence on the line and he could imagine the fellow at the other end thinking. No whispered conversations, no discussions though, so maybe he was acting alone, same way as McCann. Maybe it was just the two of them facing off against each other.

'Where do you want him? Give us a time and place and we'll be there,' McCann found himself begging. Then the voice answered and McCann scrabbled for a pencil and paper.

Coming out with Tofer into a grey Belfast afternoon, McCann met Taylor coming the other way.

'Is this your man Tofer, McCann?'

McCann nodded, both men hesitating, Tofer bemused by it all.

'Where are you taking him if you don't mind me asking?'

'Taking him back to the scene of the crime,' McCann lied, but lies didn't come easily to him.

'I'd like a word with him first, if I may,' said Taylor, pointing them both back up the steps. 'He's a key lead isn't he? To the gang at the Sceptre and as investigating officer on that now I've a right to detain him for questions.'

A mad idea came to McCann that he should just push Taylor off the steps and make a run for it with Tofer. But Taylor was a big man, younger, fitter even, had seen McCann's professional glance to left and right, the way he'd clenched his fists. Taylor moved easily on the balls of his feet.

'I'd like to show him the crime scene first to see if it jogs his memory.'

'That won't be possible. Leastways you can't release him. Isn't that what you were going to do? The usual crazy freelance stuff. Jesus, McCann, Sergeant Thompson was right about you.'

'What do you mean right.'

'A real wild card. A kamikaze merchant, going out alone to meet those boyos, not telling anyone. Is it a death wish or what that you've got McCann?'

And with that he placed a hand on Tofer's arm, turned him around and began to walk him back up the steps away from McCann.

'Here,' said McCann. 'He's my prisoner. I can do what I like with him.'

'I'm afraid not, McCann,' said Taylor.

A Kamikaze merchant, a death wish? Had Thompson really said that? Maybe she had, maybe he was what she said, thought McCann as he watched Tofer disappear back into the police station with Taylor and along with him, maybe his last and only chance of getting Flannery back alive.

When he got home McCann slammed the front door so hard it cracked a pane of glass, which made him angrier still. He banged the doors of the kitchen units for good measure, but even that and a cup of tea didn't steady his mood as he watched the clock on the kitchen wall ticking on. He looked out at the wasted chaos of the back garden, where his digging and good intentions of tidying had come to naught. With nothing else to do, he slid the patio doors back, stepped out with his cup of tea into the muddy wasteland, full of nervous energy, feeling like he'd explode if he couldn't do something.

Then he grabbed a fork from the shed, made over to the back fence where the bindweed had twisted its way up the rambling roses, strangling them at the roots, took a few wild swings at the stuff, started tearing it down, ripping piles of it back till it formed a mound at his feet and he could see the rose bushes peeking through, the odd dried bloom, the first promising buds of spring. He took off his jacket and started going at the roots, rolled up his sleeves, dug down till he saw that even the roots were entwined, the two plants a mess of tendrils, diving deep into the soft and loamy soil, bindweed and rose an inseparable puzzle, so inseparable the only thing to do was to dig it all up and maybe start again with new rose bushes. Like a maniac he tore into that as the sky began to darken, ripping and gouging, tearing the plants out of the ground because if they couldn't be separated they'd have to go, until at dusk he'd finished and soaked in sweat he retired to the house for a Radox bath.

But even in the bath he couldn't let it go, the thought of the clock ticking on past the deadline for the exchange of Tofer and what might happen to Flannery after that. He swore to himself, erupted from the steaming water, dried himself down quickly, got himself dressed. Then he grabbed his car keys off the table by the phone and leaped from the house.

Chapter Nine

McCann drove with his head hunched down, barely showing above the dashboard, the headlights sweeping the road ahead across the moor. At a crossroads he took a right turn towards Antrim, passing the occasional cottage. Suddenly the headlights ranged over a straggle of twisted trees and a two-storey farmhouse where a white van was parked. McCann switched off the engine and let the car free wheel to a standstill short of the farm, extinguishing the lights. He reached into the glove compartment, pulled out his Walther. Its weight was unfamiliar in his hand and for a second he hesitated before stuffing it into his coat pocket. Leaving the keys in the ignition, he gently closed the car door and crept away, ducked through a gap in a dry-stone wall into a field where he waited. In the darkness every hedge and boulder took the form of crouching men, judgement made more difficult still by the presence of bullocks in the field, breathing and snorting.

Maybe it had been stubborn pride, vanity even, to refuse to ask for anyone's help? Or just caution after the fiasco of the day before, that help could be more trouble than it was worth? Hadn't he allowed Flannery to get herself into this situation, so surely it was up to him alone to get her out? Nonetheless, as he edged forwards across the damp grass towards the farmhouse, McCann realised how useful some intelligence paraphernalia could have been; the night vision sights, listening equipment and aerial surveillance. The moon sailed out from behind a towering cloud. He wasn't too sure if he'd trust the Branch behind his back in the dark, trust them to do the right thing in a corner. So he crept forwards alone, his trouser turn-ups soaked in the dew, right up to the hedgerow that bounded the farm, moving stealthily along until he found a path that led up to the back door and a single lighted window. He hid himself amongst the bushes, to observe for a few more minutes, looked at his watch in the moonlight and saw that it was almost time.

The door opened and a path of light streamed towards him, a figure silhouetted in the doorway. As McCann ducked back into deeper darkness a fellow stepped out. He caught a glimpse of another fellow lolling on a chair inside with a gun held like a baby in his lap. There was no sign of Flannery. And then the fellow in the doorway walked straight towards McCann, a revolver in his hand, pushed through the bushes and hid himself beside him. McCann stayed stock still, his head down, barely breathing, feeling the man's presence next to him, trying to gauge how far off he was, considering if he could take him if it came to that. The clouds rolled back over the moon, covering him in complete darkness.

Suddenly a match flared and McCann caught a glimpse of a face. The man saw McCann too, dropped his cigarette, fumbled for his gun. McCann was on him, had him over in the brambles putting his face down into them with his hand on the nape of his neck, his full body weight on the small of his back while he kicked the gun away, put his own gun into the fellows jugular. But he couldn't stop the bellow that the man let out.

The second man appeared in the doorway of the house, peering towards the source of the commotion, gun at the ready. With his knee still on the man's back underneath him, McCann fired three times towards the house, hearing the bullets ricochet off the wall. Then he saw Flannery behind the gunman.

'Let her go or your man gets it,' he bellowed, his voice wild and loud with rage. And Flannery leaped on the gunman from behind, shoved him violently off the step, off balance, his gun tangling as he fell, firing wildly into the darkness, the bullets ripping the foliage around McCann. 'There's a car on the Antrim Road,' he bellowed.

McCann jumped forwards, but the fellow he'd been holding grabbed him by the ankle and he fell with a crash into the brambles, his gun slipping from his hand.

'Give us a hand here will you,' shouted the fellow that was holding him. He saw the gunman hesitate for a split second in his pursuit of Flannery, start to turn back. McCann fought to kick the hand free of his leg, flailing to recover his gun in the darkness, but the hand held him like a vice. He heard the noise of a car starting up, the engine racing, tyres squealing on the road, just as the cold steel of a revolver was put to the back of his head and the sing-song voice of the gunman commanded McCann to lie still.

When the news came in that Constable Sinead Flannery had escaped and turned up at Division, Taylor and Thompson rushed down from Castlereagh to Division with the siren going and the lights flashing. They double parked in the pound and ran up the steps to the first aid station, where Flannery had been checked out, given tea, all the while babbling some story about McCann being taken. Thompson had helped her get cleaned up, borrowed some fresh clothes from one of the women Constables on duty and they let her have a wash before Taylor took over.

'Welcome back Constable Flannery,' said Taylor. 'Can we get you some more tea? I hear they've been giving you a hard time.'

'I'm fine, Sir, thanks.' Truth to tell she'd have liked more time, but Taylor had more urgent matters on his mind.

'So, tell us about these fellows that took you.' So she described how she'd gone up to the Sceptre, Taylor halting her immediately.

'And not clearing it with McCann? That seems a bit foolhardy.'

'I left him a note.'

'That's not the same thing, love.'

She'd tried to leave Liam out of it, but the story seemed unreal without him and Taylor picked up on that: 'So you went up there alone, did you?'

'I took another fellow up with me. We need to check if he's OK.' And she scribbled out Liam's address and phone number. 'He's just a friend. I thought we'd have more chance getting in there, informal like.' Taylor rang through to the incident room at Castlereagh to put the crime team onto it, to check him out, bring him in for questioning.

'But he only saw the Sceptre, not the fellows that took me.'

'We'll bring him in just the same,' said Taylor. 'You know it's gone, do you?'

'Gone?'

'We were going in to get you but the IRA got there first, bombed it flat.' Flannery was shocked, put her hand to her mouth. Taylor raised his eyebrows, like she had something to explain. Then he moved on, asked for a description of the man who had taken her. She described his clothes, everything about him that she could remember: 'Had an odd kind of a voice. I think he'd a limp too, sounded like he was dragging his foot. He was careful though, balaclava like he lived in it. Knew what he was doing, what he was after.' Then it all welled up and she found herself sobbing and Thompon put her arm around her shoulders for comfort.

'That's ok. Do you want a wee break? Use the toilet maybe?' Taylor asked, awkward there in the room with the two women, maybe even a little impatient.

'No, we've to find him. He's the fellow that'll maybe still have McCann.'

'Any names. Did you catch any names?'

'They were careful, but there was a young lad I think I recognised. Peter Kemp his name was. He was the first lad I interviewed when Raymond Small went missing.' Taylor paused again while she found his details in her desk, then he rang them through to the incident room again and told someone to pick Peter Kemp up too, if he could be found.

'And the farm, we need to know where it is right now. Get up there, get forensics in, track the owners, roll this one back up.' Taylor was sharp, working through the steps, Thompson noting things down as he went, fetching a map of the Antrim Plateau, helping her retrace the drive down off the moor into the city, pulling up large scale aerial photos from the office, till they'd an X on the map where she'd been. All done in ten minutes, then more calls to deploy the men out there, backed by forensics.

'Now tell us how in God's name did McCann find you?'

Flannery said she didn't know, hadn't an inkling.

'They'd have rung him. He'd have had the contacts, some backroom way round it,' said Thompson. Taylor looked unhappy.

'Doing a swap with no one to swap. Is the fellow mad or what?'

'He's not mad,' said Thompson. 'But he doesn't know when to stop.'

'And how come you got away?' Taylor had an edge of suspicion to his voice, like he couldn't quite believe that a young woman and someone like McCann could escape a paramilitary gang.

'They'd untied me. They were expecting a swap, an exchange, had got ready for it,' she explained. 'McCann distracted them, put himself in danger and I made a run for it.'

'Did you hear any shots as you were running away?'

'Only the fellow that was after me.'

Flannery looked down at her feet, ashamed at that. 'What else was I to do?'

'You done right,' said Taylor, picking up his cigarettes and keys. 'We'd best get out there then, see if McCann's there.'

'But before that they had me somewhere else,' Flannery interrupted. Taylor dropped his keys back down on the table.

'Where was that?'

'Some kind of industrial premises maybe, a storeroom. It was quiet, very quiet indeed. No traffic, no noise of machinery, nothing. I had to go down some steps to get in and out. Eighteen steps.'

'And what was there in the storeroom?'

'Boxes, cleaning materials, filing cabinets.'

'Anything on them that would give us a clue?'

'I tried to memorise anything I could see; Revic, Berned, Macquip.'

'Means nothing to me. How do you spell those?'

Thompson pushed her pad over to Sinead with the pen and she wrote the words out carefully in large capitals. The three stared at the unfamiliar trade names. Then Thompson pulled over the yellow pages, riffled through to see if the commercial directory could help.

'Berned, they do knife sterilisers. Jesus! And Macquip, abattoir machinery, there's even an advert here.' She showed them the picture of a carcass hanging.

'How many abattoirs are there?' Taylor began to reel off the places he knew of, but Flannery interrupted: 'By water, I could swear it was by water, must be the one down the Docks. Come on.' Flannery was already out of her seat.

'We'll deal with this, love,' said Taylor, hitching his trousers, standing in her way. 'I'd get yourself cleaned up, a bit of make-up, you'll feel better. McCann won't be wanting to see you in that state now, will he?'

He left the room with Thompson by his side. As the door closed and they walked away Flannery heard him say: 'Jesus McCann and Flannery are two of a kind, aren't they?' and Thompson's reply: 'Made for each other, sir.'

Where was he? McCann tried to twist his head around, to pierce the darkness, strained at his bindings, but found that he was held fast. There was a noise which for a moment he couldn't place, a soft sighing, maybe a distant slap of waves against a quayside. Perhaps he was dreaming a nightmare, were it not for the grip on his wrists – that was so tight he could feel his fingers swelling as the circulation was cut off – and the rough cord across his thighs and chest. He was cold. He could remember the journey down, had tried to memorise each turn as he lay in the back of the white van. He recognised the twists and turns descending off the Antrim Plateau, the stopping and starting at traffic lights as they entered the city, but after that he was lost until they bundled him out roughly up some steps, along a corridor, then forced him to lie down.

Suddenly his hood was pulled off and lights blazed. When his eyes accustomed to the glare he could see meat hooks attached to a conveyor belt that ran across a high ceiling. Next to where he lay there were white plastic wheeled bins stained with blood, all parked up in orderly rows for the night. He heard the sound of a door being unlocked behind him and footsteps coming nearer, footsteps with a dragging action on the stone floor. He still couldn't see anyone. The steps stopped behind his head.

'Are you ready?' A strange voice asked, high pitched and dry, like its owner had some injury to his vocal chords, like it was a strain for him to speak. He tried to tilt his head back to see who had spoken but was unable to do so. Then there was the sound of a zip, as if an overnight bag was being opened, or maybe the fellow was slipping out of his parka, or into some outfit they had for work on animals? Wild thoughts raced in McCann's mind until he heard the slow rasp of a blade being sharpened on a whetstone.

'Where's our Mr Tofer?' The gag was removed from his mouth and air rushed in, along with some blood from a cut on his lip.

'I wasn't allowed to bring him. Thought I'd do instead.'

'And you are Inspector McCann?' it wasn't a question, it was delivered like an insult, as if the fellow were inquiring the name of an insect or a small boy.

'That's me,' said McCann. The fellow sighed, almost like McCann had given him some longed for sexual pleasure. McCann wondered was this one of the fellows from the Sceptre he'd met before? Then they'd had the uniform, the regulation Milletts balaclava. This man didn't care for disguise, even stood out in the light almost like he expected to be examined. He had a fleshy face, slight double chin, a large nose and receding hair that seemed unkempt, as if he'd used the clippers on it himself. But it was the blue eyes that held McCann's attention, the irises flecked with red veins, the pupils dilated, staring at McCann like he was some kind of specimen on a petri dish in some hellish laboratory. Why wasn't he trying to conceal himself, McCann wondered? And the answer came with another dull thud of realisation; it was because he was going to die and therefore it did not matter if McCann had his description or not.

'You'll like these,' said the fellow. McCann's head was swivelled roughly to the left so he could see a wooden block and the tools being laid out there from the bag, and then each turned over so that McCann could appreciate its potential.

'The boner,' he said. 'Though not the kind of boner you might be familiar with Inspector.' He chuckled as he showed

McCann a long, thin blade on a rubber handle. 'The fillet knife. You'll know that one, seen it in the kitchen, maybe.' That blade was placed down next to the boner, like he was preparing to start work. 'And the big fellow. The Chinese cleaver.' And this one the fellow drove down deep into the chopping block, adding 'For major operations.' There was a pause and the fellow whispered in his ear, where McCann was not expecting it: 'But let's start with something special' and immediately, he felt an agonising pain in his arm, so his whole body arched against it, away from it, like an electric shock, but far worse, deep in the flesh, deep in his being. The man laughed. 'The hotshot electric prodder,' he explained. 'Useful for pigs. But you should stay still Inspector, or else I'll need to use the boning hook to stop that squirming. Then we'll be ready for a little light conversation, won't we?' And McCann felt the ties being tightened by a hand encased in white latex gloves.

Suddenly McCann understood why everyone seemed afraid, why no one told him the truth. He understood that he had found his man, though really it was vice versa, because the man had found him instead and there was nothing he could do about it. Maybe they'd even taken Flannery and let her escape because it was him they had wanted all along.

'Just a wee chat, you and me together,' said the high, reedy voice, as the pain subsided. He braced himself, all his muscles tight, testing the bands that held him to the table.

'What did our friend Tofer tell you?' The voice was gentle.

'Said you done in Raymond Small up the Sceptre.' McCann went fishing, casting the line out.

'Why would I do that McCann?'

'That's what we're trying to find out.'

'I'll tell you, if you tell us how come after that bitch of yours came over with her fancy man the Sceptre got bombed? That's what we want to know first. You sent her over McCann, to size us up, to plan the raid. You know what they say about the fish rotting from the head. You were in charge and let someone set us up for a bombing. We got your message. It's just as well we'd friends that warned us.'

'What friends?'

'We've more friends than you, McCann.' Then another agonising shot of the cattle prod, this time to McCann's right side.

'Who was that lad she come over with?' McCann caught a glimpse of steel just in the corner of his vision, heard the sound of the boner being stropped, a cold dread, a terror gripping him, rushing through him, a paralysing fear. He'd always thought that if he came face to face with death he would be glad, that it would be a release, but not pain, if it went on. He'd read somewhere that everyone broke, if there was enough pain and he was human like everyone else. Except perhaps this fellow with his boning knife.

'Just a wee incision to start with,' said the fellow with another chuckle. McCann barely felt the cut, so sharp was the knife, but he did feel the warm trickle of his own blood, down his arm along the steel tray, seeping out.

'Just a wee cut to get things flowing, McCann. Now tell us who the other fellow was. Tell us what Tofer told you.'

He saw the man's hand reach back for the cleaver, like a dentist hiding the drill from a nervous patient. Another warning light flashed in McCann's mind, that if this was the same man that had killed Raymond Small they'd be sending a memento to Division, to put the pressure on. Which part of himself might they send?

'What's Tofer been saying?'

'He's been saying nothing.' What was happening to him seemed disproportionate, inappropriate, unmeasured, whatever kind of adjective you would apply to the behaviour of a lunatic. Or someone driven mad by loss and fury in Ulster's war. The fellow drew his arm back, McCann could see the blade flash in the light. McCann closed his eyes and he brought it down with a mighty crash. McCann had felt nothing. The man was laughing, the blade embedded in the wooden block beside him.

'Ah come on Inspector don't tell us you've had Tofer in the cells and he's not been talking. Just tell us the truth, if you can, or next time I'll chop you for real.' McCann tried to breathe evenly, his breath coming in short gasps now. If he could spin out his answers, that might give them time to rescue him. But no one knew where he was except maybe Flannery, if she'd been held in the same place and had got away.

'What do you want me to say? I'll say anything.' If they were to cut him to bits, there'd be no way for them to tell what was true and false, so he'd say anything they wanted to hear because it wouldn't matter, so long as he didn't put other people at risk..

'Tell you what,'gasped McCann. 'Since you're going to kill me, let us have a last wish.'

Another chuckle, then the man reached for the chopper again, tried to wrest it from where it was embedded in the block.

'I've not the facilities for last wishes, McCann, if its bacon and eggs you want. Might be able to do you a steak.'

'None of that. What did you say your name was?'

'I don't have a name.'

'There's one thing I'd like to know before you do me in.'

'I'm not done with you yet.'

'Well you soon will be because I'm not going to tell you what you want to know, so you'll have to kill me and then you'll never know it will you? But just let me have it, that last wish. It's the decent thing, isn't it? It's what you'd want, were things to be reversed. If I'd had you up the Crumlin Road in the old days you'd be given whatever you wanted that last morning before the big drop. Any kind of big fry up, a chat with your mother on the phone, a pint of double, hear tell they'd even let you have conjugal relations, so the least you can do is let me have a last wee something.'

McCann could feel his energy draining away, could feel his fingers starting to tremble, he felt a seeping cold, spreading up from his toes.

'Cut your crap McCann and just tell me what you want and then we'll see.'

'At least you can tell us about Raymond. Where he is, why he was topped, who done it. If you're going to kill me, let me know first. It's what started all of this off. If you'd not have taken Raymond none of this would ever have happened.'

'Raymond?' said the voice. 'Wee Raymond?' A bit of a laugh again, as if the man was savouring a pleasant, perverted memory.

'What had he done that put him in the frame?'

'Like you, McCann, he'd not told us what we needed to

know. He'd not come clean. Not admitted his crimes.'

'And what crime was that? What was so important that you'd to kill him?'

He'd go out with the answer, that at least, thought McCann. He'd be gone but he'd have done his duty by the lad. He'd be on the right side with God, if there was one. They'd all be on the right side with God if the truth came out. He tried to explain that to the fellow, gasping for breath, consciousness slipping from him begging to at least be told where Raymond's body lay.

'You'll find Raymond down with the others.'

'The others?'

'Where the unbelievers go. The no hopers, the spongers, the traitors, the deceivers, the touts, all of the dross and the filth, that's where they all go.'

'But why? Raymond was no traitor.'

'Wasn't he?'

'Tell you what McCann. Tell us who the boyo was at the Sceptre and we'll tell you exactly where Raymond went.'

'I don't know,' said McCann.

'Is it don't know or won't tell?' said the man, showing McCann the blade dripping with his own blood, wiping it clean ready for action.

So for a minute or two they fenced around it, arguing, till they came to trade the details, one word at a time, where Raymond Small was buried for a name that McCann gave him, drawing it out for as long as he could until he heard the boner being sharpened one last time.

'And this Liam O'Rourke, where will I find him?'

'I don't know,' said McCann. 'I honestly don't.'

'How will I know that's true?'

'You won't. You've to trust me like I've to trust you. It's a leap of faith,' said McCann.

'And Tofer, what did he say about the money?'

'What money?' And then the lights went out.

The dockside at night glistened black in the moonlight, the slow gurgle and slap of the incoming tide audible against the quay as the officers worked their way towards the abattoir, past the steel holding pens, past two or three trailers waiting collection – their freezer units still running – then up to the doors of the abattoir itself, which were locked, the lights off.

Thompson checked the magazine on her gun, heard Taylor and other men do the same. The automatic weapon was heavy across her shoulders. They'd need them if the gang were armed as they would be. Yet she wasn't sure she could recall the training at Magilligan, remembered only the massive kick when the gun went off, the way the bullets sprayed everywhere. It'd be carnage and maybe McCann would be caught in it.

'OK,' said Taylor and they advanced together around the side of the building until they heard an eery, almost inhuman cry, like a beast in pain, yet recognisable as a version of McCann, an unearthly being inhabiting some nether world, echoing over the black moonlit waters of the nearby dock. They climbed up to a fire door at the top, that opened when they pulled. Once inside, along a steel walkway they could see a bright light. There was another cry, echoing and rolling from the walls. Thompson moved forwards but Taylor pulled her back.

'We'll do the lights,' he said, gesturing at a junction box. And then they stormed the room where McCann was held.

Chapter Ten

When McCann woke up he was in a hospital bed, tightly constrained by starched white sheets and two thick green blankets and propped up against a bolster pillow so he could see around. He was in a room by himself. Through a frosted-glass panel in the door he could see a shadow moving, as if a sentry were shifting position to rest his feet. He twisted his head. That felt OK. Bright spring light filled the room, telling him it was morning. He could just see the green mountain outside the window. He poured water from a carafe on the bedside table into a glass, drank it down in one, peered to see if he could see his clothes. Then he wiggled his toes, his feet, each arm, each hand, testing his body. Apart from the bandages, everything was OK. He tried to move himself upright, but at first felt dizzy, out of breath, recollections of the night before surfacing; the rescue, the ambulance, being stitched in casualty. He took another sip of water. His mind felt strangely sharp, as if the effects of the previous night's drugs had been to remove any extraneous thoughts.

Flannery must have got away in order for him to have been found. That made it all worthwhile. Taylor would have taken his tormentor to Castlereagh. The fellow with the thin reedy voice and the limp, the surgeon, but was he the one in command or just a technician? And there was Tofer still in custody too, that had taken Raymond Small up the stairs and started it all off. Everyone detained except for Sammy McGuigan, who seemed always above the fray, hovering just out of reach and above him Councillor Rabbie Smith. They'd be like ferrets in a bag fighting each other and hard to work out why they'd done what they did to Raymond, or which one of them had been involved, though the surgeon clearly seemed to have the skills. And why had they wanted Tofer back so badly that they'd take those risks to get him?

A nurse came in and he caught a glimpse of a Constable behind her in the doorway. Was he there for protection or something else? He got himself a coffee and a couple of rolls from the trolley the nurse had brought in, slapped on some butter and jam, made himself decent with a thin hospital dressing gown and eased himself out of bed towards the door.

'All right, feller?' he said. The Constable was a big, thickset lad that had the brawn but not the brains: 'Aye, OK Sir.'

'Who sent you?'

'Taylor said I'd to keep an eye.'

'An eye on what?'

'He didn't say.'

Despite the protestations of the nursing staff, McCann discharged himself from hospital and picked up a black cab to take himself up to Castlereagh. When it became snarled in traffic going around the City Hall he leaned forward impatiently to tap on the glass, just in time to see Councillor Rabbie Smith climbing out of a taxi up ahead, then striding into work at the

Licensing Committee with his brolly and briefcase.

'C'mon pal I've not got all day,' he muttered at the driver as the cab stopped at a crossing crowded with people, ponderous with their prams, shopping bags and walking sticks.

When they turned up the Castlereagh Road there was a roadblock in place, a Saracen and a squad of Redcaps checking cars. Two soldiers loomed up as the driver tried to jump the queue, each six feet tall in their boots.

'You can't go up there, mate.'

'I'm police,' he said. McCann realised he must have presented a sight; the bloodstained shirt under an old jacket, the shoes and trousers still muddy from the farm. The soldiers were only young lads and without their boots and their attitude they'd be five foot six at most and pimply with it. He flashed his card, but they wouldn't wave him through, so McCann thrust a banknote into the driver's hand and got out to walk the rest of the way, overtaking cars as they inched forwards. A helicopter was throbbing overhead, the noise of its rotors now receding, now returning, the wind from its downdraft blowing litter along the pavements.

Taylor greeted him at reception.

'What are you doing back here, McCann? You should be taking a rest, after the shock you've had.' Seeming genuinely concerned he took McCann by the elbow, out of sight into an empty room which hadn't been used for a while, the heating off. McCann was grateful for the coolness, to be able to sit down.

'Flannery get back then?'

'Constable Flannery? She's doing fine,' said Taylor. 'Surprising, given the risks you both took. You could both have been killed, other people could have been hurt. Arbuthnut's coming over later from Division for the post-mortem.'

Taylor looked him up and down.

'What happened to your clothes?'

'No time to stop by C and A.'

'Did they say you could be discharged?'

'They couldn't stop me.'

'Was that wise in your condition?'

'I'm right as rain, considering, thanks.' Relative to what he could have been if he hadn't been rescued, he was fit as a fiddle. 'Thanks to you and Sergeant Thompson. I'm grateful to you both.' Taylor nodded, accepting McCann's thanks.

'I'll get someone to sort you out some clothes.' He went to the door, leaned out into the corridor and shouted for Thompson. Then when that didn't have the desired effect, he grabbed a passing Constable and got him to bring her from the incident room. She arrived in a rush, worried too that he'd discharged himself. She was out of uniform, in tight blue jeans, a white summer shirt.

'Never knew you were such a dab hand with an automatic,' said McCann, feeling a rush of gratitude and pleasure for her presence there in the room.

'And how are you?' She asked. McCann assured her he was OK, but saw her discount that with a slight nod and a critical glance, knowing that it was what he always said even when he was in a bad way.

When she had gone Taylor sat down opposite him and swept the empty table between them with his hands, as if clearing the decks prior to battle.

'You've got the fellow from the abattoir that done this to

me?' McCann got his question in first.

'Stephen John McKittrick, his name is.'

'I'll need to see him. He's now the prime suspect for the murder of Raymond Small, as good as admitted it.' There was an awkward silence. Taylor tapped his fingers on the table, like a difficult question had arisen.

'You're not fit for that McCann and anyhow it's not Division's case any more. That's a serious crime and you need our resources for it. First things first, man. Let me put him away for what he's done to you and that Flannery woman. Put your feet up. You can't have a victim investigating a crime against himself. I'd stand back from this one because it's way beyond your remit, beyond your capacity.'

'But I've to talk to these fellows, try to work out who done what, who gave the orders in the murder of Raymond Small.'

'First let us get them off the streets, McCann, get them bang to rights for what they done to you and Sergeant Flannery.'

McCann tried to argue the toss until Thompson came back into the room carrying a bundle of fresh clothes.

'I'd to raid the jumble for the next fundraiser,' she said, laying out the clothes she had managed to find. 'The least we can do is to smarten you up a bit.'

'Nice pair of worsted breeks there,' said Taylor, fingering the fabric of the trousers she had brought.

'Looks like one of Paper Clip's castoffs,' said McCann, turning the trousers over, looking inside. 'Best check for skid marks first.'

Thompson smiled, asked Taylor if she could sit in while he debriefed McCann and settled opposite with her notepad before Taylor could refuse.

'Tell us what happened then McCann, before you go AWOL again.'

So, McCann described how he'd been taken prisoner during Flannery's escape, the hood they'd had on him as he was moved to the abattoir, the interrogation by the man called McKittrick and the questions he'd asked.

'And did you tell him anything?' McCann hesitated, a little shamefaced: 'I had to give him the name of Flannery's boyfriend that was up at the Sceptre with her.'

'Anything else?'

'They wanted his address but I didn't know it so I couldn't give it to him.'

Taylor frowned.

'We're looking for him too. He wasn't at the address she gave us.'

'But in return he told us where to find Raymond Small's body.'

'And you believed him?'

'In so far as anyone can believe anything.'

'We'll need to warn the man.'

'We've got McKittrick in custody, so he's in no danger.'

'For now we have. But it could still be a risk for him that they've got his name.' McCann could see that, tried to think if there'd been any way that McKittrick could have got Liam's name out before Taylor's team had stormed the abattoir.

'No other questions then?' Taylor asked.

'He asked about money, if Tofer had told us anything about money.' Taylor frowned. 'But I think he was interested in the bigger picture.'

'What bigger picture?'

'Well if I knew that I'd be Lenoardo,' said McCann. 'Or maybe Goya, he would have liked the blood. That fellow could do it justice; Saturn devouring his own children, the look of horror on the fellow's face as he bit into the infant arm, the blood pouring down.' He'd been to the Prado in Madrid with his ex wife once on a Spanish package holiday and now the night with McKittrick had brought Goya's painting vividly to mind. McCann suddenly felt sick, dizzy again. Taylor started to look bemused, Thompson concerned. He realised he was rambling. Maybe it was concussion, a blow to the head somewhere along the way, some injury to his vital faculties? 'I've got to get out of here,' he said, pushed away the table, tried to stand, staggered out into the corridor, placing his hand against the wall for support, Thompson following. He met Paper Clip coming the other way, his step faltering when he saw McCann: 'I didn't expect to see you up here, McCann.' His eyes hovered over McCann's clean shirt which was a size too small, chest hair bristling from between the buttons, then descending lower to the trousers, held suspended by Paper Clip's own red, white and blue braces that he'd recently given away to jumble.

'All worked out well in the end then, I gather, thanks to Inspector Taylor's swift action. Cleared up what could have been a very nasty situation. Lisburn are still livid, demanding a high level review. I don't mind telling you it's not been good for Division. Though I am pleased you are both OK. Mind you both get checked out by occupational health and complete your return to work form.'

'Just doing it right now, Sir.'

'Good, good, I'm glad to hear it. You're wearing my

trousers you know.'

'Takes a big man to fill them, Sir,' said McCann, still leaning against the wall to halt the unpleasant sensation he had of the floor rolling beneath him.

'I need you down at Division then, if you're well enough. I'll need a full report, with learning points and action plans. There'll be retraining involved too. The chief's worried about our failure to share the plate on all of this.'

'Share the plate, Sir?'

'Not enough teamwork, not enough communication between the teams. I'll be scheduling everyone for a two-day event at Connswater. It'll be informal, loafers, cords, smart casual wear. Get on to Deirdre and she will diary it in for you. You'll be well enough for that?'

'Look forward to it.'

'And remember our D.O.C.'

'What's that?' McCann squinted with the pain of listening to Paper Clip's jargon, like he was trying to understand some foreigner speaking bad English.

'Yes, yes McCann. D.O.C. is really important just now. Duty of care. For each other and for our citizens. A force that cares for citizens cares for itself and one that cares for itself can care for its people.'

'Very true, Sir,' said McCann as Paper Clip accelerated away up the corridor. Behind him he heard Thompson's voice: 'So, you know where Raymond Small's body is? Traded Liam for it?'

'Aye,' said McCann. 'I couldn't do anything else.'

There was a silence.

'And where's that?'

McCann began to murmur then, like he was reciting something from a work of literature that he'd learned by heart: 'A pebbledash cottage with red chrysanthemums on the left hand side of the Kilkeel road, a turn opposite down a lane to Nicholson's strand. There you can look out to sea and find the Hellyhunter light flashing at the entrance to Carlingford lough. If you put the light at your back and walk into the dunes fifty paces from the high tide mark, you'll find him there.' It was all of the detail he'd teased out from McKittrick as he had lain under the knife. 'Those kind of fellows always like to go back,' he explained, like he was in some kind of faraway trance. 'Go back to gloat. Or maybe because they think one day it'll be useful to know where the bodies are, that one day Raymond's body might be more valuable than Raymond himself ever was alive. His people would want Raymond's remains. It'd be something of value, that bag of bones. So they'd keep the records, make themselves important forever.'

'Or maybe they just thought that when this was all over Inspector, there'd be a reckoning, and it'd be only fair for people to know, to get their loved ones back.'

But McCann took exception to that: 'When this is all over? When will that be Sergeant?' And he pulled himself away from the wall and began to walk towards the fresh air outside, leaving her behind. At the door he turned back and barked at her: 'Are you coming or what, Emily?'

'Where to?'

'To get Raymond.'

Outside the barracks it was raining, stray drops building in intensity; the kind of weather where you think it's only a shower and leave your brolly behind, but as the drops grow larger and it starts to pour, you realise it is too late to go back to fetch it.

'I'd take it easy Inspector. Here, let's get a coffee shall we.' Thompson was two steps behind him.

A coffee and a hug would be just the ticket, thought McCann. But instead of agreeing, he asked: 'Can you get us a vehicle, Emily.'

'What for?'

'Newry. We've to get away down to Nicholson's Strand.'

'Now? Sure you can leave that, can't you, Inspector? Do you not want to sit in on the interview?' McCann turned back towards her: 'Taylor warned me off, said he'd do the charges for the assault on me and Flannery. Said he'd appreciate it if I'd stand back, that it would be better if I did. The murder of Raymond Small was a serious crime now, not a matter for C Division any more. He said it was beyond our remit, beyond our capacity.'

'He said that, did he?' She stood close to him, so close she could almost hold the lapels of his jacket.

'He said it wasn't appropriate for a fellow that's been the victim of a violent assault to investigate the crime himself, it'd be against the regulations.'

'Paper Clip must have got to him then,' she said, joining him as he walked towards the vehicle pool.

Flannery still felt jangled, on edge, after her ordeal and Paper Clip had sent her home to rest, telling her to take a few days off until she felt ready to return to duty. The place was safe of course, a line of solid detached police houses in a respectable area, well defended, but while that was reassuring, it wasn't what she needed. She wished there had been someone else in the house with her, but the woman she'd shared with had been transferred to Armagh to be closer to her family and they'd not found a replacement yet. The heating was off, the bare beige walls marked by myriad sellotapings, even her room that she'd tried to cheer up – with warm throws of colour, family pictures, a clothes rack stuffed with going out gear for every occasion, a poster of the beach at Marbella at sunset – all of it suddenly seemed tawdry and cheap; the home for some teenager that had aged ten years in the day that McKittrick had held her.

She felt exhausted and collapsed on her bed, wrapped the duvet around herself and tried to sleep. But she was restless; as she tried to doze images of McKittrick's face floated before her, along with memories of Peter Kemp's clumsy slap, the escape from the farm. She tried to ring Liam's number, but there was no reply. She padded to the kitchen, made herself jam on toast, a mug of hot chocolate, padded back to the phone, tried again. This time one of his flatmates answered. Liam was out he said. Had he seen him at all, she asked? He said he hadn't, he'd been out himself, didn't know where he could be. She gave her number, asked for Liam to ring her when he was back, said it was very important. She sat in front of the television, not caring what she watched, the images moving on the screen meaning nothing to her. At around midnight, Emily had rung to say they had found McCann, that he was safe, that they'd arrested both the men that had held her. That was great news. Emily had asked how she was, even offered her a spare bed for the night if she needed it, which she had refused. That didn't solve the problem of where Liam was.

Flannery had a restless night, woke early to find there was heavy rain slashing the concrete driveway, drumming on the roof and the cheap PVC skylight. The house had warmed up with the heating on, condensation streaming on the windows. She flicked on the television, put the kettle on, listened to the English news that was always strangely reassuring in its ordinariness. Then the local news came on. There was no mention of the recovery of McCann or how it had been done. If it had been on the TV it would be because someone had been killed or seriously injured. If it wasn't, it meant the raid had gone well.

In the police house there was nothing for her to do, she was no longer with the investigation. It was as if she had been untied from the thing that kept her sane and she felt herself losing it there alone in the house. At eleven she got herself dressed, went to the police house next door to borrow sugar, had a friendly chat with one of the Constables there, but it didn't help. If anything she felt awkward, embarrassed to be wasting time, unwilling to burden him with her problems, so she just murmured that she'd the day off and might spend it doing some shopping, but she set off for Division instead.

But as she went out of the front door, the phone rang and she unlocked, ran back inside to hear a familiar voice on the phone.

'Sinead? OK?' Liam said and asked her what she was up to and did she have time to see him, just as if nothing had happened.

He pushed open the passenger door for her, leaning over from the driver's seat while she got in, not giving him a kiss, but putting her bag down between her knees, until he'd turned the car round and they were driving away, then she said: 'Did you not get my messages?'

'Had things to do, had to see the folks to help move some furniture and stayed over.' He turned towards her, picking up her sharpness of tone, the tension. She couldn't even think how to begin telling him what had happened to her, because the whole experience of the last twenty-four hours didn't seem to exist for him.

'After you left me, I was rolled by a fellow and they took me.' Then she started to tell him haltingly, the story already seeming unreal in the front seat of his Ford, with its laddish clutter under the dashboard, the radio playing softly, the smell of his cigarettes.

'What do you mean? Jesus, are you OK? Rolled? They done nothing to you, did they?' She hadn't expected that he'd jump straight to the assumption it was something sexual, that he hadn't grasped that most people didn't think of sex when they'd warfare in mind.

'Nothing like that, no. They weren't best pleased though. They'd worked out we weren't the full Orange ticket. It seems like your line about the Model School rocked their boat for them and near got me killed.'

'We should never have gone up there. I'm sorry, it was my fault.'

'It was my idea.'

'But I agreed to it.'

'We both did it. Anyhow, they've got the fellows that done it. Inspector McCann's safe too. They'll be wanting to speak to you. You've not heard from an Inspector Taylor?'

'No, should I have?' They were driving up the Lisburn Road now, the small shops bustling on either side, the road busy with traffic.

'He'll want to ask you a few questions about what you saw.'

'Ach Christ,' he said, taking out a cigarette, not offering her one, lighting it with one free hand.

'You've nothing to worry about. It'll just be a formality,' she said. Then, exasperated by the turn that events seemed to be taking, the way the trip to the Sceptre had somehow come between them, she blurted out: 'Couldn't we just do something normal, like go to a film, just for now,' almost pleading with him.

'Aye, OK. We'll go up the Majestic, shall we?'

'What's on?'

'There's Bugsy Malone. It's a film about gangsters, but played by kids.'

'Oh very nice, that is.' She found herself laughing then, a touch of hysteria in it.

When they came out of the cinema it was dark, just a handful of cinema goers making for their cars or walking briskly home as the City was already shutting down for the evening, the traffic thinning, the shutters coming down on the shops and bars, the pavements emptying. She held onto his arm tightly.

'Liam?' She began to ask the questions that had been on her mind: if he'd told anyone about their visit to the Sceptre, anyone on the other side. If he was connected in any way with the people that had bombed it, maybe by accident, by a chance remark, if he'd let that slip, and along with it let slip that he was walking out with a Catholic policewoman?

'I'm not an eejit, Sinead,' he said and put his arm round her shoulders, guided her to his car. 'I'll never put you at risk.'

Then they were driving towards his flat.

'You don't mind if we drop by a fellow's place up the Ardoyne first?' he said. 'Maybe we could just kip down there till all this blows over.' And he accelerated, past the turning.

'Take us back to yours, Liam. You've nothing to worry about with Taylor. It's just routine. Maybe there's something you saw that can help us get Raymond's murderer. You could help identify the barman maybe. Let's go to your place, Liam, please.'

'Aye, Ok,' he said, and swung the car round.

They had barely got through the front door and up the stairs – Liam had put the kettle on, she'd taken off her coat – when there was a loud knocking. She saw Liam go to the head of the stairs and call out: 'Who is it?' cautiously, because everyone in the area knew you'd not stand behind the door where you could be sprayed with bullets.

'Inspector Taylor. RUC.' The knock became a hammering, the voice became a shout.

'Just a minute, hold your horses. We'll be right down.' Liam went down and opened up.

'Are you Liam O'Rourke?'

'That's me.'

Taylor came up the stairs into the living room, followed by three Constables. Taylor seemed surprised to find Flannery there lounging out of uniform, her shoes kicked off, a cup of coffee steaming on the table. She pulled herself upright, stubbed out her cigarette.

'Flannery?'

'Sir.'

'We've been looking all over. You could have told us where this fellow was, asked him to come in. It would have saved us a lot of bother.'

'I couldn't reach him, Sir.'

Taylor's eyes ranged around the kitchen. He nodded to the three officers to check the other rooms, now looking straight through Flannery like she was invisible.

'We need you to come down to Division to answer questions about the Sceptre, Sir.' Taylor was formal, but not polite, the 'Sir' with the special tone police deployed for hoodlums. Flannery found herself a seat out of the way.

'Can you not do the questions here? I'm happy to tell you anything.' One of the Constables was at the bookcase now, running his eye along it, starting to pick out books.

'Have you fellows a warrant?'

'Don't need a warrant for this kind of thing,' said the Constable, Taylor nodding that he'd to continue. Flannery watched for a moment as the books and papers started to form a pile on the floor. There wasn't a lot that was surprising: Robbins' *The Carpetbaggers*, well thumbed, most of James Bond, a wee bit of Le Carre, a fair bit of Irish literature, beginner's Gaelic, Haynes guide to the Ford Cortina, complete with oil stains on the cover. 'It'd be easier if you come with us, Sir.'

'I'm not coming with you unless you arrest me,' said Liam. Just as a flutter of papers came out from the bookcase; a history of the IRA, papers from the Sinn Fein *Ard Fheis*,

An Phoblacht.[11] Taylor moved over, shifted the pile of papers around with his foot.

'Have these bagged up,' he said. 'Clarke will be interested. He'll be the boy for this kind of material. Then he turned to Flannery and said: 'Did you know your feller was a Shinner[12] then, love?'

The wipers were going back and forth, barely coping with the deluge that was coming down the flat windscreen, across the armoured glass. They drove out of Belfast across the sodden landscape beyond Comber, a grey sky overhead, a silence between them. They passed through another road block, manned by the Wiltshires in green army capes. They made McCann wind down the window, get out to open the back in the rain.

'Thought we were on the same side, son,' he said.

'Only doing my job, mate,' said the lad, fed up with the rain, the routine, fed up being a target out there all day in the open. Then they were nodded through, away out onto the Newry Road .

Thompson smiled as they left the city behind and the weather began to clear; at first the cloud grew lighter, almost translucent, the darkness began to lift, the rain thinned to drizzle, mist hanging in the hedgerows, steam rising from the backs of cattle in the fields. Then a stray beam of sunlight made liquid silver from a lake that lay between rolling hills of

---

[11] *An Phoblacht* is an Irish Republican Newspaper and the *Ard Fheis* is the annual conference of Sinn Fein, the Republican Party

[12] A Shinner is a member of Sinn Fein, implying active Republican and the possibility of IRA membership.

luminous green. But the light flicked off again, as if showing two faces of the same country. But there would be light, thought McCann. The bad weather was breaking up. There would be another of those rays soon enough, the air would be sparkling and fresh and maybe there would be a rainbow too over the Mournes, before the sun came through and the day broke up into spring warmth, a gentle breeze and light scudding clouds over the sea.

'Good to get away, Emily,' he said, scrabbling around for a cigarette for each of them and lighting up.

Chapter Eleven

In Newry McCann turned right over the old level crossing, then left into the abandoned railway yard where the Warrenpoint line used to run. Now it was given over to a builder's merchant, a timber yard, a machine hire depot with a couple of JCBs. He parked the Land Rover and they both climbed out. The yard seemed deserted until they spotted a man in blue overalls tinkering with the hydraulics on a digger, a neat toolkit carefully laid out on the ground alongside a can of hydraulic fluid, pipes part dismantled and dripping onto the gravel.

'Georgie!' said McCann. The fellow was in his fifties, stout, but with the fitness of a hardworking man, nimble as he got to his feet, wiped his hands, shook McCann's hand like he was an old friend, nodded to Thompson.

'How are you son?'

'Keeping well,' McCann replied. 'And how's Anne and the kids?'

'Grand, grand. Our eldest is away at Uni now in Dublin.'

'Get away,' said McCann, amazed at the years that were racing by.

And then they went for tea in his cabin, with a packet of biscuits and a cigarette.

'How's business?' McCann asked.

'Slow, I'd be lying if I said things were good. Demolition is all there is. If there was a market in hardcore I'd be a rich man.'

McCann nodded in sympathy. There'd been a spate of bombings that had left the centre of the town gap-toothed and derelict. Almost progress, given the state much of it had been in before, but not for the people killed, the businesses destroyed.

'There's digging too,' he said. 'But not the kind of digging you'd be familiar with.'

'I heard tell you'd been doing some work for the police?' McCann asked.

'Aye, that's right.'

'So you couldn't help us out at all? Just for an afternoon?'

The clouds were beginning to pile up again over the mountains on the south side of Carlingford Lough as McCann turned right off the Kilkeel road and down a rutted path that ended at the sea. He parked the Land Rover next to the beach. The wind was blowing the sand across the tarmac in thin streaks, making a soft trickling noise, blowing over the toes of McCann's shoes, tickling his ankles. The yellow JCB came to a standstill beside them.

'You can follow me,' said McCann.

The sea glittered in the distance, the waves curling far down at the tide line, their noise barely audible. There were a few people on the beach: dog walkers throwing sticks and balls for their pets, scampering and barking in and out of the sea, or parents supporting small children as they teetered tentatively into the water with their trousers rolled up, the occasional jogger running in the waterline on the hard white sand. Across the bay lay the Republic, the same green hills as the North but a country and more away. McCann trudged on, Thompson a few paces behind and the yellow JCB behind her with its digging arm swinging and clanking.

'Keep walking,' said McCann, casting a glance around, but all he could see was a woman with her grey skirts flying, striding along behind them with a boisterous Jack Russell on its lead. Behind that three young lads with a football had come onto the beach and were laughing and yelling, kicking the ball into the sea and watching it being washed back towards them by the waves.

McCann scanned the ocean for the faint flicker of the Hellyhunter light.

After a few minutes walking he was able to pick it out and turned so it was square on his back, walked into the dunes in large strides, almost like he was counting yards out in his head like a surveyor, the digger and Thompson following his black form. From time to time he would stop again and look around, change direction, as if quartering the ground or sniffing for a scent. At one point he cut off right, further into the dunes and waved back towards them that they should come, pointing to a spot set back from the beach with a view of the blue-black ocean and the waves of the Irish sea breaking on the white strand, a spot where the light would be directly at his back and fifty paces from the high-tide mark.

'This is it,' he said. The digger revved, swung itself in position, lifted itself up on its hydraulic haunches and the clawed arm began to pull the sand away, while McCann smoked and watched.

'You sure of this?' shouted the digger driver after an hour.

'I'm sure,' said McCann. Then, after another hour of digging, just when the light was fading and they were thinking of giving up, the claw dislodged the last remains of Raymond Small.

The following evening Hannigans was standing room only, the angled mirror behind the bar giving an erroneous impression of space. Clarke was there, Taylor too with a line of pints queued in front of him on the bar. The whole of the Castlereagh crime team was celebrating a result; the men that had been out to the farmhouse and the abattoir, the fellows that had gone to bring in Liam. Taylor waved at McCann and Thompson as they pushed through the doors, ushered them through the press of bodies.

'McCann! Come over here, man. We've charged that fellow for what he'd done to you and Flannery. Stephen John McKittrick. Said he was doing it in self defence. Would you believe that, McCann? Defence of Ulster, he said, against her enemies.'

'I've done nothing to that man.' McCann laughed. 'That's what they all say. *For Ireland, for Ulster*, always the same jungle juice when people lose their heads.'

'Did you bring in any of the others?' Thompson asked, pressed up to him in the crush. 'What about the farm?'

'We've a lad called Peter Kemp in custody too and Flannery's fellow, Liam O'Rourke.' What'll you have?'

'Flannery's fellow? What's he supposed to have done?'

'Being a member of a proscribed organisation, his flat bunged with Republican propaganda.' Taylor was on a roll now, his face smug and red and sweating, shouting the order for drinks over the heads of the other drinkers to the barman.

Then Clarke eased forwards, inserted himself between Emily and McCann with a mineral water in one hand.

'He's a cousin done time in Crumlin Road, active in Civil Rights himself. Sinead's not been a clever girl at all.'

'But that can't be right,' said Thompson. 'I know he's an RC but there's no way she'd go out with a terrorist.'

'It might not be right, but it's happened,' said Taylor, over his shoulder from the bar. 'Thanks to Clarke's intelligence here we were able to find the guy, do a proper search. And that's not all, we found fourteen thousand pounds behind the panelling in his bathroom.'

'She's not involved. It's a mistake.'

'I doubt that love,' said Taylor, draining his pint, slapping the empty glass down on the wet bar, miming to the barman above the noise that he'd need a tray for the fresh drinks. 'Now what are you two having?'

'Aye well,' said McCann quietly. 'That is a surprise.' He drained the pint he'd taken when he came in, put the empty one down on the counter for Taylor's attention.

'And Thompson will have a double Jameson, since it's you that's paying Taylor.'

'Emily and I are away,' said Clarke, intervening to halt the order, placing his hand on her elbow.

'Why not another?' said Thompson, nodding to Taylor she'd have the drink anyway.

'Clarke?' said McCann, 'You'll stay for another?'

'I'm done,' he said, putting his empty glass of mineral water there on the counter. 'Emily, I'll catch you later.'

When the fresh round of drinks had been distributed, the empties loaded onto the tray, McCann slipped up closer to Taylor, gripped his arm.

'Just one wee thing.'

'What's that McCann?'

'We've still the murder of Raymond Small to deal with. I've a body now, down the strand just like McKittrick said. I'll be wanting access to those fellows tomorrow, to Tofer and McKittrick, Peter Kemp too. They're still all in the frame and it's nothing to do with what those boys did to me and Flannery. Nothing to do with what Liam O'Rourke may or may not have done. I've a right to see them.'

Taylor stared at him, Thompson moved in to back McCann up, whiskey in hand. But Taylor was in a generous mood: 'Come up to Castlereagh tomorrow and we'll see. You take it easy now McCann,' he said.

And McCann raised his glass to him to thank him for the drink and to show that he would do just that.

'I should go,' said Thompson, seeing Clarke pushing out through the crowd towards the door. Her double whiskey stood on the bar, caught in a golden light.

'Knock that back first,' said McCann. 'I've to get my things from Division later. We could share a cab back. I could give you a lift.'

'Share a cab over?' she said, hesitating, reaching for her glass, downing it in one sharp medicinal gesture.

'I'm afraid I can't do that tonight, Inspector.'

And later, lying on his back in the bed it nagged McCann that she'd chosen Clarke and that he was still alone. It worried him too that Flannery was in trouble because of what Clarke had said about her boyfriend. But at least Liam was safe for now, detained by Taylor, where McKittrick's gang couldn't get to him. It still vexed him that he'd given Liam's name to McKittrick. Maybe he was no better than any of them, willing to betray people for his own survival? For a long while McCann lay there looking out through a gap in the curtains at the trees soughing in the moonlight outside, like they were sighing some timeless wisdom about how a man might lose his soul.

Chapter Twelve

McCann was slumped in the cab, wrapped in an old jacket with the collar up, his head pulled down. It was still early, just a few commercial vehicles on the road, an occasional bus with a scattering of passengers. He wondered if Taylor would really let him in to see McKittrick. McKittrick had known where Raymond Small's body was, had the methods and the tools of his murder, so it should be but a short stretch to get him charged for that on top of his other crimes. But what about Tofer? McCann had heard evidence from the lad Patsy Kidron naming him as a suspect too, so someone was lying about the murder. And he'd still no idea why Raymond Small had been killed, nor why Tofer was so important to the gang. McKittrick had asked about money, but what money?

He looked out of the window as the suburbs opened up, at the neat, ugly bungalows, each one different yet each somehow the same; the small plots, the brick garden walls, the rose bushes, concrete driveways, wrought iron gates, all neat and tidy but the opposite of the way people were living now. Then they were cutting through the lights, up past the sangar, pausing to show his pass as the minicab u-turned in the road outside. He walked on into Castlereagh headquarters, with its

Nissen huts and blockhouses, its exercise yards and stores, its administrative offices and interrogation suites.

Turning a corner McCann was surprised to find Clarke's familiar figure on the step of the custody suite, in a fawn corduroy jacket, muffler on against the morning chill.

'Morning Inspector,' said Clarke. 'Taylor said you'd be coming over.'

'Have you been in with McKittrick?'

'Aye,' said Clarke.

'Did he open up at all?' McCann asked, as he signed him in to J Block. Inside the building it was warm, glass bricks covered with iron grilles letting in the light, green rubber nonslip floors that muffled their footsteps, a smell of disinfectant and heavy doors like you'd find in a high-security prison.

'Open up? In what way?' Clarke looked tired, like he had been up half the night.

'What did you talk about?'

'We talked about his UFF unit,' said Clarke. 'About what they were up to.'

'Did he admit anything about Raymond Small?'

'You can ask him yourself, McCann. It's your turn now. But I'll sit in just the same.'

When the cell door opened McCann was surprised to find Stephen McKittrick tucking into a good cooked breakfast, a white napkin at his throat, wearing a smart shirt open at the collar, his hair well brushed, clean shaven, as if he'd had a night in a good hotel. And Clarke greeted McKittrick like he was an old friend, a professional equal in some way. But maybe that was just the respect that police anywhere had for serious criminals, people at the top of their game. They'd already had some time together, built a bond that Clarke would have been using to tease out information, not that he seemed willing to share it.

'You'll know Inspector McCann,' said Clarke.

'We've met,' said McCann and sat himself down opposite, the victim in the interrogator's seat, Clarke beside him. McCann didn't recognise the solicitor, a painfully thin young man in a cheap grey suit, with a pudding basin haircut.

'This here's Sam Buller, off the rota,' explained Clarke. Buller nodded, fumbled nervously with a pad and pencil on his lap, using his shiny attaché case as a desk top. McCann found himself wondering how come McKittrick only had the services of a young duty solicitor, while Tofer had Brindley, the best man that money could buy? McKittrick eyed McCann, masticating the last piece of bacon from his breakfast, before wiping his lips carefully with the white napkin, folding that over the remains of the breakfast, over the knife and fork, leaving the tip of the blade sticking out. Clarke nodded to McCann that he should get started, bent to brush a bit of fluff from the toe of his shoe.

'Tell us about Raymond Small. How come you knew where he was buried?' It was time for his revenge on McKittrick for what he had done to him. But he wanted it to be a useful revenge.

'We keep the records,' said McKittrick. 'For the next of kin. When all of this is over they'll want to know.' There it was again. *When all this is over*.

'That's very generous and humane, but if you'd not killed

him first you'd not need to do that.'

'I didn't kill him.'

'Fine piece of butchery though, his finger off with, what did you call it? The chopper? Forensic will be matching the cut with the blade right now.' McCann raised his eyebrows so that McKittrick would get his meaning, know he had found the body, but McKittrick laughed. McCann tried to ignore that, the same way he was trying to block out the images that kept floating unwanted into his mind of his own time spent on McKittrick's operating table

'Well they'll be disappointed then Inspector.'

'What happened on the night of 10th April?'

'Let's see Inspector. That would be Linfield-Glentoran away, the blues won 3-nil, with a goal by McPartick, two by Willie James. It was a good night I can tell you. I've the tickets on the mantelpiece back home I could show you. You could talk to the fellows I was with. Here, I'll give you their names.' And he clicked his fingers at Buller, asking for a sheet of paper and a pencil.

'No need for that just yet,' McCann stopped him. Then he let McKittrick stew, knowing from experience that those kind of people found it hard to sit still under someone's gaze, if at all. They suffered from restless agitation, unease, like they were never at peace, always moving, never settling, always blaming, always angry. Not so different to himself in fact, it was why he could see things their way. And sure enough McKittrick began to fidget, fiddle with the corner of the napkin, turning it back to expose the tip of the knife, a sly grin pulling at the corner of his mouth, like he was enjoying thinking about what he could do with it if he could just move fast enough.

'You've nothing connecting me, nothing at all. Its Tofer you'd best be seeing about all of that.'

'You hacked the fellow's arm off.'

'Where was it he worked? Engineer at Harland and Wolff I gather? They'd do a neat job wouldn't they? Hear tell he wasn't too popular down there.'

'He was taken upstairs at the Sceptre. We've witnesses.'

Buller gathered his courage to pipe up: 'What's wrong with that, Inspector? Are stairs illegal? And my client has made no admission he was there, in fact he's given you a robust alibi.' And when he'd finished he glanced over nervously for McKittrick's approval. McKittrick, sensing McCann's weakness, added: 'Anyhow, no one would hack an arm off on a Saturday night in a pub full of people. Boy, if that happened it must have been some floor show.'

'Not just his arm but his finger too and not in the bar. You took him the same place you took me. What was it you wanted him for? What had he done for something so disproportionate to happen? Maybe you were sending a message, start with the finger, then when you didn't get what you wanted you did the arm?'

'Why stop at the arm? If they were dismembering him it makes no sense.'

'Maybe you were interrupted, got disgusted, had a wee glimmer that what you were doing was wrong?'

'Inspector, with respect this is all maybe's and mights, all speculation. My client won't respond to that.' Buller piped up again, more confidently now, starting to enjoy what was maybe his first major role. He was followed by McKittrick piling in behind with: 'What makes you think it's me done Raymond in? It could have been anyone. Everyone knows the methods now. You fellows are as good at it as we are, from what I hear about Magilligan,[13] what you've been doing to your prisoners up there; sleep deprivation, hung up by the arms, mock execution, none of it any different to what I've done to you. Don't tell me the police are any different now. And the Republicans? We learned everything we needed from them; power tools through the kneecap, fellows tied to lampposts dipped in hot tar, even dumped in shallow graves. Isn't that where you found Raymond Small? Maybe that's where you should be looking then? Don't you go climbing up on the moral high ground Inspector, because there's none of that left. Don't you go making assumptions about who done for Raymond Small. But see when I had you on the slab there was no way I'd have done anything serious to you. I'm no murderer. It was you believed I'd do something terrible. To be honest Inspector, I was surprised when you caved in, how quick it came. There's no telling is there, if a fellow has the fibre or not? And loyalty? You were pretty quick to give me your man O'Rourke's name in return for what you wanted.'

'So how come you knew where Raymond's body was?' McCann stuck with the key question, like driving through a heavy rainstorm with his eyes fixed on the road ahead.

'Tofer's the Intelligence Officer, you'd best ask him because he gave me the information. He keeps the records.'

'So you're saying Tofer done it?'

'I'm not saying him in particular. There's Chinese walls;

---

[13] Prisoners were mistreated at Magilligan army camp during the early phase of the Troubles.

every piece of information is fragmented, like you're tearing up a history book,' and here McKittrick made a gesture with his hands of tearing something into smaller and smaller pieces and letting the fragments float down to the tabletop like snowflakes, like he was apprising McCann of some simple process that even a schoolboy would know. 'Each man has only a part so the whole can never be seen. It'd take you a lifetime to get to the bottom of that and how much time have you got Inspector? How old are you? Sixty I'd say, by the look of you. Have they not pensioned you off? Or hold on, maybe they can't afford to let you go, a man of your skills, the things you know?' McCann looked at the ceiling, let McKittrick blather himself into silence.

'And why would they do it? What had Raymond done wrong?'

'It'd be an infringement, a breach of the code.'

'What breach? What code?'

'It'd have to be serious for him to be treated like that. As I say I wasn't there, so I wouldn't know. You'd best ask Tofer.' Surely there couldn't be another torturer? The paramilitaries from what McCann knew of them had only a handful of enforcers between them, responsible for discipline. He turned back to McKittrick to find him in the middle of a big yawn and stretch, like he was both bored and tired.

'What was it about Tofer? Why did you want him back so much?'

'Well you wanted your Constable back and we're the same, McCann, its called loyalty.'

'Just out of loyalty? You mentioned money. Was there money involved?'

'No comment.'

McKittrick was quiet, no snappy riposte this time, his arms folded.

'OK,' sighed McCann. 'Let's go further back here.' He reached down under the table to the folder he'd brought with him, keeping his eyes on McKittrick in case he made a move, thinking maybe it was crazy to worry. He pulled the folder out onto the table, slipping the photos from the dead files out, laying them in a line, like he was turning up cards in a game of patience. Each time he turned up a photo he said a name. When there were half a dozen photos on the table there was no more room, he took McKittrick's breakfast tray and put it on the floor, filled the space with more photos, more names, until there were so many photos that he had to stack them two deep.

'And finally these ones,' he said, putting the last two photos down in the centre of the table. Two young teenage girls, in the full bloom of life, he could hardly look at the pictures now himself. McKittrick let his glance skim over them, faced McCann: 'Recognise any of these?'

Buller sat forwards, anxiously attentive: 'No comment, I'd suggest.'

'Nope, can't say as I do,' said McKittrick.

McCann slid the photographs back into the folder carefully, one by one, taking his time.

'I'd never touch them, Inspector. I'm respectful of women; see when I'd your Constable I never touched a hair of her head. There's far worse could have happened to her if she'd fallen into the wrong hands, you know that. Inspector Taylor's got me bang to rights for what I done to her and to you. And I didn't ask much of you either, did I? Interesting that you come out with all that about having your last wish, I'd not expected that. I thought you'd be wanting the priest.'

'I don't believe any of that. Is that what they all ask for?' But McKittrick dodged the trap McCann had set: 'What do you believe in then, Inspector?' Suddenly, he faced McCann head on, like he was in the right and McCann in the wrong. 'I believe in God and the holy scriptures, McCann.'

'I believe in the law.'

'What law? Sure there is no law, only the rule of the righteous.'

'And that's why we've got you banged up here is it?'

'For now. With the passage of time and our victory there'll be a get out of jail free for all of us. We'll be there in your retirement, McCann, heroes. In the supermarket, on the beach, there at your children and grandchildren's schools. We'll all be there with our get out of jail free cards and where will you be?' McCann shook his head in disagreement. 'You'll still be snarking around trying to stir up old bones that no one wants to hear about, that's what you'll be doing. Everyone else will want to move on and you'll be spoiling it like some dreary old Auntie harking back to past slights. You'll be standing in the way of peace.'

McCann let him finish. There was no sense to it, no truth in what McKittrick was saying. There was only today and now and the need to stop McKittrick and his gang, regardless of how it might all be seen in ten or twenty years or however long it took for the people to forget his crimes. 'And Sammy McGuigan? I think you were his cleaner-upper, his useful fixer.'

McKittrick scoffed: 'Well he would say that, wouldn't he,

to shift the blame?'

And Buller chirped in with: 'I'm sorry Inspector but I can't see where this is leading. Are there murder charges or not? Are there any further charges for my client at all?' McCann treated him as if he hadn't spoken.

'Were you working for Sammy McGuigan when you done this to me?' He rolled up his sleeve, to show the bandages on his arm.

'What do you think?'

'I think you were. I think you were all part of the same game.' But McKittrick interrupted him: 'You should get your head looked at McCann, thinking like that. Sammy's done more for this City than you or any of the other jokers that have been standing in our way.'

'Has he now,' said McCann, wiping the back of his neck and his face with a clean white handkerchief, then his hands, like he was trying to wipe away some infection that might have stuck to him closeted there with McKittrick. He nodded to Clarke and they both stood, nodded to Buller too, a minimal gesture of thanks. Outside the cell door, he blinked in the bright fluorescent lights. Even in the enclosed confines of the custody block the air now seemed clean in comparison with inside the cell with its reek of bacon, sweat and fear. He turned to Clarke: 'Lock that fellow up. Throw the key away for good measure.' They both began to walk towards the exit. 'Plastic knives and forks too, for Christ's sake.'

Outside on the step he pulled out a cigarette. The sky was suddenly blue overhead, between the grey barrack buildings. He drew in the smoke deeply, then exhaled. There was barely a puff of wind, so the smoke funnelled upwards in a column into the early summer sky.

'Do you want to see the other lad they brought in?' asked Clarke.

'Not now. I've had just about enough of this shite that I can take,' said McCann and walked away.

He took the bus down into the City Centre. It was full of shoppers, a chatter of conversation around him, the fug of cigarettes on the top deck. The bus crossed the bridge over the river, the seagulls wheeling around the overnight ferries that had come in from England and Scotland, gobbling slops thrown from the galleys. On impulse, McCann got off the bus and stood looking down at the water with the traffic rushing backwards and forwards over the bridge behind his back. The tide was in, most of the slick and filth pushed upriver by an inrush of fresh seawater. He found his eye drawn out towards the open sea, seeking the flat horizon beyond the City. For a long while he leaned on the parapet looking out and then he walked on into the centre of town, through the security gates with their iron clanking rattle, like they were chains he was dragging, into the narrow thoroughfares beyond. He strolled among the shoppers, amongst normal people ebbing and flowing like the waters in the estuary, pausing to consider if he should take a coffee, then ambling away down the Queen's Arcade to his favourite shop. He came up to the window where a display caught his eye, of fish drawn to a certain new kind of bait. There were all kinds of fish there in the illustration; bream, carp, eels, pike, roach, tench, salmon, far more fish than you would ever see in one place together. The advertisement was cunningly drawn as if from the fish's viewpoint; you could see the angler foreshortened on the shore and his baited line falling through the surface of the water to the fish below. For a minute or so McCann peered at the illustration, admiring its skill, wondering what could have attracted so many different species of fish together; predators, bottom feeders, all after the one thing. Then he walked on.

The light was on in the dead files room and the door unlocked when McCann pushed it open. He was surprised to find Flannery there on the phone, with the cord wound around one wrist like she'd been there a long time and had got frustrated with whoever she was speaking to. She caught sight of McCann, started to put the phone down with a quick 'Sorry, I've to go, the Inspector's back.'

'Didn't expect to see you in today, Flannery,' he said.

'Neither me to see you,' she said and stood up, awkwardly formal. 'I'm grateful for what you done and don't say it was nothing, because it wasn't.'

McCann was embarrassed, but also pleased: 'Couldn't leave you with them boys. You done well to get a break. And we've caught a few of them as a result of what you did.'

'You too Inspector. And you're OK yourself?'

'Aye, fine,' said McCann, busying himself for a minute collecting messages that had come in, throwing circulars and memos in the bin. 'Taylor said your fellow's in some trouble. What was all that about?' he murmured gently, guessing she'd been on the phone to Emily about the arrest of her boyfriend.

Flannery was suddenly angry: 'He's in no trouble at all, it's Taylor's imagination that's the problem. He'd some Republican literature in his place that made Taylor suspicious, so instead of doing what he come for he starts to tear the place apart, finds money that Liam was holding for the Athletic Association. And dear God apparently only some of the serial numbers match up from the bank job.'

McCann lit a cigarette, taking his time, saying nothing at first, then: 'That's not good.' He knew the way it could go when an ambitious officer like Taylor had enough to charge a suspect and put pressure on his back to get results. He knew it could cast a shadow over Flannery's chances in the force. She saw his hesitation: 'Ah for God's sake there's no way Taylor's right, Inspector, it's just ridiculous.'

'Well he's right until we can prove him wrong,' said McCann.

'But aren't people meant to be innocent until proven guilty?'

'Not here they're not,' said McCann. 'It's safer to assume everyone's up to something till you've proof of the opposite.' But he still looked worried, staring away into space.

'There's just one thing I should give you,' she said, reaching into her pocket where she'd kept the beer mat from the Sceptre with the phone number on it. 'Though God knows the way Taylor's treated Liam I'm inclined not to.' She handed the beer mat to him. 'It's the number of the fellow that booked the upstairs room.' McCann placed it on the table in front of himself, then dialled. For a while the phone rang at the other end before it was answered: 'Yes, McGuigan speaking. Who's this?'

'It's McCann.' There was a pause, both men surprised to find the other on the line.

'McCann you've some balls ringing me after what you

done up the Sceptre. You said you'd clean it out for me, not bomb it flat.'

'I thought you said you had finished with the boys at the Sceptre, Sammy? So how come it was this number that was used to book the upstairs room where Raymond Small was taken to be murdered?'

'Ah well that would be historical,' said Sammy's voice, not missing a beat, 'I should've told them I'd not want anything to do with it. They've no right to still be giving out this number. But tell me again, how did the IRA get in to bomb the Sceptre?'

'I'd not be so sure it was them, Sammy.' Then McCann gave him some flannel about investigations continuing, evidence being gathered, security being tightened in future, till McGuigan lost patience and hung up on him with a few choice expletives.

Chapter Thirteen

'Anywhere I can put these where they won't be nicked?' McCann heard a loud, entitled voice and stepped outside the dead files room to find George Brindley – Tofer's solicitor – manhandling his golf clubs. 'Can't leave them in the car. I suppose they'll be safe in your room at least Inspector?'

'It'll be at your risk, but you can put them in my room for now. I suppose you're here for our Mr Tofer?'

Brindley made a little speech about the absence of charges against Tofer, the length of time his client had been detained and even some grandiose threats of a Habeus Corpus application as they walked along the corridor and down to the cells where Tofer was held, only falling silent when the door was unlocked.

'I'm within my rights under the Emergency Powers, George,' said McCann. 'As you well know.' Then the interview started: 'Who's Stephen McKittrick?'

Tofer looked tired and seemed unwilling to co-operate: 'Stephen who?'

'He knows you, he confirms that you were the Intelligence Officer at the Sceptre.'

'Excuse me Inspector, but I think you're relying on

hearsay there,' said Brindley, putting his oar in the water early on, ready for a day's rowing.

'McKittrick says it was you that told him where Raymond's body was to be found.' McCann reached into his pocket, rootled around, pulled out the paper on which he had written the co-ordinates and started to read them out, almost like they were some kind of spell that would break Tofer's silence. Then he paused, looked inquiringly at Tofer. 'Does any of that sound familiar?'

'What's all this about Inspector? Carlingford? I've never been there at all.'

'You've never heard those directions? McKittrick says you wrote them. It's where we found Raymond Small's body. Poor Raymond Small seems to have known something they were prepared to torture the fellow to death for. And you say it's McKittrick did the killing?'

'I never said that. If it's Carlingford, that's where the IRA do their killing.'

'You're not denying it neither. So what was he punishing Raymond for?'

'That's him that would know that, not me.'

'You were in the Sceptre when he was brought in, taken upstairs, judged and found guilty.'

'I'm sorry, Inspector, but you've no evidence for that. If my client is to be charged the evidence should be presented. He should be given the opportunity to challenge it.' Brindley took a quick gulp of air but McCann interrupted him before he could continue: 'Maybe you and McKittrick could get together and get your stories straight,' said McCann. 'The who, what, where, why and when of it. Get your ducks in order and stop wasting my time and that of Mr Brindley here. Maybe you and McKittrick could share a cell up at Castlereagh, sort it out between yourselves. Who's to pay the price? I'm sure you two are familiar with that kind of conversation.'

'I'll have to note that my client is being encouraged to fabricate a defence with another prisoner when he has already provided a reasonable and credible denial to allegations for which there is no evidence.'

'I'm just consulting with Mr Tofer if there might be more suitable detention facilities available for him, where he'd be in the company of his own people and better able to prepare his defence? How would that be, Mr Tofer?'

'That'd be all right,' Tofer replied halfheartedly, like Castlereagh was the last place in the world he'd like to be and McKittrick the last person he'd want to be there with.

So McCann left the cell, made the arrangements to move Tofer to Castlereagh, to place him side by side with McKittrick, whistling thinly between his teeth as he dialled through to prisoner transport.

'I just can't believe this place,' said Sinead. 'Look at this shite.' McCann took the paper that Sinead held out to him on his return to the dead files room.

'*Stage 1 Disciplinary hearing, pre-enquiry.*' McCann read out the words, like he didn't believe them either. 'Ah dear God,' he said, ran his hand through his hair, sat down. Then he read out the charges: 'Not following orders, endangering other officers and oneself, having inappropriate relationships.'

'There are these too, Deirdre said I'd need them.' Sinead pointed to a weighty set of volumes which lay on her desk.

McCann bent down to take a closer look: *'The Disciplinary Code. The Annex to the Disciplinary Code. An Officer's Guide to Disciplinary Procedures.* I'll tell you what you can do with these.' He lifted the volumes one by one and dropped them into the bin, along with the letter that had come with them, made for the door and leaped up the stairs to Paper Clip's office.

McCann should have been warned by Deirdre's cautious and barely audible closing of the door behind him that Paper Clip was not in a good mood. He was seated at his desk, his face carrying a mild, understated frown. His hand hovered across the desktop like a small, predatory bird, from time to time diving to pick up a paper, glancing at it, then with a loud bang stapling it to another and slipping it into one of the folders laid out on the desk.

'You've Constable Flannery on a disciplinary?'

'Yes, I've had to start a PR4 disciplinary on her McCann, I've no alternative. Castlereagh have been on at me about it. It's a matter of disobeying instructions, inappropriate friendships that undermine force security. As her direct superior you'll be able to make representations of course, there's space on the form for that. But for the moment she's suspended till we can convene a disciplinary panel. You'll pass it on to her?'

'She's inexperienced Sir, and it's me that should have supervised her more closely. I don't know a lot about this fellow of hers, but I doubt very much she'd be hanging around with an IRA man if you look at her record. I need her on the team right now, I've no one else.'

'You don't need people now that Taylor's taken on the case, do you? Let's just get the process started, because the sooner it's started the sooner it'll be over.' Paper Clip interrupted, then he returned to the pleasant predictability of the papers on his desk, one hand making a gentle shoeing movement, indicating to McCann that he should leave before he found himself in trouble. McCann was inclined to argue, but thought better of it and instead turned on his heels and clattered away down the stairs.

Flannery looked up as he came through the door of the dead files room.

'Come on, get your stuff. We're away to Tofer's place.'

'Why to Tofer's?' But McCann was so angry he couldn't answer till he was in the Land Rover outside.

'There's something that doesn't add up,' he said, crunching the gears and spinning the wheel as they bounced over the ramps out past the sangar and away into the city.

Chapter Fourteen

'Mrs Tofer I've a warrant to search,' said McCann, holding the warrant that he'd asked for when he'd first brought Tofer in, that had come through that morning.

The woman read the warrant, holding it with her one free hand, jiggling the baby up and down on her hip all the while, blocking their way.

'Search for what? What's my Billy meant to have done ? Can't you just leave us alone?' She glared past him at Flannery standing behind, as if she was blaming her too for taking her husband away. 'When's he coming back anyway?'

'We're investigating the murder of Raymond Small and he's still some questions to answer.'

'Raymond?' The woman looked baffled, amazed even. 'Murder Raymond, my Willy?' And then the amazement turned to outrage and contempt for McCann: 'Billy wouldn't harm a hair of that boy's head,' and she even looked to the baby as if for confirmation. 'Sure Billy looked after him after what the lads did to him down the shipyard. He used to say he was his right-hand man, to tease him, cheer him up. He was just a poor wee lad lacking confidence.'

'He told us he didn't know Raymond,' said McCann, all

the while wondering how Tofer could have been blamed for something he probably hadn't done, more than ever convinced it was McKittrick that had set him up, that somehow lay near the centre of it all. Tofer's wife looked worried then, like she'd given away one of Tofer's secrets, adding: 'Well Willy probably had his reasons for not telling.' Like they all had, thought McCann.

'We'll need to have a look around all the same,' he said, starting to push past gently into the open hallway. Mrs Tofer stood aside, closed the door quickly behind them – once Flannery was through – so the neighbours wouldn't see that the police had called again.

Inside the house there was a smell of newly laid carpet and fresh paint. In the lounge there was a large colour television, the box it had come in pushed behind the sofa, an older child lying watching. It was not what McCann had expected, that prosperity, the sense of improvement that was at odds with Tofer's record, the young wife, the fine children. Suddenly he felt ill-at-ease, like an interloper that had wrecked something fine, and he found himself apologising for the intrusion.

'Has he any special room where he keeps his stuff. We could start there? '

'Start where you like. We've nothing to hide,' she snapped. 'C'mon Timmy!' She grabbed the older child by the arm and hoiked him away before he could do any more gawping.

In the kitchen and bathroom there was all the paraphernalia of washing and drying that you would expect in a house with two young children. Only in the master bedroom did they pause at a new wardrobe that was full of clothes, Flannery pushing the dresses back on their hangers, two new suits, shoes still in their boxes.

'Been on the spend,' she said thoughtfully. 'Like Raymond Small.' McCann asked her what she meant then and she described the suits, the Fender Stratocaster in Raymond's locked cupboard. McCann looked out through the bay window at the grey day outside, at a fellow walking his dog, lifting its leg against the gleaming hubcap of Tofer's new Rover.

He paused by the bedside. On one side a Mills and Boon novel was open on the table, on the other he was surprised to see a copy of Tim Pat Coogan's 'The IRA,' and beneath that a well thumbed copy of the 'A Short History of Ireland' by a Professor J.C. Beckett.

'Right little intellectual,' he said. 'Let's take a look out back, shall we? And then that's it.'

He stuck his head round the door to the kitchen, explained to Mrs Tofer. The backyard had a drying line, more children's clothes blowing there, a concrete yard cluttered with an old trike, a bicycle, an abandoned push chair. There was a coal bunker and beside that, a small wooden shed.

'You got the keys to this?' asked McCann, trying the padlock.

And when it was unlocked he stepped inside to find power tools, a rack with different chisels and screwdrivers, drill bits, all neatly organised. McCann poked a little at the back of shelves, lifted a paint pot or two, a couple of rolls of gaffer tape. Sniffed the drill bits for the scent of blood, chucked one of the rolls of gaffer tape in his hand, released a bit from the drill, popped them both in an evidence bag.

'I'll just borrow these, OK?' he said.

'Mind you bring them back. Billy doesn't like people

touching his things,' said Tofer's wife as they went back through the house.

But he thanked her all the same, winked and grinned at the older child and chucked the younger one under the chin as he pulled the door closed behind him.

'And now we'll do McKittrick's place.'

'I'd have thought Taylor and the crime team would be doing that.'

'Always worth another look, even if they did.'

'You'll be taking a risk with that, won't you?'

'That's good, coming from you, Flannery,' said McCann, giving her a grin.

He turned down towards Duncairn Gardens, swerving and accelerating past burned-out cars, round the shell of a bus with the ribs of the coachwork bare like the carcass of a whale picked clean by sharks, the tarmac bubbling and scorched underneath. She was silent then beside him, tapping her foot, looking around like she wanted away from his Land Rover, away from the police force.

'Tiger's Bay, that's where McKittrick lives. You'll be OK with me,' said McCann.

McCann looked up at the house while they waited for the door to be answered. It was one of those big Victorian piles that had fallen on hard times, with peeling paintwork, a broken upstairs window patched with cardboard and sellotape, a line of bell pushes with the names running in ink or crossed out, wires trailing. He stood close on the top step ready to put his foot in the door if they tried to close it on him. There was no answer at 5B, so McCann rang the ground floor number. If there was a Landlord, he'd likely have the ground floor from where he'd be able to hear the tenants doing a runner or smuggling girls in. But it was a woman that came to the door, middle-aged, prim in a housecoat, with a neat blue rinse.

'Sorry to bother you, but we're after a Mr McKittrick and there's no reply at 5B.'

She peered through the gap in the door, opened it when she saw his warrant card.

'I've not seen that fellow for weeks,' she said. 'What's he done?'

McCann stepped inside and Flannery followed.

'Still pays his rent does he?'

'Aye, always regular.' Maybe that meant it was a safe house, thought McCann, always free for whovever needed it, paid for by anonymous banker's draft.

'I'll need to see his room.' McCann was already looking up the stairs, edging past.

'I'm not being funny, but I'm not sure he'd be OK with that.'

'It's up here is it?' McCann ignored her objections and started up the central stairwell, with its numbered rooms, a faint light filtering down through a glass skylight at the top, the smell of old breakfasts, damp plaster and stale smoke in his nostrils. The Landlady flicked on the lights, started to sort through the keys she held on a long chain. Flannery followed, peering up to see where he had got to, the Landlady behind still murmuring protests, before relenting and letting them into McKittrick's room.

Inside, it was the smell that hit him and the sense of

solitary abandonment, of somewhere a man might try to sleep if he could not live a life. The food had started to go off where he'd left it on the drainer, the unwashed dishes to stink, the low drone of a couple of bluebottles circling over the detritus. The bed was unmade, the sheets grey. He opened a cupboard and a pile of pornography fell out. He flicked through, disgusted. It was the kind of material you could only acquire if you looked hard in the sort of places that were difficult to find.

He went to the windows and tried to open them up but they were painted shut with clogging layers of cracked emulsion. There was a small bathroom with a tiny space for a shower, a plastic curtain, a basin. A thin green towel was crumpled over the towel rail, a red one dropped on the floor, used disposable razors in the overflowing bin and scum around the sink. In the end the closeness and the smell that came with it, and the difficulty of opening the windows to fresh air forced him out down the stairs and outside onto the step, to light a cigarette, fill his lungs with something other than that smell.

On the step he turned to the landlady.

'No one else been round for him?'

'You're the first.'

'And anything outside, up the back?'

'There's the yard. We keep the alley door locked. The tenants are not allowed out there except to dry their washing, thems that does it.'

'Let us have a gander at that then before we go,' said McCann, following on behind her up the alley out to the back of the house where there was a patch of muddy ground leading to a walled backyard set with a clothesline, a coal bunker full of slack, a disused outside toilet with a rotting door. On the line were a few items of clothing; mens' underwear, a string vest but they were already blackened by coalsmoke and rain, like they had been abandoned by their owners.

'Would these be his?'

'How'd I know? Sure I wait a month or two then chuck anything that's not collected.'

He pushed open the toilet door, peered inside in the gloom.

'It's none too nice in there, Inspector,' the Landlady warned. Cobwebs, spiders, old rusting boxes on shelving, a box of yellowing newspaper, a smell of Jeyes fluid, he looked around as best he could, saw the trace of a footprint in the dust that lay on the toilet seat.

McCann climbed up, matching the footprint in the dust with his own. He put one hand on the lowest shelf and levered himself higher so his head came level with the top of the cistern, cobwebs across his face, lifted the cistern lid off and handed it down to her. He ran his hand around inside and felt something there, floating on the water, something like a tobacco tin. He brought it out and down into the daylight, jumping down. The tin was new, with no sign of rust. He reached in his pocket for a coin to prise open the lid. Inside were the remains of a finger, the flesh creeping from the bone, attached to a chain like it was a pendant or memento. And underneath the chain were several locks of human hair swimming in the sludge of putrefaction.

While they'd been inside a thin drizzle had come in off the Irish Sea, up the lough, enveloping Belfast in grey dampness that seeped everywhere; even in the front seat of the Land Rover McCann's clothes felt damp, the controls slippery with condensation. Out on the street the shoppers in the city centre had their umbrellas up, wrapped in plastic macs, the women with their perms protected under headscarves, the men shrouded in hooded parkas or flat capped with their collars up against the rain. They drove over the bridge but the view was obscured by mist on the windows, mist outside.

'Why did he keep it?' Flannery asked.

'A memento, like a souvenir he'd have of his travels, the places he visited, the people he'd killed,' said McCann, the tin in an evidence bag on the seat between them. Sinead's features puckered in disgust. 'But why the chain?'

'Maybe wore it round his neck,' said McCann. 'Better to keep it on him and then he could keep it forever and use it on whoever needed it most. He'd use it to terrify, that's what he'd do.'

Flannery had expected McCann to be elated at the end of the road, with revenge for what had happened and justice for the victims within his grasp, but he was still grim faced, his jaw set, turning a matchstick over and over between his teeth.

'So you've got him then?'

'McKittrick, aye, I've got him at least,' he said.

Afterwards McCann barely had time to get home, wash, shave, pull on something reasonable; an old jacket that didn't quite fit over a clean shirt he'd quickly ironed, a pair of too tight trousers and his brown shoes though he'd not time to do the laces up as the cab was tooting on the driveway. He was fifteen minutes late by the time he came into the cafe, Thompson already seated there by the window fiddling with the menu. She waved at him as he came in, the place deserted in the early evening. McCann apologised for being late, sat down.

'What's up McCann, you look like you got the cream?'

'I wouldn't say that,' said McCann, thinking that you couldn't describe the rotting finger in his fridge at home that way. 'But I had a good day all the same.' And he told her how the new evidence should help convict McKittrick. She leaned forward, listening, gravely thoughtful.

'That'll change the dynamic then,' she said.

'How do you mean?' Now he was baffled; she had got ahead of him, quicker off the mark. The waiter hovered to take their orders, but McCann hardly saw him.

'Those lads Flannery interviewed might tell you the truth now. You'll be able to get further up the tree, maybe right to the top.' Then McCann grasped what she was saying, too tired to have worked it out for himself.

'I'll need Tofer to open up too,' he said. 'He's higher up, knows where it leads,' he said, ordering up a plate of beans on toast and tea for two.

'How's Sinead bearing up?'

'Paper Clip has her on a disciplinary.' Thompson let out a cry of frustration.

'Jesus, could he not just leave it alone for once? That was Clarke done that, I told him he'd to keep his mouth shut.'

'What did he say about her fellow Liam?'

'He'd all this intelligence on him; he has a cousin was in the South Armagh ASU, put inside in 74. Liam's a smart boy, a trainee solicitor, not in his cousin's steps at all, but connected. Gallaghers is the outfit he works for, used to instruct chambers in the Republic in some IRA trials: O'Dwyer, the Cork Examiner job, McFadden, the Eniskorry bank raid. They'd connections, according to Clarke.'

'Sure lawyers go where the money is, they don't care. I'd not worry too much about that. Poor Sinead though, if she's wrong about him. She gave me a number for the fellow that took bookings at the Sceptre by the way. Turns out it was Sammy McGuigan.'

'Not him again.'

'Went jogging with him. Nearly killed me.' She smiled, tried unsuccessfully to suppress a laugh.

'What? Do you not think I'm up to it?'

'I'm saying nothing.'

'Sammy denies all knowledge of the business at the Sceptre. *Whatever you say, say nothing*, as the saying goes.'

He looked at her for a moment, then asked: 'And you? How's the bank job coming on?'

'Taylor's doing his nut. He's stolen money pouring out everywhere, bubbling up so fast he can't stop it since he put the serial numbers out in the papers.'

'Like where?'

'Well he says some of Liam O'Rourke's money came from it. But not just there, you'd not believe the places they're finding notes. I even hear tell one of the Sergeants at Castlereagh got a stolen Ulster Bank tenner in the change at the bar of the police social club.'

'You're joking.'

'Straight up, there's cash in the Presbyterian tea rooms, a car showroom in Cullybackey, even a member of the General Synod handed one in and then more of them in the collection plate of the Saint Joseph Church of the Assumption. It's a proper non-sectarian thing. What we've always dreamed of. Money talks, doesn't it, brings people together?' Emily Thompson was smiling the special Ulster would-you-believe it smile, that was needed more and more as the Troubles worsened and the barely credible became normal, the unthinkable just a mildly disappointing surprise. But it made her attractive; dimples at the corner of her mouth, legs crossed, reaching for her tea while McCann tucked into his beans on toast.

'I've been looking at this,' he said, reaching into the inside pocket of his jacket, pulling out a coloured brochure, spreading it out on the table in front of her: 'Get away, when all of this is done, get away for good.'

'Royal Canadian Mounted Police? The mounties?'

'They'd a recruitment event a while back and I picked these up,' said McCann sheepishly.

'You, in the mounties?'

'D'you not think I'd look the part? See!' He grabbed a brochure, showed her the picture of a handsome, chiselled fellow with a jutting jaw and perfect teeth on horseback, wearing a mounties hat, a bright red uniform, looking out proudly into the far distance with a snowcapped peak in the background.

'You're not serious?'

'Just taking a look,' he said. But he felt her eyes on him.

'You could come over too.'

'For God's sake what would I do in Canada?'

'You could be a mountie too.'

'I hate horses, hate snow. I'd be homesick. What would I do with my daughter?' She became suddenly serious. 'And you're not finished here yet, are you Inspector? You've not closed off that old case of yours have you?' Her eyes were concerned, she could see she'd hurt him. 'You don't think this

McKittrick could have done those girls too, do you?'

And that was it really, thought McCann. They were all mired in it, this troubled life. He would like horses and knew how to handle them, had had them on the farm. He had loved it when he'd woken as a boy to find the mountains thick with snow, glittering on a January day like they were newly made. In Canada there'd be air, clean in your lungs, good money in the pocket for a policeman, almost like it had been when he'd first joined up. It would be a new start.

'You'd not be able to leave all this behind, you'd bring it with you anyway. I know you McCann, you'd regret not finishing what you started, wouldn't you? You'd be running from it.' She paused. Always sharp as a knife when she needed to be, that Emily, he thought. Then she seemed to change the subject: 'Do you see anything of your wife now by the way?'

'Nothing,' said McCann. He didn't want to, didn't need to with the divorce that had come through the year before. Thompson had her social worker face on now, he thought, like he was a case that needed attention. She didn't realise it was her that he wanted, not the woman who'd left him for another man. So he stood up abruptly, jangling change in his trouser pocket, leaned over the menu, calculated the bill and counted his share out on the table in front of her.

Chapter Fifteen

'We've Stephen McKittrick in custody, so you can tell us the truth now.' McCann started with Patsy Kidron – the most malleable of Raymond Small's associates – surprising him on his own doorstep as he set out to work. At first Kidron was silent, walking beside McCann like he was pretending they weren't acquainted.

'Was it Stephen McKittrick told you to say you saw Tofer take Raymond upstairs?'

'No one told me to say anything. What I told you was God's truth.' A shrill schoolboy lie, turning up the volume in the hope it would persuade McCann.

'It was Stephen McKittrick that done for Raymond. We've got him up at Castlereagh right now. But we need to know why he did it and who else was involved.' McCann could see Kidron didn't fully believe that McKittrick was in custody and that he was safe. Even when you had the bad men to rights people were still afraid, no matter how securely they were held. That was how deep their rule went and McCann's methods just didn't compare.

'He's overreached himself,' said McCann. 'C'mon son, I know it's a shock for you. We'll away and get some breakfast shall we? Bacon and eggs, I know a good place and I'll treat you.' And he guided Kidron along the pavement to a quiet café nearby where he knew they'd not be overheard.

'So, tell us when McKittrick first turned up down the Sceptre?' McCann asked, pouring ketchup on his breakfast and waving his fork at Kidron's loaded plate to indicate he'd best tuck in too as they'd be there till he had heard the full story.

Kidron bent low over his plate in the café, suddenly talking fast across the steam rising from the fresh cups of tea, hardly touching his food.

'McKittrick come down the Sceptre just the once before, give us all a wee speech about how there was things going on that had better stop, that he was sure we all knew what he was talking about. That he'd his eye on us.'

'And the night of 10th April. What was it that happened?'

'It was a normal night like any other, just the week after. All of us lads went down the Sceptre.' McCann reeled off the names then that he'd got by heart, Kidron nodding confirmation.

'The meeting started at seven upstairs but McKittrick brought Raymond up first. When the meeting started he said there was someone taking a cut and he didn't know who it was, but he'd heard tell there was money being spent and he wanted to know where it was coming from because it certainly wasn't there in the takings. He had us all up the front in turn, shouting at us that if there was money Sammy needed it, the fighting men needed it. If there was anyone taking an unauthorised cut, well they'd soon learn what a cut meant.' I hadn't a clue what was going on, thank God. I'd no money, nor any of us as far as I knew. And that's when he took Raymond away, him and Peter Kemp did.'

'You saw him do that?'

'Aye. I'm sorry Inspector, I couldn't tell the first time you came on account of…'

'Account of what?'

'He came to see me individual like, came to see all of us.' Kidron had stopped talking, like he'd been struck dumb by the memory of seeing the severed finger of his vanished friend.

'It's OK son, we've got him inside now,' McCann said.

'He showed me Raymond's finger. Said I'd to mention Tofer if I was asked by the police, to keep his own name out of it. Said I'd to SFU, for Ulster.'

'SFU?'

'Shut the fuck up.'

Afterwards he took a cab up to Castlereagh. Once inside the detention block he made his way to Peter Kemp's cell, hoping to confirm Patsy Kidron's story. Now dressed in a clean pair of jeans and a grey school shirt – that his mother had maybe brought in for him – Peter Kemp seemed less than the nineteen years his charge sheet showed. His feet were pushed into trainers from which the laces had been removed. He was slumped over the table with his head in his hands, but looked up as McCann entered.

'Mr Kemp?' said McCann. He nodded warily, sat up, suddenly alert.

McCann busied himself at the table with the paperwork, carefully laying out the charge sheet, a notebook, biro, pencil, eraser, ruler, pretending not to be satisfied until the biro was perfectly aligned with the ruler and then he looked up.

'Peter William Kemp, nineteen years and four months. Charged with the abduction and attempted murder of an RUC Constable.'

A knock came at the door, gentle and tentative. The duty solicitor's head appeared.

'Sam!' McCann greeted Sam Buller like an old friend. 'You'd best come in because we're just getting started,' pulling forwards an extra chair for him, waiting while he fumbled his notepad and pencil from his briefcase before resuming: 'We're holding Stephen McKittrick, so you can tell us all about him now.'

Kemp leaned forwards on his chair scowling, shaking his head.

'I'm saying nothing.'

'Where'd you meet him and when?'

'I can't remember.'

'You know he can't get to you now, nor even later. You and him will be separated, we'll see to it. And if you tell us the truth sonny we could go easy on you, maybe have you on a lesser charge.' Buller sat forwards at that, but Kemp spoke first: 'I'm not interested.'

'He's offering you a chance, Peter, and you're not taking it.'

'I'm still not interested.'

'What alternative charge had you in mind, Inspector,' Buller asked, before turning to Kemp to say: 'It might just be worth hearing what the Inspector has to say before rejecting it.'

'I think your client just said he wasn't interested,' said

McCann wearily, but before he could say anything more there was the sound of an altercation outside, of furniture being thrown, the footsteps of heavy men running in the passageway. McCann apologised, said he'd be just a minute, pulled the door ajar, stepped outside to find the corridor full of uniforms.

'McKittrick went for me.' Tofer was still panting, a rough gash over one eye. In the background McCann could hear the noise of a continuing scuffle as the officers struggled to separate McKittrick from him. Big, burly men held him from behind, lifting his feet from the floor, dragging him back.

'Taking them out for exercise and this kicked off,' explained the officer in charge, retrieving his hat as McKittrick was manhandled away to his cell.

'Any idea why?'

'Said I was a Lundy,'[14] said Tofer angrily, wiping the blood away with one hand as the first aider came in with his kit, sat Tofer down on a chair under the light, fussed over him putting on disinfectant, lint, a big sticking plaster, while McCann waited.

'Why would he say you were a Lundy?'

'That fellow sees Papists everywhere.' Tofer shrugged the first aider away with an impatient gesture, like he'd be happy to have another scar to add to his collection, to show what a man he was. McCann ran his hand through his hair.

'But that's not the real reason, is it Mr Tofer. I've an idea now why McKittrick was after you, was after Raymond Small,

---

[14] A Lundy is an Ulster term for a traitor. Lundy was the governor of Londonderry when it was besieged by Catholic forces in 1689 and ordered the city gates to be opened.

done for him, would maybe have done for you too if we'd not stopped him.'

'Oh yes and what idea would that be, McCann? You're a regular brainbox this morning, aren't you?'

'We'd better wait till your man Brindley gets here. So everything's official, the way you fellows like it.'

'Nice little earner for you Roger,' said McCann, greeting Brindley at reception, leading him through, noting that the solicitor had swapped his golfing kit for a smart Italian suit that glistened and shimmered as he walked.

'It's regrettable McCann that my client Mr Tofer is still in custody without any charges.'

'Other than yours,' said McCann, signing him through into the detention suite.

'I do hope you'll have something new for me this morning.'

'Oh aye, I've that all right,' said McCann, as the Custody Sergeant opened up and let them in to see Tofer.

'God in heaven! What have you done to him?' Brindley rushed forwards to examine him with a look of concern on his face like he was a doctor too on top of being a dodgy lawyer. 'I'll need an independent medical report right away. I objected at the time when you suggested transferring him to Castlereagh and now he has suffered the inevitable consequences.'

'He was set upon,' said McCann, 'not by us though, by another prisoner.'

'How come? That's prima facie negligence in my book. You've a duty of care to people McCann.'

'Hard to keep to that when they've a desire to kill

each other.'

Brindley settled himself down, adjusting his buttocks on the hard Formica chair. McCann turned back to Tofer, offered him a cigarette, apologised for the assault he had experienced. Tofer took a deep draw and blew the smoke out.

'Nice new Rover you've got yourself,' began McCann. Immediately Brindley started up, like a steam locomotive chuffing: 'I'm sorry but I really can't see the relevance of this at all.'

'And the television set too. I went round to yours last night to search your property, met your wife and lovely children. It's a wonder a fellow like you is mixed up in all of this Mr Tofer.'

'You've a nerve McCann, harassing my client's family in their own home.'

'All legal and proper,' said McCann, flicked the warrant over to Brindley without taking his eyes off Tofer.

'How much do you earn then Mr Tofer?'

'What's it to you?'

'New Rover, nice wee house newly decorated.'

'I come into some money. Is that a crime?'

'What kind of money?'

'Had a bereavement, a wee bequest.'

'And your friend Raymond Small too? Seems like you and him were close, not strangers at all. Seems like you've not been open about that, that there's something you didn't want us to see.'

'I didn't want to get dragged in.'

'But you knew him well, looked out for him. Was that what McKittrick was interested in? Was that why he was sent in?'

'This is just pure speculation, wasting my client's time,'

chuntered Brindley, 'Invading his privacy with ill-founded intrusions and enquiries about his private finances and personal life.'

'I'd not be worried about any intrusions I'd make,' said McCann. 'But by what'll happen to him if you manage to get him out of here.'

Brindley's round face sagged a little, like a small puncture had been made through which hot air was now escaping.

'Not just to him but his family too, now we know he's in danger.'

McCann paused there, saw Brindley's mind working on that, Tofer's too, let the two of them ponder for a moment before he said: 'We could maybe make him an offer that keeps him and his family safe, if he tells us all about Stephen McKittrick and who is in charge and what this is all about.'

'Morning!' said McCann, striding into the incident room afterwards like it was his own. Taylor was up at the front, deep in conversation with Thompson. In the background there was a whiteboard – like Taylor was the star in some TV crime production – complete with photographs, maps, lines drawn from suspects to the victim. He caught a glimpse of Flannery's face pinned there before Taylor swung round.

'What're you doing up here, McCann?'

'You'll be interested in this,' said McCann, and handed him the evidence bag with the finger in its tin inside. 'A wee something for forensics we found down McKittrick's place.'

Taylor set the evidence bag aside on the desk, walked McCann to one side of the room, lowering his voice.

'What were you doing down there without my say-so?'

'There's something else,' said McCann, ignoring the question.

'And what would that be, McCann?' Taylor loomed over him, looked at his watch then glanced back at his colleagues to show he'd work waiting.

'Seems like Raymond Small and William Tofer were both in the money,' he murmured. 'Tofer's a new two litre Rover, colour TV as big as his living room, Small's bedroom I gather a regular Aladdin's cave.'

'What're you suggesting, McCann?'

'Maybe your Ulster bank job wasn't just the IRA involved? Seems like Tofer and Small may have been in on it and all.'

Taylor was incredulous, let out a loud involuntary scoff at McCann.

'I'd say it was worth a look at least.'

'You been up at Tofer's place as well? I'd appreciate it if you'd stay off my patch, McCann, otherwise there'll be crossed wires, duplication. That's what I agreed with Arbuthnut. Wasn't that what got you into trouble the last time?'

In the corner of his eye, McCann caught sight of Clarke pretending to sort some papers in the incident room, a bit of a smirk on his face like he was enjoying McCann's discomfiture.

'Just thought I'd mention it, that's all,' said McCann, slipping away before a real argument could break out, giving Clarke a nod of the head on the way out that he'd like to speak with him privately outside.

In the corridor McCann told Clarke that he needed a favour.

'Now why would I do that, McCann?' Nonetheless McCann could see Clarke was curious to know what the favour was.

'Tofer may have a story to tell, with the right incentives,' he said. 'Hear tell that's something you boys can fix.'

'I'd not be so sure about that McCann. What's he offering us?'

'Not sure yet. If I know we can get him immunity and protection, I can offer it to him, then we'll see what he says.'

Clarke took McCann's arm gently, leading him around a corner out of earshot of the open door of the incident room.

'That's not the way it works, McCann. You've to get the story first, see what sort of a story it is, then we'll see if we can do a deal and protect him.'

'Could be a nasty one,' said McCann. 'Goes up from the Sceptre, ties it all up, goes way back.'

'Does it now?' Clarke was thoughtful, concerned, unsure what to say, like he already knew the story but was worried that McCann did too. 'And its not one of your fantasies?'

'Fantasies no, but nightmares maybe,' said McCann.

'And this lad Tofer. Is he worth anything?'

'I'd say he was, better than the others at least,' said McCann.

'I'll see what I can do. There's no promises mind, no guarantees.'

'I'd not expect that from you,' said McCann. 'But thank you all the same.'

Then it was Saturday. McCann nodded to the fellow at the water's edge next to him as he set up his rod and line, the folding stool, his thermos beside that, the sandwiches wrapped in tinfoil, the bait box. The other man was going through the same motions; pushing the squirming bait onto the small barbed hook, casting out onto the reservoir, the float bobbing there on the water, then setting the rod on its stand with just the right slack upon the line. When that was done McCann poured himself a cup of tea from his Thermos and strolled over to chat, cup in hand.

'All right Jackie?'

'McCann.' The man was bundled up against the slight morning chill, a woollen cap pulled down to his eyebrows. He gave a reluctant nod, then took a glance to left and right checking they'd not be seen together nor overheard.

'How's retirement Jackie? Must be grand,' said McCann.

'Well out of it.' He watched the float bobbing on the bright morning water for a minute, a breeze rolling off the green hill above scurrying on the water.

'There was something I wanted to ask you about the Crumlin Road.'

The other fisherman sighed as a pair of swans paddled majestically past with a clutch of cygnets in tow. McCann shook out two cigarettes, one for himself, one for Jackie, lit both.

'You were a warder in there in '72, yes?'

'I was.'

'Would there have been any contact then, between the Republicans and Loyalist prisoners?'

'Not unless it was fighting. Except the hospital, that was the only place they'd be together.'

'They'd not kill a sick man then?'

'Not then, no. You couldn't have two sick bays anyway. The fellow's were in there sometimes side by side. I was on there from time to time, to keep a watch out for any trouble.'

'Did you have a lad by the name of Tofer in there by any chance?'

'Tofer? Oh I remember him right enough. The Professor, they called him.'

'Why'd they call him that?' McCann was genuinely bemused. Anyone less like a Professor would be hard to imagine.

'The fellow was into books, always his nose in them, reading stuff out to the lads, starting arguments. He had a bad time I gather, cut up and then had some kind of infection. It was a right mess and him only just married, a wee one at home. I think it turned his head, so it did.'

'Turned his head?'

'He was the only one of them had any time for the Micks in there, arguing the toss about everything. I can tell you I was glad when he was well enough to go back on the wing.'

'Was he pally with anyone in particular that you saw?'

'Fellow by the name of Ruaraidh O'Malley. I think he was done for killing an RUC man back in '74. Broke out soon after, never recaptured. A big man in the IRA. You'd not expect them to get on. It wasn't the done thing to fraternise.'

'O'Malley? You're sure it wasn't O'Rourke?' Jackie nodded, said he was sure.

McCann looked at the sky. The sun was breaking through. A tumble of clouds illuminated along their edge were blowing down over the water.

'That's great, Jackie,' he said, clapped him on the arm.

'Glad to be of help.' He nodded back up the bank towards McCann's float, which was jigging and jerking before disappearing with the strong pull of a fish he'd hooked underneath.

And then that afternoon he had a session with Flora McKeown in the Dunmurry Arms.

'How's things?' said McCann, sliding in on the seat beside her. He'd known her almost since his first days in the force, before the Troubles, when there was all the time in the world to sit and chat in bars like the one he was in; to watch the foam on the Guinness settle and have a smoke listening to the soft platter of the rain against the windows. Back then the forensic service was hardly scientific and Flora was pretty much all there was of it. But now it had expanded, developed arms, directorates, divisions and subdivisions like some kind of headless octopus. Flora had remained the same, though her post now lay near the bottom of what was an impressive hierarchy of new positions.

'I'm surprised McCann that you're taking time out to talk to the likes of me,' she said, eyeing her hot whiskey greedily as he brought it over to her on a tray, the steam rising from it, the stirrer standing in the golden liquid, the faint scent of lemon wafting upwards. 'No doubt there'll be something you're after.'

McCann tucked his coat tails under him and sat down beside her.

'Good to see you again Flora. How've you been keeping anyway?'

'I'd say I've been fair to middling, McCann.'

'That's two of us then,' said McCann, taking the first sip of his pint, Flora doing the same with her whiskey.

'By jove that's good,' she said. 'Start as one means to go on.'

'What do you know about sticky tape?'

He pulled a roll of black gaffer tape from his pocket – the tape he'd taken from Tofer's house – put it down on the table between them.

'What's that, McCann?' she said, eyeing it from each side and above, taking her whiskey stirrer to push it to and fro on the tabletop like it could explode at any moment.

'Hoping you could tell me,' said McCann. He noticed her glass was already empty and went to the bar and waited while the barman put the kettle on, sliced another lemon, put a double shot in a fresh glass, two spoons of brown sugar. While he was doing this McCann looked over at her. She was reaching into her bag, taking out a small black book that McCann recognised. She called it the 'Book of Kills', after the Book of Kells that rested in Trinity College Library, an illuminated gospel that was Ireland's most famous manuscript. The Book of Kills however contained the distilled wisdom of a lifetime in murder. More references than in any encyclopaedia, the repository of Flora's vast knowledge of the myriad ways people could be done to death.

'Thank you for bringing me this,' she said. He wasn't sure if she meant the whiskey or the sticky tape. 'A tricky one but I'd say this is Samson tape, made by O'Gorman's in Cork. You'd not normally be getting it up here in the North, though it's been used in tarring and feathering. No doubt someone has been up to no good with it?'

'You'd be right there Flora,' said McCann, draining his pint, frowning, wondering how Tofer had got hold of tape from the Republic, amazed but not surprised that even such everyday material could have partisan affiliations.

'And a box with a finger in it? Has that come your way yet?'

'Your Inspector Taylor brought that in late Friday. It's away to fingerprints, then biology for analysis. I'd doubt you'll get a whisper on it for a while.'

'But you took a look at it, did you?'

'Just a wee glance. There was Swarfega, carborundum powder and he'd had some injuries from swarf. Maybe the fellow was at Harland and Wolff or the Sirocco works. That kind of thing is very common for lads working on machines.'

'Lads?'

'It's a young man's finger.'

'And the tools that were used?'

'Come on Inspector I think I've done enough for one day. You'll have me on double time.'

'I can get you another?'

'Aye all right then.'

But she gave him no more. Only a couple of stories about lost fingers stretching way back, some of them handed down from before partition,[15] that she'd been told by her predecessor. All of the stories were darkly amusing, but none of them relevant or even believable. When they stood to go he asked her again, hoping perhaps that the whiskey might have oiled the cogs of her wondrous intelligence.

'I'll see what I can do McCann.'

And McCann went out, surprised to find that while they'd

---

[15] Ireland was partitioned in 1921, with the northern six counties remaining under British Rule.

been talking night had fallen. On the step she called him back.

'Just one wee thing though. The cut was very clean, like he'd used a chopper, not a Black and Decker like they normally use.' McCann thanked her. Already the traffic was emptying on the streets outside, the pavement deserted, a sharp rain slanting down in the light of the one streetlamp that was still working.

'And the hair? Any chance you'd a match for that?'

'Match with what?' she was suddenly sharp, suspicious even.

'Elizabeth McCabe and Mairead O'Shea. The two girls in the dead files,' he said. She shook her head.

'You're not still on about that Inspector, are you?'

'I am. I'll never give up. Can you just ask for us?'

'OK, since it's you,' she said.

McCann said goodbye to her, pulled up his coat collar, lit a cigarette, drew hard on it and lifted by that, strode off into the night.

Chapter Sixteen

On Monday morning they were kept waiting outside Paper Clip's office for the disciplinary hearing. Flannery had turned herself out as if she were on parade, or attending an interview; in full uniform, newly cleaned and her hair clipped back in military style under her hat. Taylor had arrived a little later, smart too, with a briefcase, grunting at them both before turning his back and staring out through the frosted glass window, while Deirdre busied herself with the papers on her desk. McCann tried an encouraging grimace, but it did nothing to break the tension.

'You'll be on soon,' said Deirdre. But the wait continued. McCann could hear voices behind the closed door and then finally they were ushered in. The Superintendent's room had been re-arranged so there was now a row of upright chairs facing his desk, which was occupied by the Chief Constable. Paper Clip and a woman he did not recognise were perched on either side, like china dogs at the ends of a mantelpiece. McCann could see a newly printed copy of the disciplinary papers on each chair as they filed in. He sat down next to Flannery, with Taylor at the far end of the row of chairs, facing the panel.

The Chief Constable looked at his watch, welcomed

them all with practised urbanity, introducing the grey-haired woman on his right as a Mrs Curtice from Establishments and explained the procedures. Then he said: 'We'd better crack on,' and asked Paper Clip to run through the charges against Flannery, swivelling towards him in professional listening mode. Paper Clip started to outline the case against her. Mrs Curtice took assiduous notes in a large black ledger and from time to time studied Flannery and McCann with a bored and slightly insolent stare. Then Taylor was on his feet explaining how they'd wanted to bring Liam O'Rourke in urgently, but despite knowing that, Flannery had still spent the afternoon at the cinema with him, and gone back to his flat afterwards. When they entered the property they had found Republican journals and literature. Taylor explained that it was these that had led him to search the property and to the discovery of the stolen banknotes.

'And Constable Flannery was present throughout?' asked the Chief Constable.

'She was there when we arrived, well settled in,' said Taylor, hesitating just long enough to ensure the panel would understand his inference.

And then it was Flannery's turn to answer questions.

'How long have you known Liam O'Rourke?' Paper Clip asked her.

'Two weeks.'

The Chief Constable hesitated, licked his lips: 'And was it a physical relationship?' Flannery blushed and hesitated, began to say that with respect, that was a private matter.

'The panel have a right to know if one of our officers is sleeping with the enemy,' said the Chief Constable and repeated the question. McCann could see the prying beginning to take effect in the way Flannery gripped her hands tightly by her sides, Mrs Curtice peering down at her pruriently, like an inquisitive bird as she answered: 'Yes.'

The questioning was swiftly over and an oppressive and satisfied silence descended on the panel for a moment before the Chief Constable asked McCann if he wished to add anything.

'Tell us again how you know Liam O'Rourke was in the IRA?' McCann turned to Taylor, setting himself the task of appearing reasonable, a colleague to colleague, professional question. Taylor gave his reply in the same tone, outlining the family connections that Liam O'Rourke had, the panel seeming bored, disinterested, even mildly irritated that there should be a defence at all.

'Yes, yes, we've heard all of this,' said the Chief Constable tetchily.

'Does reading books make you a terrorist?' asked McCann.

'Them kind of books, yes,' said Taylor.

'They're freely available. *An Phoblacht* is a newspaper like any other but you might not agree with it, is all. And having family members in the Republican Movement doesn't mean you are a terrorist either.'

'No, but it's a good guide. It means you're likely tarred with the same brush. And there's the stolen banknotes too,' Taylor replied.

'Are you charging anyone else for that?' asked McCann. 'Inspector Morrison for example, who had notes in his pocket I gather at the police social club, a member of the General

Synod too, notes in church collections. Isn't it the case that everyone in Ireland has stolen money now? That it's bubbling up everywhere. It's not just Liam that has it. And Constable Flannery tells me there's a reasonable explanation for that too.' He looked over towards her, summoned her to speak. Paper Clip whispered something to the chair, but the chair allowed her to reply with a grandiose wave of the hand, like he was doing her some special favour, demonstrating impartiality in the face of Paper Clip's reluctance to hear any more from her.

'He was the treasurer of the athletic club, kept the takings till they could be banked. There was nothing illegal. If he'd known the money was stolen he'd not have touched it. Like Morrison, like the other fellows.' Flannery was suddenly confident and strong in Liam's defence.

'His cousin was in the South Armagh active service unit. But Liam's a lawyer, an articled clerk in a solicitor's firm. He's not in his cousin's steps at all. The fact a fellow's from a family that's been active doesn't mean he's involved. Though I gather he's been in the Civil Rights movement, none of it was terrorism. If you've nothing more than circum-stantial evidence we can't be sure there's a link, or a risk to the force.'

'I think we've heard enough of that for now,' said the Chief Constable. Mrs Curtice paused in her scribbling, pen in hand, to give Flannery what seemed like a special glare of disapproval.

The Chief Constable looked at his watch again, consulted the panel in a low whisper, then announced: 'We'll move on shall we? The second matter please, Superintendent.'

'And McCann forbade you to go to the Sceptre did he?'

'Not in so many words.'

'What were his words exactly?' asked Paper Clip.

'That it was no place for a woman.'

McCann was on the edge of his seat, his hand up like a fellow at school with the right answer to something puzzling everyone. He couldn't stop himself and like a dam bursting he was up on his feet shouting: 'It wasn't an order. It was an observation. I wish it had been an order. But let's just look at the results; we've caught a dangerous gang, three of them. Stephen McKittrick, William Tofer, Peter Kemp. McKittrick and Kemp charged with assault, abduction, other charges to follow. Instead of having Flannery in here today you should be congratulating her for having a go.' And then McCann had a brainwave, adding: 'It's the 'Way Ahead', isn't it? The RUC handling things ourselves, not relying on the army. It's real policing for once.'

And he could see the Chief Constable nodding, Paper Clip anxiously shuffling documents in his folder, Mrs Curtice writing down his words in her black ledger.

They had a long wait outside, Taylor again standing where McCann had often stood, looking out at the frosted glass. Flannery sat by McCann, not speaking, each trying to catch the gist of any small snatches of conversation from behind the closed door as the panel deliberated. The refreshment trolley was delivered into the room carrying continental pastries, a silver coffee pot and bone china cups, real napkins, the kind of luxury only the high-ups could command. McCann caught a glimpse of them relaxed inside in shirtsleeves, the papers spread around them before the door closed once more. Eventually Taylor looked at his watch, turned to McCann as if to say something, stopped himself, then blurted out: 'You said there was more to come?'

'Aye,' said McCann. 'I've been speaking to Flora McKeown.'

'Come on McCann you'd not trust that old biddy would you? Sure forensics have come a long way since her day; there's new techniques, new systems, materials. Even the way we investigate now has changed. All of that is old school, old Ireland, village Ireland, went out with the horse plough and the curragh, all of that Men of Arran malarkey, all of that tough but fair honest decent hardworking folk that never existed, that never happened, that was some Papist fantasy bollocks.' Suddenly Taylor's frustration at McCann seemed to boil over, all of the tension of the last week and he raised his voice: 'Because you know what McCann? We can do better with science and systems and modern methods. You're old school McCann. You're all washed up. Nothing you do will ever stand up in court, because its full of the vapours, the banshee howl of old Ireland, full of bollocky wish-list fantasies and whispers, all of that.' Taylor's voice had risen to a shout now, his face red, his jowls quivering, spittle spraying McCann's face.

'We're back on,' McCann interrupted him, nodding back towards the door to Paper Clip's room which now lay open, the heat from the panel's deliberations wafting out, mingled with the smell of the fresh coffee which they had recently enjoyed inside.

Could he keep Flannery in the force after what they'd put her through? McCann was worried. It had been a result of sorts; a reprimand, the loss of a month's pay. He'd had the feeling they'd wanted her strung up, but couldn't bring themselves to do it. The 'Way Ahead' required a police force that represented everyone, Catholic and Protestant. So it wasn't his arguments that had clinched it, it was the politics of the situation as usual and as like as not the Chief Constable would have overridden the others to give expression to that.

'Thanks again, Inspector,' Flannery had said. But it had seemed half-hearted, her eyes downcast. A dispiriting day for all of them for which McCann's offer of a drink in Hannigan's seemed no answer and had been politely rejected.

'Come on, come on,' he chivvied her, but it felt close to the bullying he'd just seen her put through, he realised it was something he needed more than her, so he let her go her own way.

McCann went home without a drink. He rang Emily Thompson to give her the news of Sinead's reprieve.

'That's great,' she said. 'I'd not have expected that.'

'Had to do a bit of pushing,' said McCann. 'How's Taylor getting on with finding the money by the way?'

'Not far. We're recovering notes all over like I said but the bulk of it is missing.'

'Have you access to accounts.'

'Aye Taylor's got an order for it, so we can follow through on that.'

'Any chance you could check William Tofer for me? And

there's a Republican too, a Ruaraidh O'Malley. You could have a look at Raymond Small too, though I doubt he'd even have an account.'

'What are you after McCann?'

'Ah well now that would be telling.'

'You were in an awful bad mood when you left the other night, you know.'

'Was I?' said McCann. 'I asked Clarke a favour and he's not got back to me. D'you think you could jog his memory?'

And then he heard her calling to him in the background and felt another surge of jealous pain that Clarke and Emily were still connected.

Ten minutes later the phone rang in the hallway and McCann padded to it.

'Is that you, McCann?' He recognised Clarke's voice. It was late now, past eleven o'clock.

'You're clear to go,' he said. 'You've till five tomorrow to speak to Tofer and if he gives you nothing the deal's off, no immunity, nothing.'

He turned on the radio; classical music this time, something soothing. He'd no musical taste, could never remember if something was Brahms or Mozart, but from time to time there was a concert that would do the trick while he thought things through. He put on the kettle, glanced outside into the garden where the light from the kitchen showed the black hole where he'd torn out the rose bush and the bindweed. He'd not found the time to fill it in nor replace the plant and the mound of earth was like a gravedigger had been at work and was just awaiting the corpse.

'Ah, McCann, McCann,' he breathed to himself an admonition, popped the tea bag in the cup, waited for the kettle to boil when he caught a glimpse of a movement, a shadow in the garden outside in the darkness, the notes of the classical music still playing, rising and falling, winding their way through the empty rooms of his house, like the accompaniment to some B movie.

He flicked out the lights, crouched down, held his breath, heard the kettle click off. He knew the door was locked, – they all were – he made sure of that. On all fours, like some kind of scuttling animal, he made his way to the bedroom, found the Walther in the darkness, the classical music still playing. He fumbled some shells into the chamber, cursing as he did so. Why had he told them there might be more arrests, that he was going above McKittrick? Maybe that's just what they didn't want. The music stopped, the needle bumping, then silence. He crouched in the darkness, hearing his own heartbeat in his chest, his own breathing. Then nothing; no hand on the doorhandle, no sound of breaking glass, just the sighing of the wind outside.

Afterwards, he made himself a double, sat in the living room sipping it with the lights on.

If they offered Tofer immunity, then whatever Tofer said would seem tainted and might be picked apart by the defence. Far better that Tofer's story was freely willed and then it would be more likely to be true and to be believed. It was ironic that McCann – who had always fought against such dirty tricks – should now find himself on that slippery path.

But how else could he get proof, of who had ordered the killing of Raymond Small, get the story of what had really happened? Reel in the line till he got right to the end of it, to the deep-lying predators? Because McKittrick would be acting on orders and those kind of orders were always deniable; given one to one down the backstreet, in the darkened alleys, the empty toilets behind the bar, out on the strand, where they'd not be overheard, where there'd be no record. The person delivering the orders could always deny it, so it would always be one man's word against another's, one criminal against another, so the top man could almost always walk free.

There was one man that could maybe still help and McCann had resisted any temptation to go and see him again until that moment. What had Deevery meant when he had talked of Sammy McGuigan having set the dogs on people? Deevery had played with McCann for an hour or so at Purdysburn that day, but not been specific. Maybe with one last push, Deevery could tell him more, maybe with McKittrick inside he'd feel free to talk, like Patsy Kidron? Maybe it was Deevery that could – freely willed – still tell him what he needed to know? But Deevery was in Purdysburn, meaning Deevery was mad. Nothing he said could be believed. Or could it? Maybe the world was so upside down, that the mad were the only sane people, the only people who could tell the truth?

Chapter Seventeen

Deevery broke off from a game of cards he'd been playing with a group of other patients to stand and greet McCann, shaking his hand like he was an old friend. He had regained some of his colour; the red veins in his nose had re-appeared, the grey tinge to his lips had faded. McCann wondered had he heard news of the arrests through the grapevine?

'Can I get you a coffee, McCann?' He gestured to a new fangled coffee machine that was burbling gently on a table by the window and McCann accompanied him while he poured them both a cup, offered him biscuits from a tin.

'Hobknobs, McCann. Right up your street, if I remember.'

And when they were settled together at a table at the far end of the lounge – by a big picture window with a view down over the lawn to a line of trees – McCann asked: 'Did you ever hear tell of a fellow called Stephen McKittrick? We'll charge him for the murder of that lad I asked you about, that Raymond Small, up the Sceptre. He'll go down for twenty.' And as he said this, he felt Deevery let out a small, barely audible sigh, an exhalation of breath, like somehow his body was releasing some pressure that it had been holding in for years.

McCann pulled out the most recent mugshot of Stephen

McKittrick. It was a black and white print that had been enlarged and somehow the photograph gave off an air of evil; the eyes were unnaturally large, the pupils strangely dilated, the hair awry, an expression that combined truculence, malevolence and pride in equal measure as he glared straight into the camera. He caught a tiny shiver in Deevery's hand as he put his cup to his lips. It was a reaction that even Deevery's professionalism could not hide. He took a sip of his coffee, placed the cup down on the saucer deliberately.

'Would have known Barney McGuigan, been a rising star in 1975, maybe before that,' prompted McCann. 'Cast your mind back to them days, Deevery. When you and Barney McGuigan were up to your dirty tricks. Was there this fellow hanging around?'

'I seen him,' said Deevery. 'I wish I never had,' shaking his head with regret.

'When did you last see him?'

'Around the time Barney had his place up the Shankill Road, before he moved, he'd be hanging around.' And then Deevery seemed to be wrestling with the memory, before he started to speak: 'I told Barney that we'd been having problems with the girls, that there'd been complaints, not just about him, but about me too, that it was affecting the information we could get, could affect our reputation, so we'd need to end our arrangement. The girls and their families were starting to kick off, like you found out. I remember the night clearly, we were up the Sceptre having a few beers and that fellow McKittrick was there. At the time I thought he seemed like a vicious, evil cunt, but him and Barney seemed close.' McCann fumbled for a cigarette, offered Deevery one but he was so far into his tale he refused. Was it true or was it just a convenient yarn, a yarn that every criminal would tell, hanging every crime on the back of Stephen McKittrick?

'They went out to the loo together after we'd had our wee talk and when they came back Barney seemed pleased, rubbing his hands like he'd set up a good deal. That's when he said it.'

'Said what?'

'Don't you worry Inspector, Stephen here will fix it for you.'

'Why didn't you tell me? That's convenient for you to have him to blame.'

'Because you wouldn't have believed me, McCann. If you had, it would have put me in the frame too. I was there, you see. I wanted it cleaned up. But when it was done the way he did it, there was no way I could talk about it. I'd supped with the devil, you see. I didn't believe it myself when the two girls were killed. I didn't believe it when he came to see me after.'

'Who did?'

'This fellow.' He tapped the photograph with his knuckle.

McCann knew from personal experience what a visit from Stephen McKittrick could be like.

'But we've other evidence links you to the murder of those girls, not McKittrick.' There'd been Deevery's lapel pin in one of the vans that was used in the murders.

'I lost the pin and the fellow must've picked it up, used it against me,' said Deevery, rueful, aware of the weakness of his case.

'And you'll put this on paper for me.'

'Aye, if you promise me he'll be inside for good.'

'He will if you give me it all in black and white, Barney's role too. I want all of it this time.'

'You can absolve me now?'

'Give us the statement and we'll see,' said McCann.

Then it was on to Castlereagh. The lights were still burning in the block where Tofer was held, a permanent daylight in the rubber floored corridors, the full complement of staff on at reception and security. McCann showed his pass and asked to see Tofer, but at first the Sergeant refused.

'I've been left instructions by Inspector Taylor that you're not to be let in.'

'I've orders from the Branch,' said McCann, got them to ring through to Clarke and then grudgingly he was let through.

Tofer was dozing and had to be roused with a shake of the shoulder, blinking in the sudden bright light.

'We need to have a wee chat about our Mr McKittrick,' said McCann.

'Brindley not with you then?'

'It's just us two that need to hear this.'

'Hear what?'

'I can make you an offer Mr Tofer. You can walk out of here now with nothing on your record, protection, a new life in England for you and your family. There's just one condition.'

'And what's that?'

'That you tell me everything you know about Stephen McKittrick and Barney McGuigan.'

The police house where Flannery lived was one of four identical concrete homes, with spalling cement, peeling paint on steel framed windows, but otherwise substantial enough for the mostly young officers that were allocated accommodation there. McCann parked the car, and rapped the knocker, standing with his back to the door until Flannery opened up, surprised to see him there.

'There's something I want you to do for me,' he said.

'Come on in, Inspector, it's a bit of a mess I'm afraid.' But of course it wasn't a mess; the house was starkly clean; a thin carpet over a worn parquet floor, a galley kitchen with a serving hatch into a living room with an ugly three piece suite – black vinyl with orange cushions – facing an old Bakelite TV.

'Can I get you some tea?' McCann stood, ill at ease on the threshold of the living room, fidgetting with the Walther in his pocket, feeling the weight of it there.

'I need some cover, for tonight,' he said.

'Cover for what?'

'I'm going after Sammy McGuigan. I'd like you to have this.' He placed the gun down on the coffee table in the living room.

'Why me? Isn't there anyone else?'

'You're the one I'd trust to help me bring him in,' said McCann.

Chapter Eighteen

McCann stood in the shadows, tucked back behind a steel stanchion, watching the crowds milling around the second-class gangway and the slow trickle of departing passengers climbing up. To the rear of the dock offices the road was full of taxis and private cars dropping passengers for the ferries. Beyond the dock building lay the quay and the high steel sides of the *Ulster Prince*, its red funnel belching grey smoke into the evening sky.

There was a tug at his elbow, a whisper in his ear from a figure that had slipped up beside him.

'Is that you, McCann?'

'Aye.' He caught a waft of Guinness breath in the evening air, felt a clumsy fumble of a handshake. He could barely distinguish Tofer in the dusk, dressed now in a heavy black coat, a new trilby, a red muffler up around his mouth.

'Did you bring it?'

'Aye,' said McCann and handed him a thick Manilla envelope. 'There's everything you'll need. There's your ticket – first class – money for the train. New papers you'll need if you're asked. There's a Mr Johnson will meet you at Lime Street, platform three. Your family's arrived safely. They'll meet you over there.'

McCann relayed the instructions he'd had from Clarke.

'And on the boat?'

Tofer was nervous, despite the drink he'd had to stiffen him.

'I'd go straight down below, take your cabin, don't go to the bar, leave your breakfast till you're on the train.'

'Good man,' said Tofer, clapped McCann on the arm, like he was a friend.

The ship's siren sounded, one enormous mournful blast that drowned out the rest of what he said, then the tannoy advising those not sailing to leave the ship. The flow of people started to reverse on the gangplanks, the last few travellers pushing past and up.

'Best be off then,' said Tofer and vanished in the crowd. A moment later McCann saw him striding up the gangplank, a new suitcase swinging on his hand, stepping down on the deck into his new life. Then the gangplank was untied and swung down to the dock. McCann kept watch until he heard the ship's engines rev, saw the water boiling at the stern, the lines cast off. Only when the ship began to drift from shore did he turn away back into the city.

It was a fine evening, the flowerbeds filled out with fresh growth since the last time McCann had been up to Sammy McGuigan's, the new lawn now almost grown in. On the patio the barbecue was alight, a column of blue-grey smoke rising up and leaning away slightly to the west. Down below the lough was a delicate shade of silver-pink along the horizon and blue-black in the centre where the night ferry to Liverpool was making its way to sea, its lights starting to twinkle in the dusk.

'McCann! Over here, son!' Sammy McGuigan waved the barbecue tongs at him, dressed in new white trainers, shorts, a rugby shirt open at the collar as he turned the burgers and sausages, a can of beer in hand. At the table he could see Amy, her long blonde hair moving as she mixed and tossed the salad. He could hear the low murmur of conversation, the occasional big bellow of laughter from the fellows that were there, a wee shriek from the ladies, all dressed to the nines but casual with it.

'Glad you could come,' said Sammy, pressing his arm, drawing him in. 'Beer's over here, or you could have a wee short.'

'I'll take a beer,' said McCann.

'Amy!' shouted Sammy. 'Get McCann a beer will you?' And shortly he had an ice cold Guinness frothing in one hand, a burger on a paper plate in the other.

'How've you been you big cunt?'

'I'm fine,' said McCann.

'Didn't expect to see you up here.'

'Neither did I,' said McCann and left a pause while McGuigan raked the barbecue coals back and forth to bring the heat up, sending sparks flying into the darkening air.

'I'm grateful for what you done up the Sceptre, clearing that McKittrick out,' said Sammy.

From where they stood they could see far down to the Mourne mountains, even distinguish distant spires on the Ards Peninsula in the deepening dusk. The scent of cut grass mingled with the smell of the barbecue. 'I'll be able to get in there now and make the writ run. There'll be order and discipline there now, Inspector, you can be sure of that.'

'Well that's the first bit of thanks I've ever had from you,' said McCann, then paused. 'But I'm afraid I've a bit of bad news for you Sammy.' And McCann bit into his burger, the sauce flying out, spraying red ketchup down the front of Sammy's shirt. 'Ach God Sammy, I'm sorry,' said McCann. But he wasn't sorry at all. He let him get his own napkin to try to clean off the red stain dripping down over where his heart should have been.

'I've had a statement that goes way back,' he began. 'Three statements in fact, signed and sealed.'

'Whose statements?' Sammy's voice was sharp, as he tried to wipe down the ketchup.

'Patsy Kidron, William Tofer,' McGuigan threw his head back and laughed. 'Ach McCann you'd not believe them wasters would you?'

McCann enjoyed the moment. 'I said there were three.'

'Aye, so you did.'

'And I've William Deevery too, Sammy, pointing the finger at you. Because it was you that wanted the Sceptre cleaned out and you that sent in that knifeman Stephen McKittrick to do it. We've all of it down in black and white. You couldn't leave it alone when the new gang started to take over, William Tofer, smart lads like Raymond Small. And when they had the money from the IRA bank job it made them stronger still, so you'd to get your hands on that. Killed Raymond to find out who had it, then went for William Tofer didn't you? But the problem was I'd already arrested him, hadn't I? Then you had one last brainwave, once you'd picked up my Constable you'd a way of getting Tofer, hadn't you? A way of getting your hands on Tofer's money?' McCann hadn't realised he'd been raising his voice, that there was a lull around him, guests paused with glasses and burgers in their hands, everyone looking towards him and Sammy McGuigan,

'And I've just had the call from forensics. McKittrick done them girls too. He'd kept locks of their hair, along with Raymond's finger, as mementoes. He was your cleaner-upper, wasn't he, Sammy? We've Deevery's statement now to prove it.'

Sammy Mcguigan's eyes flicked from the burger in one hand to the pint in the other, then back to McCann's face and a thought struck McCann that he might be deciding if he'd time to finish them both before the cuffs went on him. Or break for the pigeon loft, where he kept his gun. Or laugh, because his fat face twitched with half of a grin, half of a snarl and then he broke away diagonally across the lawn, his cheeks puffed out, his legs pumping like he was jogging for his life towards the place where he kept his .45.

McCann started after him, called out: 'Sammy, don't be an eejit.' But Sammy had disappeared around the corner of the house, all the guests watching. McCann hesitated, knowing if he followed around the back there'd not be witnesses, but then thinking maybe these guests would be used to people being killed in cold blood. If he waited for Sammy to come back they might just stand there with their burgers and white wines and let it happen. So he stood there on the lawn amongst the trestle tables, with the smoke from the barbecue drifting through the summer trees, the lough still silver below in the last light of the evening. Then Sammy re-emerged, the gun dangling from his hand like it was a fresh can of beer he'd just picked up from the freezer, cocked it and aimed at McCann. Behind him, he saw Flannery closing on McGuigan with silent steps across the fresh grass, just as he'd arranged, heard her order him to put his gun down as she trained her own gun on McGuigan's head.

McCann looked down beyond the boundary fence and saw a blue flashing light, heard the sound of doors slamming. The crime team – Taylor, Clarke, Thompson in the lead – came running up the steps. By then he had McGuigan against the wall, the cuffs on him.

'Clarke told us where you'd be, McCann,' Taylor said, panting with the exertion. 'He was watching you all the time.'

Clarke stood back scanning the crowd for faces, like he was looking for someone.

'Thought it was best,' he drawled, like the explanation was obvious. 'I'd a guess you'd try to close things down when you had Tofer's statement. We'd a tail on you and Tofer to make sure everything went off all right, that Tofer got away.'

'Tofer got away? What the fuck is this all about?' Taylor erupted, swung round towards Clarke.

'Munton cleared it, the brass cleared it. I'm sorry you weren't kept informed,' said Clarke smoothly.

There were more men from the crime team in the garden now, coming down through the woods above. Sammy McGuigan was protesting, being patted down against the wall of his big new house. The guests tried to slip away with quiet apologies, or stood to watch in shocked silence, awaiting their turn to give statements, finishing up the drink in the meantime.

McCann talked fast, the story coming together in his head, getting it all out before Taylor could pour cold water on it. Taylor sat down at one point on a folding chair, looking like he'd decided to endure McCann's tale politely, only because McCann seemed so keen on it he knew he wouldn't stop.

'Why was there no intelligence on this?'

'Because McKittrick had scared everyone off. He'd even Raymond's finger that he'd wear round his neck on a chain, to encourage the others. That's why none of the lads would say anything, why the Branch never picked up what was going on.'

'And the bomb?' Taylor raised his eyebrows, humorously, like he was expecting another funny explanation from McCann.

'Part of the same operation, a big fat 'don't fuck with us' message to the landlord at the Sceptre, to Tofer and everyone involved in the bank job, from Sammy McGuigan.'

'And the IRA, nothing to do with it I suppose?'

'That's your patch Taylor, that's all to prove. I'd imagine they were the crack delivery team for the robbery. From what I hear it was sophisticated and – say what you like about the UFF and the boys at the Sceptre – that's not their forte. It's Tofer was the really smart lad who saw what the IRA lacked, the capacity to launder out fantastic sums of cash. He had contacts with the IRA from his time in the Crumlin Road gaol, buddies with Ruaraidh O'Malley, a top man. It seems like he had some sort of an epiphany in there. And the way it was done, there'd be no questions asked, not like if the Republicans had tried to launder the cash themselves. As a Protestant Tofer would be trusted anywhere, by the Branch, the police too.'

'How do you know this, McCann? How do you know any of this?'

Thompson, who until then had been silent, spoke up: 'We did what you wanted Inspector; we followed the money-tree back down to its roots. You said yourself you'd just scratched the surface, that there were millions missing.'

'Aye, still are love,' said Taylor ruefully.

'Not any longer,' said Thompson. 'We did a little more digging around on the quiet, checked the lads at the Sceptre too. All of them were broke except for the two of them McCann told you about, William Tofer and Raymond Small.'

McCann butted in: 'Tofer said there'd been bequests. Gifts from the dead you might say.' Taylor waved his hand impatiently, annoyed by McCann's interruption.

'They'd each had big cheques.' Thompson looked at her notebook where she had written the figure down: 'Three million, four hundred thousand, three hundred and twenty two pounds in total. And there's more,' said Thompson. 'George Brindley's name was on them.'

Now Taylor seemed baffled.

'Brindley? Sure he's a solicitor.'

'So what?' said McCann. 'Sure there's bent solicitors same as there's bent coppers.' Now it was Thompson's turn to be irritated, anxious to get to the end of her story.

'The long and the short of it sir is that the bulk of your Ulster Bank money, stolen by the IRA, was laundered out through Brindley's firm and Tofer was the link man with the IRA.'

'And Raymond Small was his messenger boy, his runner.'

'The link man?' Taylor tipped his head back and let out another laugh at that.

'You've been spending too much time with McCann,

you've gone off your head too. The two sides, IRA and UFF working together? Your head's cut, love. They'd never trust one another.'

'Shape of things to come,' said McCann.

'But here's the thing,' said Thompson, ignoring his interruption. 'Brindley had the means; sure they're one of the biggest firms in Ulster, must hold millions on account for clients, big property deals, business transactions, estates held in escrow, it'd be easy for them to wash through those kind of sums a little at a time. I went up there and found these.' She pulled out an evidence bag filled with new twenty pound notes, placed it on the table in front of Taylor. 'It was his firm that worked the trick for Tofer. That's why McKittrick wanted Tofer dead. That's why McKittrick tortured Raymond, because he was the weakest link and he knew he was close to Tofer, so he could find out what Tofer was up to and where the money was.'

'Oh yes, and I suppose you can prove all that too,' said Taylor.

'As a matter of fact we can. But that's not all McKittrick done, because Flora McKeown got me a match for the hair we found at McKittricks house, with Mairead O'Shea and Elizabeth McCabe. I had a call from her just before I came up here. Seems like he killed them too.'

'But how's Sammy tied up in any of this?'

'Sammy gave the orders all along. Tofer confirmed that McKittrick was Sammy's knifeman, since way back. Deevery confirmed that he'd discussed the two girls with Sammy and McKittrick, and he'd said he'd sort it. But he'd no idea he'd go so far.'

'He would say that, wouldn't he? Diverts the blame, they all do it.'

'But McKittrick *is* a knifeman, that's the difference. We've the evidence to prove it.' And here, McCann showed his bandages, the marks on his arms, like they were stigmata.

'And that Sammy ordered it?'

'Tofer and Deevery came clean about who gave the orders to McKittrick.'

'Deevery, came clean?'

'Aye,' said McCann. 'He's changed. Some people do.' He tapped his pocket, where he had their statements side by side.

'I've another serious matter to discuss with you, McCann,' said Paper Clip first thing the next morning. It would be his return to work form, McCann was sure. Either that or the PR5 he'd need to sign off from Flannery's disciplinary, the top copy and the duplicates for the records.

'I hear tell from Castlereagh that your Mr Tofer has been released, despite being heavily involved in laundering the proceeds of the bank job?'

'That's correct, Sir.'

'On whose authority was that done? I wasn't notified, I've not had the paperwork. It's not been through Lisburn.'

'I gather it was Clarke's boss that cleared it.'

'Why would he do that?'

'You tell me, Sir. The Branch has its own logic.' They had needed Tofer's testimony to close down McKittrick and McGuigan's rogue UFF unit that had got out of control and turned into a monster that was laying waste to the City. 'Tofer was ahead of his time. I think the Branch will need folk like him to work with one day, people that can talk to the IRA, work across the divide.'

'What utter nonsense!' said Paper Clip. McCann raised an eyebrow. Nonsense could be true. Nonsense could happen. It was not so surprising after all; wasn't getting the two sides to work together better than letting them kill each other? They'd need men on the ground that saw the sense of that one day.

'And the money. I gather the fellow had millions from the Ulster Bank that you're letting him away with.'

'No Sir,' said McCann. 'I've a PR 8 right here to confiscate the proceeds of crime.' And he slipped the neatly completed form across the table towards a surprised Superintendent. 'If you'd just sign here, here and here,' he said, indicating where his signature was required. And when that was done, he asked him if he could borrow a paper clip to hold the sheets together.

McCann entered Stephen McKittrick's cell. He'd smartened himself up for the big day – a new light blue poplin shirt open at the collar, a pair of chinos, crisply ironed, even a new pair of black shoes with leather soles.

'Morning Stephen!' he said cheerily, sitting down opposite him. McKittrick was once again eating breakfast, but now it was the standard menu; a white roll, thin instant coffee, jam and margarine in plastic tubs, plastic cutlery, paper plates.

McCann placed the folder down on the table, McKittrick eating cautiously, discomfited by his uncharacteristic good humour.

'Stephen McKittrick,' began McCann. He stopped eating. 'I am charging you with the abduction and murder of Raymond Peter Small.' He paused then took a breath and added: 'Also

Mairead O'Shea and Elizabeth McCabe.'

And then he looked over at the duty solicitor and said: 'Write that down, son.' Then McCann lay back in his seat like an enormous dark weight had been lifted from around his heart. He smiled at McKittrick, whose mouth had dropped open, revealing bad teeth and a half-chewed white roll with strawberry jam on it.

The radio was playing *Afternoon Delight* as the road rose and fell ahead of Liam O'Rourke's car, Sinead Flannery beside him in the front seat, the window open a crack to take away the smoke of his cigarette. On either side the trees were starting to show a slight fading of the green and some of the patchwork fields were brown with stubble, an occasional tractor ploughing the land with birds following in its wake. Up ahead she could see Slieve Donard low down on the horizon and the brightness in the sky that only proximity to the sea could bring.

'Amazing they let you off,' she said. 'I'd never have believed that.' He smiled, puffed on his cigarette.

'Sure I never done nothing, did I?' He said, still smiling.

'Nothing, is it?' she said. He took his eye off the road for a moment to look at her.

'That fellow Tofer said I'd nothing to do with the robbery, apparently, or so they said.'

'Who said?'

'Gather it was McCann took the statement off him. Your boss, I think he must have had a soft spot for us both.'

'Maybe he did.'

A further silence.

'Where are we going anyway?'

'There's a nice wee strand I know past Kilkeel, very quiet, secluded too. You'll like it down there.'

McCann was looking at the brochures again, the finely chiselled figure of a man, lightly tanned, in his mounties uniform, the clean white snow of the winter Rockies in the background, fresh snow dripping like icing sugar from the pine trees all around. What would it be like to be that man, he wondered, with the scent of that air in your nostrils, that horse snorting and tugging at the reins beneath you, ready for the off? What would it be like to be reborn like that?

'Aye that's just a dream, isn't it' he said to himself as he tossed the brochure in the bin. Just as much a dream as that peddled by the men in the IRA and the UFF, that dream of purity, of being better than anyone else, that dream of an impossible freedom.

Just then a knock came at the front door, a light tapping.

'McCann, are you in there?' A woman's voice. McCann hesitated, peeked from the kitchen to try to see who it could be.

'Come on, McCann. I know you're in there. I've something for you.'

Then he realised who it was.

'Aye, right. I'll be right there,' he shouted and rushed to unbolt the door, turn the deadlock, and open up to a bright spring day and Emily Thompson standing on the front step to see him.

At the ship's rail, the passengers had stood two deep, clutching pints from the bar, the red tips of their cigarettes glowing in the night air. The sky above was scattered with stars. The lights on the Irish coast gradually becoming less distinct; at first it had been possible to make out individual landmarks; the headlights on the motorway, the lights at the head of Samson and Goliath, Carrickfergus, lit like a fairground, its castle floodlit. The ship had gathered speed out into the lough, out towards the Isle of Man and Liverpool beyond, the lights of Ireland becoming just a glow on the sea.

Tofer had stayed on deck watching a fellow's back. He was a young, fit lad with a short haircut, brown mac on against the evening chill, the tails fluttering in the wind that passed along the deck. The lad was neither drinking nor smoking, in fact had stayed quite still, with none of the conviviality of the passengers either side that were remarking the fineness of the night, or the beauty of the stars, some holding hands, some with their arms around each other. Tofer wondered who the lad was and why he'd been following him since he came on board, why he was pretending disinterest. Tofer realised then that it wasn't all over for him yet, regardless of how fine the night.

Recommended Reading

If you have enjoyed reading *The Redemption Cut* you will probably have read the first Inspector McCann novel *Dirty Old Tricks* and should try Pat Gray's other novels:

The Political Map of the Heart
The Cat

If you like novels set in Ireland you should try:

The Failing Heart by Eoghan Smith
A Provincial Death by Eoghan Smith
Le Fanu's Angel by Brian Keogh

If you like your crime novels with a great sense of place you should try Leo Kanaris' Athens trilogy:

Codename Xenophon
Blood and Gold
Dangerous Days

And the two novels by Andy Oakes set in Shanghai:

Dragon's Eye
Citizen One

For further information about Dedalus' titles please visit our website: www.dedalusbooks.com
or email info@dedalusbooks.com for a catalogue.

Dirty Old Tricks by Pat Gray

A chilling noir novel set in the Belfast of the Troubles in which Pat Gray introduces us to the flawed but dogged and honourable policeman McCann.

'Belfast in 1975 provides a gloomy backdrop for this murder mystery, which opens with RUC officer Michael McCann lying awake, half-expecting to be kidnapped and killed, setting the tone for the discovery of 15-year-old Protestant schoolgirl Elizabeth McCabe, murdered and dumped in a Catholic area. It's a grim enough crime as it is, but the constant presence of armoured cars and automatic weapons adds a further layer of bleakness to the oppressive mood. Even the routine business of door-to-door enquiries becomes a military operation with the potential to escalate into violence. McCann has to consider the possibility that the paramilitaries have sunk low enough to sanction tit-for-tat schoolgirl murders, and it's "not easy to detect clues, in a hard country where men never cried". Creepily compelling, Gray's fourth novel probes deeply into darkness, weaving an atmosphere of tension and distrust that permeates every part of McCann's investigation, including his relationships with colleagues. It's masterfully done, but chilling and hard-hitting stuff.'

Alastair Mabbott in *The Herald*

£9.99   ISBN   978 1 912868 26 1   270p   B. Format

The Political Map of the Heart by Pat Gray

A tale of doomed love, set against the backdrop of Ireland's Troubles. Brutally pessimistic and agonisingly romantic, Pat Gray's novel recaptures the spirit of a lost Ireland. It follows the fortunes of an English family, stranded in the apparent backwater of Ulster at the end of the Second World War. Bernard, the flawed and eccentric father, who was injured in the war, Eileen his wife, and their three children, are all torn apart as the troubles engulf them.

'Absolutely wonderful! There's a strange tension about it, almost like a melodrama. Beautiful, the way it links the history of Ireland with the troubles in the family. I loved it.'
Lynn Barber in *The Sunday Times*

'This convincing and evocative novel may lack the terrors of involvement and love across the sectarian divide, none the less, it explores the universal confusions and complexities of adolescence from an original perspective.'
C.L. Dallat in *The Times Literary Supplement*

'Pat's teenage romance with the lovely Elaine is tenderly related, their innocent relationship at odds with violence around them. With understated compassion, Gray shows a family torn apart and a love tainted by political divisions. His novel is blissfully free of sentimentality and endless rain that plagues so much Irish fiction.'
Lisa Allardice in *The Independent on Sunday*

£7.99   ISBN 978 1 873982 54 9   196p   B. Format

The Cat by Pat Gray

'Left in an empty house, the Cat previously pampered with canned food and his owners' affection – learns to hunt again, much to the alarm of the intellectual Mouse and the proletarian, politically aware Rat. As the Cat makes inroads into the garden (renting property to voles, for example, and thus discouraging their allegiance with those who would topple him), Mouse and Rat try to stave off the Cat's despotic rise. They discover the Cat's vulnerable area: he hungers not only for the deference of the various rodents he has cowed but also for the affection of humans that he once knew. Gray's satire thus at first seems to target the amorality of the ruling classes, only to turn its attention more squarely to capitalism – the hollow repast that never satisfies, the empty acquisition of material goods.'

Publishers Weekly

'Gray's reworking of the *Animal Farm* concept brings in a post-Thatcherite twist. Having peacefully co-existed with his friends Mouse and Rat (the latter carries a briefcase and wears Italian suits), the Cat's owners suddenly leave him to fend for himself. He then has to fall back on feline instincts, placating the furry packed lunches which surround him with promises of consumer goods and burrow ownership. A stylish and witty parable for the Nineties.'

Scotland on Sunday

£8.99   ISBN 978 1 910213 36 0   124p   B. Format

A Provincial Death by Eoghan Smith

Lyrical and blackly comic, *A Provincial Death* is a startlingly original meditation on solitude and perseverance, the consolations of art and philosophy, and the capacity of human beings to endure catastrophe.

It is a hot, summer morning and Smyth, a struggling writer and academic, wakes to discover he is stranded alone on a rock in the Irish Sea. As he clings on in hope of salvation, he is assailed by broken memories and the failures of his past. Fragmented images of the previous day come to him: a mysterious research institute, a dead forest, a rickety boat captained by a gruff old fisherman, an eccentric academic named McGovern who believed that the Moon was about to crash into the Earth, destroying everything. Confused, weary and sore, and with the tide rising inexorably and strange sea creatures circling, Smyth tries to make sense of an arbitrary world in a desperate bid for survival.

£9.99   ISBN 978 1 912868 65 0   150p   B. Format

The Failing Heart by Eoghan Smith

'Brilliant! Dark and atmospheric. It's a compulsive account of how it feels to be tortured and mired in anxiety.'

Sue Leonard in *The Irish Examiner*

'Reading *The Failing Heart* is like taking a trip; part escape into another consciousness, part suffocating delusion. The story – or rather the scaffolding upon which Smith displays elegant philosophical architecture – follows a young scholar whose mother has just died. Estranged from his father after stealing his money, hounded by the ominous figure of his landlord, and oppressed with images of his ex-lover's impending labour, he wanders into an existential purgatory. "All these open mouths, living or dead, they never shut up." Death is everywhere, through the needs and revulsions of the body, its smells, secretions, drives. The narrative circles in on itself in an ever-decreasing gyre, examining ancient and modern ideas about existence, subjecting philosophical scholarship itself to a sardonic inquiry using its own tools of scrutiny. The writing is self-aware and wry, with rare flashes of humour amid a claustrophobic search for meaning and desire to confess. Time expands and contracts; it is unclear what is real, what is internalised: at the end of this brief novel there is the sensation of having witnessed the dark dream of a stranger.' *The Irish Times*

'I was exhausted after each chapter, drained and spent but I devoured every single word of this truly exquisite debut.'

Dymphna Nugent in *The Waterford Star & News*

£9.99   ISBN 978 1 910213 91 9   152p   B. Format

Le Fanu's Angel by Brian Keogh

'Kieran Sheridan Le Fanu, Dublin advertising executive and namesake of the famous author, wakes from a coma following a serious car accident, but even concussion can't explain what's going on around him. He's attacked by an intruder no one else sees. Events of a full day seem to be compressed into the space of two hours. A patient who was never there dies in his room, and he gains the protection of a beautiful guardian angel. Kieran begins to suspect that he's actually died, and what he is experiencing is some limbo world between life and death. Keogh's debut novel is a gripping and audaciously effective supernatural thriller, which pits his protagonist against savage spectral entities from a realm of the dead in conflicts which toughen him up for the equally crucial battles in the boardroom of his advertising agency. Through all the mayhem and gore, Keogh's tongue is never far from his cheek.'

Alaistair Mabbott in *The Herald*

'A thought provoking novel about death and a possible afterlife with Gothic overtones.'   Sue Leonard in *The Irish Examiner*

'Most importantly, Keogh tells a good story – both at the level of the individual episodes as well as the larger stories – and tells them well, making for a thoroughly engaging novel and enjoyable read.'   M.A. Orthofer in *The Complete Review*

£11.99   ISBN 978 1 912868 45 2   368p   B. Format

Codename Xenophon by Leo Kanaris

'Blessed with all the virtues of a traditional murder mystery, this debut novel has a sharp political edge. Three years in Athens left Leo Kanaris with a loathing for the self-serving parasites and bureaucrats who 'had paralysed the country for decades'. In *Codename Xenophon*, this insider's view of a paralytic society is seen through the eyes of George Zafiris, a private investigator who does his best to tread the straight and narrow, while those around him are too greedy or plain scared to take responsibility. It is the apparently motiveless killing of an elderly academic that embroils Zafiris in political machinations at the highest level. But, as his dogged perseverance begins to pay off, he comes to realise that even the best intentions can have tragic consequences. With vivid characterisation and a plot that thickens without obscuring the essential threads, Kanaris emerges as a sharp new talent in crime writing.'   Barry Turner in *The Daily Mail*

'The narrative flits from a frenzied Athens to the idyllic islands as politicians, Russian crooks, corrupt (and/or incompetent) policemen thicken the plot, the world-weary Zafiris nimbly negotiating a Byzantine culture in which morality, truth and justice are malleable concepts. The first in a proposed quartet to feature George Zafiris, *Codename Xenophon* is a bleak but blackly comic tale that does full justice to its laconic, Chandleresque heritage.'   Declan Burke in *The Irish Times*

£9.99   ISBN 978 1 909232 83 9   255p   B. Format

Blood & Gold by Leo Kanaris

'The everyday deprivations of the Greek financial crisis provide the background to Kanaris's second George Zafiris adventure. The private eye travels between Athens and the islands, becoming perilously enmeshed in a web of mysteries involving the disappearance of a body, the death of a musician and the disappearance of her husband. Anglo-Greek Kanaris keeps it light and characterful amid the dishonesty and corruption.'   *The Times/Sunday Times Crime Club*

'In Kanaris' assured sequel to *Codename Xenophon*, PI George Zafiris looks into the suspicious death of Mario Filiotis, the mayor of the island of Astypalea. According to the police report, Filiotis was riding a bicycle when he lost his balance and was hit by a truck. Zafiris, who was a friend of the deceased mayor, soon discovers that the police have done everything possible to erase any evidence. "The bicycle has been disposed of," an unhelpful official tells him. "Also the truck driver's file." During Filiotis's funeral, a mishap with his coffin reveals not a body but a trove of archeological treasures. Filiotis's appointment book provides some leads for Zafiris and his raw but eager helper, Haris Pezas, to pursue. Meanwhile, Zafiris takes on a worried new client, Anna Kenteri, who wants him to locate her missing sister, violinist Keti Kenteri. Both cases turns out to be complex and dangerous. Kanaris depicts a troubled Greece with compassion and precisely observed social commentary.'   *Publishers Weekly*

£9.99   ISBN 978 1 910213 10 0   332p   B. Format

Dangerous Days by Leo Kanaris

'This book has all the ingredients of hard-boiled classic crime: the mean streets, poverty and corruption and an upright private eye challenging the iniquities of a broken society. Except that this is not the California of the Thirties, but modern-day Greece. Reduced to pushing leaflets through letterboxes to drum up business for his detective agency, George Zafiris reluctantly takes on a family-connected job to recover a stolen necklace. But other problems close to home soon crowd in to threaten his marriage. Were this not enough to occupy him, a senior policeman hires him to track down the files of a murdered lawyer, while seeking those responsible for the death of an illegal immigrant. It all adds up to a fast-moving thriller played out against a backdrop of political bedlam – an exciting, provocative read.'   Barry Turner in *The Daily Mail*

'Leo Kanaris' addictive Greece thrillers are guaranteed to take your mind off your own troubles by empathizing with someone else's, namely, George Zafiris, the intrepid Athenian private eye who'll keep you turning the pages well into the small hours. Those familiar with *Codename Xenophon*, the first of the George Zafiris tetralogy, will pounce on the second and third, *Blood and Gold* and *Dangerous Days*. In these two Kanaris definitely qualifies as a global-class thriller writer. Razor-wire dialogue carries you through the action at jet-ski speed, descriptions jolt us with rueful recognition, such as the Greek potholes that multiply as fast as the government's debts.'   John Carr in *The Athens Insider*

£9.99   ISBN 9781 910213 71 1   297p   B. Format